———————— ★

"Oh my God!"

The watch was gold, expensive and it gleamed in a ray of sunlight that shone on the trash bin. Unfortunately, it was wrapped around a wrist. The hand attached to that wrist was large, masculine and well kept. The fingers had tightened almost into a fist. A dark suit jacket covered the arm from just above the wrist to where it disappeared beneath a layer of trash. Near the metal sidewall of the container rested a shoe, a black wing tip, nearly new based on the condition of the heel. An appalling inch of pale skin shone between the dark sock and the bottom of the dark suit trousers.

Then I saw the red stain that soaked a sheet of cardboard not far from the wrist. The smell hit me about the same time.

"I think we just found Grant & Bethel's missing executive." My voice sounded strange to me. I stepped back and fumbled for the cell phone, but my hands shook so bad it took three tries to flip it open.

———————— ★ ————————

A
GIFT
FOR
MURDER

KAREN McCULLOUGH

W❂RLDWIDE®

TORONTO • NEW YORK • LONDON
AMSTERDAM • PARIS • SYDNEY • HAMBURG
STOCKHOLM • ATHENS • TOKYO • MILAN
MADRID • WARSAW • BUDAPEST • AUCKLAND

As ever and always for Jim, who still believes,
and for Liz, Joe and Sarah, who make me proud

Recycling programs
for this product may
not exist in your area.

A GIFT FOR MURDER

A Worldwide Mystery/June 2012

First published by Five Star

ISBN-13: 978-0-373-26804-7

Copyright © 2011 by Karen McCullough

Printed in U.S.A.

CAST OF CHARACTERS

Market Center Personnel:

Heather McNeil, assistant to the director of the Washington, D.C., Commerce & Market Show Center

Janelle Addison, the Commerce & Market Show Center's director and Heather's superior

Scott Brandon, former police officer, newly hired security officer for the center

Craig Vincelli, head of security

Jo Sterling, marketing director

Tina, receptionist

Mark Templeton and Sam Boresi, maintenance

Howie Harper, security officer

Carl Roney, executive vice president, Market Centers and Events Inc., MCEI, owner of the C&M Show Center. Janelle Addison's superior.

Exhibitors:

Stan Grantwood, co-owner of Grantwood & Bethel, a supplier of gifts and decorative accessories

Tim Bethel, co-owner of Grantwood & Bethel

Ellen Spencer, executive vice president of marketing for Grantwood & Bethel

Vickie, Jason and Taylor, sales reps for Grantwood & Bethel

Sue Savotsky, owner of Trimstates

Andy Tarantoro, VP of sales, Gruber's Exchange

Dave Powell, CEO of Gaviscelli

Irv Kirshorn, owner of Kirshorn's

Martin Chang, co-owner of Chang & Fitch Associates

Dan and Joanne, owners of Stanaker-Wells

Others:

Detective Peter Gilmont, the police detective assigned to the murder investigation

Lisa Willamont, independent sales rep and Heather's friend

Tom Rupika, designer

ONE

IF I'D KNOWN how bad Wednesday would get, I would've—what? Stayed in bed? Not likely. The show must go on and all that. But I would've at least asked for another shot of espresso during my morning stop at Starbucks. Maybe two.

My workday went from peaceful beginning to chaos within half an hour. This wasn't just another day at the office. The start of the annual Washington, D.C., Gifts and Decorations Show, our biggest show of the year at the Commerce & Market Show Center, was always the worst day of the year for the staff who organized it.

By nine-thirty, blizzards of paper covered my desk, my cell phone hadn't quit buzzing, and the landline phone rang continuously. The computer constantly chimed the arrival of new email messages. A strange man stopped at the office door and stood there watching me.

The triple-shot latte was already struggling to keep my sanity in place.

I recognized the number on the cell-phone display and reached for it first.

"Heather?" Janelle, the Show Center's director and my boss, sounded disturbed. Unflappable Janelle sounding disturbed was worse than most people shouting or having hysterics.

"Problem?" I asked, trying not to stare at the stranger, who lingered near the doorway. A quick glance said he was worth a look.

Until Janelle said, "Find Mark and tell him aisles three

to five don't have power. He's not answering his pager. Then call Truffant Shipping and ask them to fax copies of the manifests for their deliveries to Brent-Cooper. A couple of their boxes are missing. Once you've done that, can you get down here? Lots of ruffled feathers over the power. Oh, and Grantwood & Bethel is missing one of their key people. They think he may be lost somewhere in the city. And Sue Savotsky of Trimstates doesn't like her location—the carpet's not clean, and the people across the way are playing loud music."

"Her again?"

"'Fraid so. But she likes you, so if you wouldn't mind— What's that?" The last two words were directed at someone else. "Gotta go. Need you ASAP." Janelle ended the call.

I reached for the latte getting cold on a corner of my desk. Someone else yelled, "Heather!"

Jo startled me so badly I almost splashed coffee on my white silk blouse. That would make a really good impression on the clients down on the showroom floor. Or the hunk in the doorway.

I turned toward her office. "What?"

"I can't find the latest press accreditations list."

"I put a copy in your inbox this morning. Did you look there?"

"Yes. It's not… Oh, wait. Here it is."

How did our marketing director manage to get her shoes on the right feet in the morning? I rolled my eyes, momentarily forgetting I was't alone.

A warm, masculine chuckle reminded me. "You must be the person who runs the place." The voice was deep and rich, sexy as a Milky Way bar—the kind with dark chocolate.

I turned to face the stranger, who'd taken a couple of

steps toward my desk. Tall, lean, around thirty, blond hair cut short, light eyes of indeterminate color.

"I'm Heather McNeil, the director's assistant," I answered. "I do my part. May I help you?"

The right side of his mouth curled into the beginnings of a smile. For a moment there was a delightfully predatory gleam in his eye, but then the light went out, as if he'd shut it off. Damn!

"Scott Brandon. I had an appointment to apply for the security officer's position you're advertising," he said.

"You need to see Craig Vincelli, down the hall. He's the security chief."

"He wasn't in his office. Someone directed me up here. There wasn't anyone at the receptionist's desk, either."

Jo came out of her office, shuffling an armload of papers. "Gotta take these down to the press room. Back shortly." She paused to admire the newcomer, then raced down the hall when she heard the elevator bell ping.

"God knows where Tina is," I said, as much to myself as to the man standing there. "Craig's probably out running down the missing boxes. Or the missing executive. Just a minute." I picked up the phone and dialed Craig's cell number.

He answered on the third ring, breathless and in a hurry. "Yeah?"

When I explained, he said, "Crap, I forgot. I'll be there in ten minutes. Give Brandon the paperwork."

I said I would and hung up.

"You've mislaid boxes and *an executive?*" Scott Brandon asked. "The boxes I can understand, but aren't executives kind of hard to lose?"

"Not in D.C. They manage to lose themselves all the time. In traffic, in museums, in the Metro, in the halls of power…"

He frowned. "You're too young to be so cynical."

"There's an age limit? No one told me."

"Real cynicism takes bitter experience."

"And you're so ancient?"

Something flashed in his eyes, something dark and dangerous. "I've walked the walk and—"

"Turned the talk into a lecture. Come with me." I stopped at Tina's desk to get the application forms and led him to the small conference room. "Sit in here and fill these out. Bring them back to me when you're done."

I spent a few minutes on the phone trying to track down Mark, our resident electrician, but he didn't answer pages or his cell phone. No one had seen him. I swore quietly to myself, then called the shipping company about the boxes. They promised to fax the manifest.

I needed to get down to the show floor but I couldn't leave Scott Brandon up here alone, so I called a few more people around the building, trying to locate Mark. On a hunch I dialed down to the snack bar and nailed my target. I asked the manager to put him on the line and gave Mark an earful about turning off his pager and cell phone. Then I told him about the power problem. After a couple of insincere apologies, he promised to get right on it. As I was hanging up, Scott Brandon emerged from the conference room.

He brought the forms back to me. I had time for a quick glance at his date of birth before the elevator pinged again and disgorged Craig Vincelli into the lobby.

"Here's the man you need to see," I said.

Was that a flash of regret in Brandon's eyes before he turned to face Vincelli? I hoped so.

I reluctantly turned Scott Brandon over to Craig, but I couldn't help watching them leave. Brandon looked just as good from behind as he did from the front. Nice shoulders, nice butt. Great ad for tight jeans. I did the mental math on his age and came up with thirty-one. I hoped he landed the job.

The phone rang again. "Heather, where are you? We're going nuts down here." Janelle sounded even more upset than she had earlier

I explained why I hadn't been able to leave and told her I was on my way down.

"Go straight to Grantwood & Bethel's booth. Twenty-two eighteen. They're about to have a cow. No one's heard from Tim Bethel since last night. See if you can calm everybody down, maybe make some suggestions—" A crash sounded in the background, followed by several excited voices. "Oh, damn. Gotta go."

The call ended abruptly and I headed for the elevator.

What the heck was I going to tell Grantwood & Bethel? Even in D.C., a twelve-hour traffic jam wasn't likely. And people got lost all the time, but they usually found their way or asked for directions within an hour or two. Even the most stubborn, most all-powerful masters of their universes eventually threw in the scepter and consulted a map. Or a cop. Of course, people went missing periodically. Most of them showed up, eventually, with a good excuse. Those who did usually wondered what all the fuss was about. Some showed up with a solid blush and a lame excuse, but, sadly, a few turned up in the morgue.

I wasn't going to mention that to the G & B people.

When the elevator doors slid open at ground level, noise slammed into me like a hurricane-force wind. A thunderous concatenation of shoes on tile, rolling bags squeaking, and, above everything else, thousands of people talking and conducting negotiations, rose from the showroom floor. The engine of commerce makes an enormous racket.

The woman at the registration desk waved at me as I

passed. The missing Tina was there, too, gossiping with one of the temps handling check-ins. "There's no one in the main office upstairs," I told her. "If Janelle gets back there before you do, your ass is fried."

I saw Tina jump up but didn't watch her race for the elevator. Two other people stopped me to ask questions before I even reached the show floor, but I dealt with them quickly.

Commerce—or was it chaos?—was in full cry. I had to push through crowds of people to get to aisle twenty-two and then halfway up it to twenty-two eighteen. It was one of the medium-sized booths, taking up six spaces on the floor. When I handed my card to the sales rep who greeted me, he looked relieved and said he'd get his boss.

Two people emerged from a curtained-off area in the center of the booth: a man in his mid to late fifties and a woman in her late forties. Both had the polished professional look and engaging demeanor of long-time sales execs. The woman's hair was an elegant shade of chestnut, and her suit hung beautifully.

"Heather McNeil," I said, extending a hand. "I'm Janelle Addison's assistant. She asked me to get some more information from you. About a missing person."

Relief and annoyance crossed both faces. The man said, "Stan Grantwood, Co-CEO of Grantwood & Bethel. This is Ellen Spencer, our executive vice president of marketing."

I shook hands with both of them.

"Come back here where we can talk privately," Grantwood said.

I followed them into the curtained-off area. The rear of their display unit formed one of the walls, and it helped dampen some of the noise outside. I declined the drinks they offered but pulled out a pad and pen to take notes.

"One of your people is missing?" I said, getting right to the point. I really didn't have time for small talk.

Both nodded. "Tim Bethel, my partner," Grantwood said. "We can't contact him. He checked into his hotel yesterday afternoon and came by here last night to make sure everything was in order. No one's heard from him since. We can't raise him on his cell phone, but it might be broken. The hotel doesn't know anything about him and he doesn't answer the phone in his room. We left a message there but it hasn't been returned. He hasn't contacted anyone back at the home office, either."

"Has anyone knocked on the door? Maybe he overslept?"

"It's not likely he overslept, but who knows? He's not staying at the same hotel as the rest of us."

"What hotel is it? I'll have someone go and check."

Grantwood gave me the name. When I asked for a room number, Ellen Spencer pulled out a piece of paper, glanced at it, and said, "Six-thirty-eight."

I wrote it down before continuing. "You're based in Cincinnati? Did he fly in?"

"Tim flew in from Seattle yesterday. He had a meeting with one of our suppliers there. Then he came straight here. His wife's flying in this afternoon, to meet him. That's one of the reasons he's not at the same hotel."

Something flashed across Ellen Spencer's face so quickly I nearly missed it. A frown or a sneer? Ellen didn't like the wife, or was it something else? Not that it really mattered, but I filed it away for possible future reference.

"So he got in yesterday, checked into his hotel and came here," I said. "What time was it, and who saw him here yesterday?"

Grantwood looked blank. Spencer said, "I don't know what time he arrived or checked in. It was about seven when he got here last night. We were putting the finishing touches on the booth and getting some last-minute items hashed out. We're going to be making a big announcement Saturday night."

"So you were here," I said to her, watching her reaction carefully. She didn't give anything more away. "Who else?"

"Two of the reps, Vickie Hanifan and Jason Welston. If you're looking for others who saw him, a couple of people were still in some of the other booths."

"Do you know what time he left?

"About eight, I think. They were shutting down the building."

"Did he say where he was going or what he planned to do?"

She shook her head.

"Where was everyone else?"

"In the bar at the Shelton where the rest of us are staying, I think. We had a dinner meeting at six. Tim didn't attend. After the meeting I came back here."

"Most of us went to the bar for some relaxation before the circus started," Grantwood said.

I nodded, looked at my notes, and sighed. A bad feeling about this had begun curling deep in my gut. "I'll have someone make inquiries right away," I said. "But if we don't find him pretty soon, we may have to bring in the authorities."

As I expected, alarm showed on the faces of both Grantwood and Spencer.

"I hope we don't have to do that," Spencer said.

At the same time, Grantwood said, "You think something might have happened to him?"

I merely said, "I'll get on it right now," then left the booth and searched for a quiet corner to make a call.

Craig answered on the second ring. "Did you hire Scott Brandon?" I asked, knowing he'd recognize my voice if not my number.

"Yeah. He starts tomorrow."

"Good. He doesn't have to work out notice?"

"He's currently underemployed."

"I wish he'd started today."

"Why? You interested? Not a good idea. Don't let the pretty face fool you."

I wanted to respond to that, but I had too much else on my mind. "Actually, I need the help. Did Janelle tell you one of the Grantwood & Bethel partners is missing? His name is Tim Bethel. I've got a bad feeling about it, and I need someone to knock on the door of his hotel room."

"Sorry, babe. It's just me and Randy supervising all the temps and rental cops. Not enough of them, either. We've got our hands way too full."

"I know, but maybe one of the temps?"

"Not likely."

I swallowed my annoyance as I ended the call. Throwing the phone at the wall would *not* be a good move. What now? My watch showed eleven o'clock. It wasn't that far to Bethel's hotel. I could walk there and still have plenty of time to smooth ruffled feathers when I got back. Maybe I could grab lunch from some place on the floor. A good thing my shoes were reasonably comfortable, despite the two-and-a-half-inch heels. Hated walking on concrete in them, though. On my salary I could only afford a new pair of good shoes every couple of years.

The day had turned mild for March, so I didn't bother to retrieve my coat. The three blocks would have been an easy walk if it weren't for two major streets and a construction zone. I debated stopping at the hotel desk, but I doubted they'd give me a key or tell me anything about the occupant of the room. Instead I went right up to the sixth floor.

I found the room and knocked several times. There was no answer. I pressed my ear to the panel but couldn't hear anything from inside the room. A glance along the corridor showed a service cart two doors down, with an open room door behind it.

I entered the room. "Hello?"

A woman in a maid's uniform leaned out of the bathroom. "You looking for someone?"

"Not in this room. Two doors down. Have you cleaned six-thirty-eight?"

"Yes, ma'am. Just a few minutes ago."

"There wasn't anyone there?"

The woman hesitated then shook her head.

"A man named Mr. Bethel is supposed to be staying in that room, and he didn't show up for work this morning. We were hoping he overslept."

She walked out of the bathroom. "Wouldn't think so. Don't look like nobody slept in that room last night."

"What do you mean?"

She glanced around, as if scared someone might leap out of the closet or from behind the drapes. "I ain't supposed to talk about the guests with anyone, but... Bed was still made up. Towels mostly all folded like I left them yesterday. Don't think he stayed there last night." She drew a breath. "Now, don't you go telling no one I told you this, you hear?"

"I won't. One more thing. Were there any suitcases in there? Had anyone been there at all?"

"Yeah, there's a suitcase in there. And a briefcase, too, best I recall. But I can't let you in to see."

"I don't need to go in. Just wanted to know if he was there." I waited to see if she'd add anything.

After a moment, she looked around again, then nodded for me to come closer. "Soap was unwrapped and a towel was on the counter. Only signs someone had been there. Shower clean and dry. No clothes lying around. Bed hadn't been used." She glanced at the door. "You didn't hear nothin' from me."

"Thank you," I said and turned to go, then dug in my purse and left a ten on her cart.

Now what? Where did an executive go if he wasn't in his hotel or at the trade show where his company would be handling millions of dollars' worth of orders? A tryst? Maybe last night, but not today. This guy was driven enough to help found a hugely successful company. And he'd left his briefcase in the room. An accident seemed more and more likely, or maybe something worse. How long did the police tell you to wait before reporting a missing person? Something like twenty-four hours?

My watch said ten to noon when I got back to the Market Center.

I phoned Janelle and told her I needed to talk to her right away. She promised to meet me in the snack bar in thirty minutes. "But first, talk to Savotsky," she said. "The woman will make a scene if you don't get her calmed down."

I sighed, ended the call, and went off to calm ruffled feathers. Sue Savotsky was a pain in the rear end, no other way to put it. But I'd watched Janelle for a while so I knew the drill. I listened and made soothing noises as Sue complained about her location, the neighbors' stuff crowding hers, the spots on the carpet, and the noise from the booth across the aisle. I figured there was no point arguing, no point in telling her that the neighbors' displays were crowding hers because her shelves sat half a foot into their space, no point reminding her that she could have— and should have—paid for a larger booth, which would have gotten her a better location. That would only bring more anger and verbal abuse.

So I let her vent, listening with half my brain, and promised to talk to the people across the way and ask them to turn down the music. I also promised to send a cleaning crew to work on the carpet stains, even though I could barely see them. Any positive action usually mollified Sue for a day or so.

I probably should have paid closer attention, but the more I thought about Tim Bethel's unused hotel room, the more worried I felt.

I was five minutes late getting to the snack shop. Janelle hadn't waited.

The manager called me over when he saw me come in. "Janelle had to go. Couple of calls came in." He glanced down at a paper where he'd scratched notes. "She asked me to tell you she'll meet you back here in an hour. Also wanted me to ask you to check on the receiving area. Someone complained about a bunch of cardboard scattered all over. It needs to be cleaned up."

I nodded. My stomach reminded me I hadn't had lunch, so I scarfed a hot dog while standing at the counter and took a bag of potato chips with me as I went back upstairs to the show floor. A mess in receiving shouldn't be as high a priority as a missing executive. I swung by the Grantwood & Bethel booth. A crowd of buyers filled the area, perusing G & B's lines of decorative statuary and picture frames. A couple of the knickknacks caught my eye, especially a pair of the most hideous little angel figurines I'd ever seen. The buyers, though, oohed and aahed over them. I've never claimed to have great taste, but I wouldn't give those chubby cherubs space on any shelf in my home.

Angels looked to be the hot item this year. I'd seen versions in a number of booths already.

I didn't see Grantwood, but Ellen Spencer stood with a bunch of buyers not far from me. She caught me looking a question at her and shook her head in the negative. Damn. We were only a few hours away from the twenty-four hours Tim had been missing. My stomach twisted into a knot.

We'd have to call the cops.

I stopped at another booth that was serving soft drinks, hoping a soda would settle my churning stomach. It meant I had to spend a few minutes talking to the people there, but since they were first-timers and excited about how many orders they'd already written, it wasn't a trial and only took up a few minutes.

The missing electrician, Mark, caught up with me at the end of aisle eighteen to tell me he'd restored power to aisles three to five and why it had failed. "Barrakind has this giant pinball game set up to get people to notice their booth," he explained. "I can't believe the frickin' things these guys do. I wonder how much that thing cost. Enough to feed my whole family for a week, I'll bet— even my brother Billy, the human garbage disposal. But they plugged it in, and ZWOOT! Shorted out and blew the breaker. Thing was a bitch to fix, too, let me tell you. Took me a couple of hours. Then I had to reset the breaker. Geez, the things these guys do." He shook his head.

I was inclined to agree with him about the absurdity of some of the gimmicks, but right then we didn't have time to dwell on the excesses of marketing notions. "Come with me. Janelle said someone complained about the receiving area being a mess."

"Sure, babe. Anything."

Damn! With all the other stuff on my mind, I'd forgotten about Mark's crush on me and his delusion that I was secretly madly in love with him. For the moment his crush was an asset, as long as he didn't manage to trap me in a dark corner for a little fooling around.

We ducked behind a curtain that walled off the exhibit area from the utility spaces. The loading dock was off to our right with the receiving area directly ahead. Two of the bay doors stood open, though no trucks were parked there right now. The openings admitted light and the fresh March air.

I plowed straight ahead into the storage area, narrowly avoided tripping over a crowbar lying on the floor, and saw what Janelle had complained about.

This was the area where most of the larger cartons and boxes were unpacked before the merchandise was loaded onto dollies and hand trucks to be carted off to the booths. The booths themselves often arrived packed in boxes, as well. There's a big rolling trash bin on the one side for packing materials, and we have signs posted all over encouraging people to take care of their own trash. Someone had a talent for ignoring signs.

Hard to describe what a complete disaster the area was. Sheets of cardboard littered the floor and stuck up at odd angles in places. In one corner, half a box formed a cozy little tent. Weird-shaped wads of tape sat like small animals traipsing through hills of torn-up cartons, and streamers of it hung off edges and corners. Slabs of Styrofoam cushioning mingled with the more environmentally friendly puffs of air-filled plastic. Bubble wrap popped loudly when Mark walked across a sheet of it.

"Day-um," he said. "Can't nobody read the signs?"

"Apparently not." I wasn't exactly dressed for housekeeping or maintenance chores, but who else was going to do it? Again I wished Vince had told that Scott Brandon guy to start today. If I ruined my silk blouse doing this, Janelle had better get the Center to reimburse me. I didn't expect my pantyhose to survive, which wouldn't be that much of a loss. At least I'd have an excuse not to wear them the rest of the day.

"Get the cart and let's start loading this stuff." It irked me to be doing this when there were so many other things I needed to do, but Janelle set the priorities. I pulled out the cell phone and called the head of maintenance to ask if he had anyone free to come help us. I had to invoke Janelle and her priorities, but he finally said he thought Sam could come down.

Sam's help was only slightly better than no help, but it was all I was going to get and I knew better than to sigh or be sarcastic. The wheels of the portable trash cart squeaked as Mark rolled it over and triggered a series of pops when they demolished another swathe of bubble wrap.

We loaded the trash into the cart. Not only did I have to take care not to tear up my clothes or get my heels caught in the junk, but I had to watch how I bent over because Mark was eyeing me all too closely.

Sam—tall, plain, and a tad slow in almost every respect—arrived within a few minutes. He surveyed the area, shook his head, and said, "Well, that's just plain rude!"

Mark said something a lot ruder about the ancestry of the perpetrators and looked up to take in Sam's reaction. Poor Sam didn't even realize Mark was baiting him. He responded by saying, "That's not nice."

"It isn't," I agreed, stabbing Mark with the nastiest warning look I could manage. I hate it when he needles Sam like that. "Get to work, guys."

For the next ten minutes or so, the three of us scraped up debris and tossed it into the cart. "Somebody was in a hell of a hurry or something to get their stuff unloaded," Mark commented as he pulled up a length of tape clinging to the floor. When the cart was full, Mark rolled it off to the loading dock where he could empty it into the big trash bin.

Sam and I continued to gather trash into a neat pile, awaiting Mark's return. It took him an awfully long time, a lot longer than it should have. The Dumpster sat on the ground outside and the dock was at truck-unloading height, so all he had to do was tip the cart and let the contents slide into the bigger trash container below.

"Hey, Mark," I yelled after a few minutes. "Find something interesting in there?"

There was no answer, so I returned to the main receiving area. Mark knelt on the edge of the loading dock, reaching into the bin.

"What are you doing?"

He jolted and nearly fell in. I leaned down to give him a hand, then froze as I caught a glimpse of what he stared at. Fortunately, he managed to right himself on his own.

"Heather," he said, his voice sounding weirdly choked, "I saw something shining...a watch, and I thought it must have fallen in there, and someone would be missing it, and—"

"Oh, my God!"

The watch was gold, expensive, and it gleamed in a ray of sunlight that shone on the trash bin. Unfortunately, it was still wrapped around a wrist. The hand attached to that wrist was large, masculine, and well kept. The fingers had tightened almost into a fist. A dark suit jacket covered the arm from just above the wrist to where it disappeared beneath a layer of trash. Near the metal sidewall of the container rested a shoe, a black wingtip, nearly new based on the condition of the heel. An appalling inch of pale skin shone between the dark sock and the bottom of dark suit trousers.

Then I saw the red stain that soaked a sheet of cardboard not far from the wrist. The smell hit me about the same time. Oh, shit! Oh, shit, oh, shit, oh, shit.

"I think we just found Grant & Bethel's missing executive." My voice sounded strange to me. I stepped back and fumbled for the cell phone, but my hands shook so badly it took three tries to flip it open.

TWO

I SPENT MORE than an hour and a half with the police, going over exactly what I'd done that morning. I related it to one of the officers who was first on the scene and then repeated it for the benefit of the detective who took charge a little later.

The only thing I hesitated over was telling them about the maid in the hotel and what she'd said to me. I didn't want to get her in trouble. But it looked pretty likely that Tim Bethel had been murdered, so I had to give it up.

They hadn't officially identified the body in the trash bin as Tim Bethel. But what were the odds it wasn't?

Janelle waited for me when I emerged from the conference room where I'd been speaking with the detective. I'd pretty much gotten over the shakes by then, but the image of the wrist and ankle wouldn't go away. I was glad to see Janelle and welcomed the sympathy on her face.

"You okay?" she asked.

"I guess."

She looked at my face and frowned. "No, you're not. Of course you're not. Let's get a cup of coffee. Unless—Do you want to go home?"

"No!" The word came out more sharply than I intended, betraying my state of nerves. "The last thing I want to do is sit around and think about it."

"Good." Janelle made no attempt to conceal her relief. "We'll have our hands full. Word's already getting around.

Damage control's sure to be a bitch. I'll find you some coffee while you hide out in my office for a few minutes."

I used the freight elevator so I wouldn't have to go through the show floor to the main ones. Tina looked up as I passed the reception desk and called my name, obviously eager to hear all the gossip, but I waved her off and continued down the hall to Janelle's office. I shut the door behind me and sank into one of her pair of upholstered armchairs.

My mind drifted, until the entry of Janelle roused me from uncomfortable musings about how the body had gotten into the trash bin.

"Got the good stuff," she said. "Triple V Designs has that big espresso maker running. I snagged us a couple of cappuccinos."

"You're a lifesaver."

She handed me one of the cups of steaming liquid. "You want some time alone to drink it?"

"No. Please, stay."

"Can't be long. I had to flip off a couple of people as it was."

"Understand. But I want to tell you about it."

Janelle took the chair opposite mine. I told her how we'd gone down to clean up the receiving area and Mark had found the body in the trash bin. I even told her how horrible it had been to see the man's wrist and ankle. And the blood. All the blood, soaking into the cardboard beneath the body.

"I'm so sorry you had to see that," Janelle said. "At least you didn't see his face. Stan Grantwood's gone to make a formal identification."

"Do they know what happened?"

She shrugged. "Cops aren't very communicative. But how likely is it he had an accident and just fell in?"

"Death by Dumpster diving? Ohmigod, that's awful. I'm sorry. But you're right. It doesn't sound like an accident."

Janelle studied me for a moment. "I won't tell you not to think about it. You can't help it. But I'm wondering if maybe you should see someone."

"Shrink?"

"Therapist."

"No. I'll get over it. It's not the first time I've seen blood. I'll work it out." I drank the rest of the coffee and set the cup down on the table. I felt better. Had more energy anyway. "I think I'm ready to get back to work. What are we telling people?"

"As little as possible. Heck, what do we actually know? We only think Tim Bethel is dead, his body found in the trash bin. My vote is to tell people we think it was some sort of accident. The detective didn't want me saying anything, but he doesn't understand that rumors spread faster than a grease fire in a place like this. It looks like an accident, but the police have to be thorough and they can't afford to make assumptions. We can't identify the victim, either. Once the cops identify him, they'll try to find his family and notify them, first."

"We're not considering canceling the show?"

"Not a prayer."

"But we're cooperating with the authorities to the best of our ability."

Janelle smiled. "You've got it." She shook her head. "I can't remember how I got along without you, Heather. But if you need time to get over this…"

"No, I'd rather stay busy. That way, when I have time to think again, I'll be able to handle it better."

"If you're sure." Janelle stood. "Time's wasting and people are talking."

HEAVENS ABOVE, were they ever talking. Janelle and I split up outside the show floor. I hadn't made it past the first booth when someone called my name. I turned to see a sales rep I recognized coming toward me. Two more people were right behind her, all with me in their sights.

"What's going on?" the woman asked. "Is it true someone was murdered? Someone we know? Who? And what happened? What's management doing about it?"

"Whoa." I held up a hand. "I see the rumor mill has been busy."

More and more people gathered, pressing in closer to hear me. I raised my voice. "Give me some space and I'll tell you what I know. It's not very much, though. Yes, someone has died. It was out by the loading dock, which is why the police have the area cordoned off. As far as anyone can tell, it was an accident, but the police always have to be cautious. We are very, very saddened by this unfortunate occurrence. No, I can't tell you who it is. The police need to contact relatives and let them know first."

A voice from the crowd called, "What's the Center doing about it? I hear someone was murdered."

I drew a breath and said, "The police have not said it was anything but an accident. But in case it wasn't, the Center is bringing in more security personnel." Well, we were. Scott Brandon was scheduled to start the next day. Then another thought occurred to me. "Keep in mind that you may not actually recognize the additional security personnel. Many of them will blend in."

People continued to yell questions at me. I can't remember how many times I said, "I don't know," but I'm pretty sure it was more than a dozen. I finished up with, "Please be assured we're doing all we can to ensure your safety and security. Now, let's get back to our real business: doing business."

I turned and walked away, pushing through the crowd and ignoring a couple who trailed after me, still lobbing questions. I picked up more people along the way, but managed to get two aisles over before I stopped and repeated my speech. I heard mostly the same set of questions, including off-the-wall ones about terrorists and bomb threats. *Bomb threats?* Where the heck had that come from?

My cell phone rang four or five times while I made my way across the show floor, covering several more aisles before Janelle and I met in the middle for one last round of reassurances.

After we'd finished our spiel, I managed to escape long enough to check my messages. The one from Janelle was probably irrelevant now. Mark had some questions about the loading dock; three calls from an increasingly frantic Tina concerned about some paperwork she couldn't find; and the last one was from my sort-of, sometimes boyfriend, Chris Horton.

I returned calls in order, told Mark to stay away from the loading dock until the cops were finished with it, told Tina where to find the papers she needed, and explained yet again to Chris that I'd be working late this week and couldn't have dinner with him until after the show ended on Sunday. Sheesh.

My phone buzzed. "We've got one more mission," Janelle said, "and I need moral support for this one."

I joined her near the end of aisle twenty-two hundred.

"Carl Roney from MCEI is heading down here first

thing in the morning," Janelle told me as we threaded our way through the crowds to Grantwood & Bethel's booth, waving off people who tried to intercept us.

Market Centers and Events, Inc., MCEI, owned the C & M Show Center and a dozen more facilities around the country. "Roney…executive vice president?"

"You got it, hon. My boss. The fun never ends." We stopped in front of the booth. "Deep breath."

Ellen Spencer was talking to someone when we got there, but broke off when she saw us and came over. "Stan's inside. This has really thrown us. We're trying to carry on, but…" Her words trailed off as her lips momentarily quivered. Ellen appeared composed, but the brittle tension of her face and the way her hands shook as she picked up a pen showed how fragile her mask was.

"It was Tim?" Janelle asked quietly.

Ellen jerked a nod as she led the way back into the curtained-off area where I'd talked to her the first time.

Grantwood was on his cell phone, but ended the call when he saw us. His eyes looked puffy and red, as though he'd been rubbing them, and his expression was strained and tense.

"I'm sorry to bother you right now," Janelle said. "I know this has to be a bad time for you, but I wanted to say how terribly sorry we all are about what happened. If there's anything, anything at all, we can do to help, please feel free to call on us."

Grantwood stared at the table between us while Janelle spoke but looked up as she finished. He focused on her face with an effort. "I'm having a hard time absorbing this. I can't believe he's gone. We've worked together for more than ten years. It's all about to pay off, too." He brushed a hand down his face, rubbing his eyes in the process.

"Are we going ahead with it?" Ellen asked him.

He took a deep breath and let it out slowly. "We'll tone down the party for the announcement. Do some sort of memorial for Tim. I can't even make my brain think about it right now. But we'll go ahead with the merger. Tim worked as hard on it as I did. Harder, in fact. This company was his baby, even more so than it was mine. It would dishonor him if we didn't go ahead with it."

"This is the party you're giving Saturday night?" Janelle asked.

He nodded. "We wanted to finish off this market with a bang. It's big, maybe the biggest thing that's happened in the industry in the past few years. I just can't believe Tim won't be here to see it. After all his work."

Grantwood's face changed, eyes and lips narrowing. He made a fist and brought it down hard on the nearest flat surface, a cheap folding table. It promptly did its namesake function. Legs crumpled awkwardly and the whole thing crashed to the floor. Papers, pencils, markers, candy-bar wrappers, and his cell phone all scattered.

We each bent down to retrieve some of the things. The phone had skidded to my left and ended up by my purse, still flipped open. I hoped it hadn't broken since it looked like an expensive model, blade-thin and gleaming.

I picked it up, along with a couple of cheap pens that bore the imprint of Grantwood & Bethel. Something sticky was smeared along the side of one of the pens.

Carefully handling the phone so that whatever was on my fingers wouldn't smear it, I was gratified to see that the screen still shone brightly and displayed a couple of numbers for incoming calls. The last four digits of one looked familiar, which wasn't any surprise, considering we worked in the same industry.

As I held the phone out to Grantwood, I said, "It's still working."

He flipped it closed without looking at it. He had control of his anger now, but it was a thin and precarious control.

"I'm sorry, ladies," he said quietly, the words a bit stretched out.

Without being too obvious, I pulled out a tissue and rubbed the sticky substance off my fingers. It looked like chocolate.

Janelle said, "We understand. And I meant what I said before. If there's anything we can do to help, please call us."

Ellen Spencer turned to Janelle and said, "Last we heard, the police still hadn't been able to reach Tim's wife, so please don't let it out yet. I haven't seen her, either, which is kind of odd. She was supposed to meet him here today."

"Maybe there was a change of plans and he forgot to mention it," I suggested.

She shrugged. "Maybe." The word was flat, toneless, maybe tired. She looked so tense it wouldn't take more than a touch to shatter her control.

Janelle and I emerged from the curtained-off area to see booths being shut down and displays locked down for the night. I glanced at my watch. Six-twenty. It stunned me. So much had happened, I'd gone into some kind of automatic overdrive that took no notice of time passing or my body getting tired. Probably the overdose of caffeine in my last cup of coffee.

It was wearing off.

I went upstairs with Janelle to get my bag. There were various "kickoff" parties going on that evening, but I probably wouldn't have gone to them even if it hadn't been the kind of day it had. I liked to conserve my party energy for the bigger, more formal and more important events coming later. In any case, tomorrow promised to be an even bigger bitch than today and I needed whatever rest I could get.

It was nearly eight by the time I got off the Metro at the Bethesda station. Fortunately, I only had to walk a couple of blocks to my apartment and the way was well lit. I normally managed to resist the temptation of the fast-food places I had to pass to get home.

But not tonight. I had no energy for preparing anything, not even pouring instant salad out of the bag into a bowl. Besides, I needed comfort food. I needed hot, salty, greasy, delicious french fries. And chicken nuggets. With lots of barbecue sauce. I ate in the store. There were only a few people in the place, but just knowing they were around brought an odd comfort.

I expected to have trouble sleeping, but I was so tired I fell into bed about twenty minutes after I reached my apartment, and that was it.

I woke at four-thirty the next morning, more than an hour before I needed to, and began to gird myself for a day that promised to bring a major headache—and probably several other sorts of aches.

THREE

I REACHED the Center a little past seven, way earlier than needed, but what else was I going to do when I was awake, showered, hair-dried, dressed, and in possession of a triple-shot venti cappuccino?

I had a key to one of the service entrances but rarely used it since the main doors were generally open by the time I arrived. At seven-ten they were locked, gated, and alarmed. Unfortunately, the entrance my key fit was on the far side of the building. Since the Market Center takes up an entire large city block, it was a long walk around.

An eerie quiet prevailed. The ever-present city traffic was beginning to increase, but the usual cacophony of motors and horns and sirens remained muted. A cool mist hung in the air, starting to dissipate as the sun brightened. Only one other person walked the sidewalk, and she was across the street.

The tap of my heels on concrete seemed to echo in the early-morning emptiness.

I felt alone in the world, an odd sensation and—given what the day promised to be like—a pleasant one. I was totally unprepared to round the corner and all but run into a man coming toward me from the other direction. I managed to swing my hand with the coffee out of harm's way, just in time.

We stopped just inches apart. He grunted in surprise, stepped back first, and said, "Heather…McNeil, wasn't it?"

"Yes. Scott? Craig said he'd hired you, but what are you

doing here so early? Didn't he tell you we start work at eight? The building doesn't even open until seven-thirty."

He shrugged, drawing my attention to the broad shoulders encased in a battered leather jacket. Something about the guy set my hormones fizzing. Sexual charisma, I suppose, whatever that is. I glanced at his face. Definitely compelling. He had a sharp, narrow jaw. His nose's lack of symmetry suggested it had been broken, and his thin mouth appeared mean until he smiled. It added up to a man who looked hard, cold, and tough. I hadn't thought that way yesterday, but maybe he'd tried to make a good impression. After all, he was applying for a job.

He held himself with a tense alertness. It gave him the air of someone always on guard against attack.

At first he didn't answer my question about being early, but I waited, and finally he said, "I like to check out places where I'm going to work. To figure the lay of the land."

"You've done security work before?"

He nodded.

"Good. We're going to need all the help we can get. Today may be a rough start for you. Did Craig tell you about—"

"The body in the trash can? I saw it on the news last night. Was that, by any chance, your missing executive?" He focused sharply on me. His eyes were neither green nor gray nor blue but some of each. Nice eyes but cool.

I couldn't handle that stare right now, so I turned and headed for the side door. "Come with me. I've got a key. Yes, it was our missing executive."

He walked beside me. "Any idea what happened?"

"The police haven't said much about it."

"The news report said it was being treated as a criminal investigation."

I stopped for a moment, surprised to hear that confirmed

so soon. "I guessed it would be," I said, more to myself than to him.

"Why?"

We reached the door and I put the key in the lock. He pushed it open and followed me inside.

"If it were an accident," I said, "why would my missing executive end up with cardboard and stuff on *top* of him?"

"God, don't tell me *you* found the body."

"I found the body. Or Mark and I did."

"Who's Mark?"

"Maintenance. You'll meet him this morning. We were cleaning the loading-dock area. He actually spotted it first. I came to find out why he wasn't doing anything and I saw it, too."

Scott had moved ahead of me in the corridor but stopped and turned. His expression softened to show regret and sympathy. A bit of warmth melted some of the ice in his eyes. "I'm sorry. That must have been brutal."

"Ranks right up there with trips to the dentist on the list of experiences I'm not eager to repeat."

His lips quirked. "I think I'm going to like you, Heather McNeil."

I rolled my eyes. "My day is made. And it's not even seven-thirty in the morning." I led the way to the elevator. "On the other hand, the day is destined to go downhill."

"Why?"

"You ever worked a trade show before?"

"I did security at one of the Christmas shows here a couple of years ago."

"Not exactly the same thing."

"How so?"

The elevator arrived. I punched the button for the third floor. "The Christmas shows are like public fairs or higher-class flea markets. A trade show is a completely different animal. It's about manufacturers and importers selling their product to the retailers. They show their latest and greatest product to the retail buyers and hope the buyers decide they can sell a zillion of them to the public. A lot rides on this show for the manufacturers. Retailers sell to the public all the time, so a bad day or even a bad weekend isn't going to kill them. But the retailers only go shopping for the stuff they sell a few times a year, mostly at these shows. They buy their product in huge lots, at the show or soon after. For the exhibitors, this is when they make the bulk of their sales, and there are only a few big shows a year. So the stakes are really high. A good show can make their business. A bad one can break it."

The bell pinged, doors opened, and we got out.

"They're going to be unhappy about anything that distracts or scares off their customers," Scott said as I worked the key into the lock of the main office door.

"You got it. Most put a huge amount of money into exhibits and parties and all that. Naturally they want everything to go perfectly. Anything that interferes with the smooth flow of the show could cost them business.

"To keep things on edge, you have a group of people who've worked in the industry a long time. They know each other. They're friends, competitors, enemies, lovers, sometimes all of those in one package. Think of the show as Vegas on steroids *and* amphetamines. Some of these people are walking a thin line. It doesn't take much to send them into a frenzy."

He followed me into the office. "You realize the police are going to start questioning people. Even if it was an accident. Without witnesses, they're going to have to treat it as a suspicious death."

"I know. And that's only one of the issues. Gossip spreads faster than spilled coffee around here. And the stories get bigger and badder along the way. Three hours after I'd found Tim, people were shouting bombers and terrorists. This morning we may be into alien invasions."

"Terrorists?"

"People love to make a good story better." I turned on the lights and put my purse away in my desk. "Want some coffee? I'll give you a quick tour of the office while it brews."

I set up the coffee maker, and I showed him the third-floor offices. It didn't take all that long. Most of us work in the big open area just off the elevator lobby. By the time he and I returned to my office, the coffee pot was full. I heard the elevator ping as Scott poured himself a cup, and we met Janelle on our way back to the front.

"You're up early," she commented as she saw me, before her gaze slid to the man behind me.

"Woke up at four-thirty and knew I wasn't going to get back to sleep," I said. Then I introduced Janelle to Scott, telling her he'd been hired to help out with security, and how I'd met him yesterday and then this morning on the way into the building.

I realized how distracted Janelle was when she barely glanced at Scott. Janelle was divorced and in her early forties, but she wasn't averse to pursuing younger men.

"I've got a statement ready to distribute," she said, "but I need to find out if the police have released an identification."

"I'll call. I've still got the card the detective gave me yesterday."

She nodded. "Warm up the printer and make sure it's loaded with paper. I want to get this out in the booths before anyone gets here."

"I'll do that while Heather calls," Scott said.

Janelle gave him a longer look this time, before she thanked him, and hustled into her office.

When I called, the detective who'd interviewed me yesterday wasn't in the office yet. They switched me over to someone who said the police had notified Tim Bethel's family and could confirm he was the deceased.

"Do you know the cause of death?" I asked.

"I'm sorry but I'm not at liberty to say."

I pretty much expected that, so I thanked her and hung up.

I relayed the information to Janelle. She, Scott, and I were the only ones in the office. We stood around watching the printer spit out copies of the statement until we had a good pile. Janelle sent Scott and me downstairs with a stack of sheets to start distributing.

The silence on the show floor was kind of eerie, given how chaotic it would become in an hour or so. Scott and I took different aisles, so we didn't get to talk as we went up and down, leaving copies in each booth. By the time Janelle handed me the rest of the sheets, a few exhibitors had begun to arrive. The clatter as they dusted, cleaned, removed covers, and set out the racks, candy dishes and baskets of pens began to churn up the quiet.

I managed to avoid conversation, but when I left a paper at Gruber's Exchange, Andy Tarantoro, their VP of sales, put down his pen and looked up at me. I swallowed a sigh as he approached. I liked him, but Lordy, he could talk. At least I'd rehearse answering questions. I figured I'd be doing it a lot in the next few hours.

"I heard a rumor," Tarantoro said. "About Tim Bethel. That something happened yesterday, and he's no longer with us."

"It's true." I pushed the paper I'd left toward him. "Our statement about it is here."

He didn't seem interested in the written words. "He's really dead?" Tarantoro was a big man, both in height and bulk, but he moved with a grace and care that belied his size. He could shuffle among the shelves of porcelain figurines and other delicate bric-a-brac Gruber's produced with surprisingly little danger to the merchandise. His soft voice and hesitant manner also came oddly from his large frame, but they were the truth of him. Last year, I'd spent an hour or so admiring pictures of the grandchildren he adored and listening to his stories of their accomplishments.

"I'm afraid he's really dead."

Tarantoro shook his head, dislodging a few strands of unnaturally jet-black hair. "I can't wrap my mind around it. And now of all times."

"During the show?"

"Yes." He looked around. "More than that," he said, lowering his voice. "The rumors said they were about to make it big. They were merging with— Well, I guess I shouldn't say. I don't even know for sure. But if the rumors are right, it's going to be big. If they still go through with it. There are some people wouldn't mind if the deal fell through, I hear."

"Really? What's the story?"

He chewed his lip a moment. "I really shouldn't spread gossip, so please don't tell anyone about this, but rumor says they're merging with Gaviscelli, which would make them the 800-pound gorilla of the trade. Naturally some competitors are less than thrilled."

"You?"

"Could be competition for us, but we've got our licensing deal with Kristian Grange all sewn up. She does such beautiful work it should take care of us for the next few years. Look here." He walked over to a glass-enclosed display case, opened it, and took out a pendant made of dozens of hair-thin strands of clear crystal woven into a graceful, elaborate, rainbow-scattering icicle. He held it up so that it twirled gently and sparkled.

"It's lovely." I wasn't lying or even stretching the truth. It was fragile, delicate, beautiful, and it probably cost more than the entire contents of my jewelry box.

He nodded and smiled. "We wrote over a million dollars' worth of orders for these yesterday," he said. "We took this pendant out of the vault the night before last. Only three people had seen it before then. No one else here has anything quite like it. Yet."

"It's going to be wildly popular this Christmas."

"And next year everyone will have a version of it. We hope Kristian will come up with another amazing design before then."

I sighed in commiseration. "Knockoffs are a real pain, aren't they?"

He nodded. "Yesterday I caught a guy trying to take pictures of this with his cell phone. He acted like he'd just stopped to answer it, but I could see what he was up to. They'll have crappy plastic imitations in the cheapo-marts by Christmas."

"But they won't be as lovely as these."

"No, but they'll still cost us sales. Not everyone will buy high-end when there's a cheap version that looks almost as good. Buyers know that. But the specialty and high-end buyers know their clients will pay for quality and a genuine Kristian Grange."

The noise around us increased. I looked at my watch and realized the doors would open in a few minutes.

"I'm sorry, but I've got to distribute the rest of these flyers before the hall opens."

"Stop by again when you get the chance, and I'll show you some other special things we have."

"I will, thank you."

"Wait. Before you go. I've got something for you." He reached into a box hidden behind a display unit and brought out a pen. "Our special pens for this year. I thought of you when I saw them."

He handed me a four-inch-long oval object that wasn't immediately identifiable as a pen. I stared at it, a bit puzzled.

"Press the black button," Tarantoro said.

When I did, the body split open into two wings over a center pen point. The wings folded back and fit together, making a sleek full-sized pen.

"Way cool," I told him.

He smiled at my enthusiasm. I was touched that he remembered how much I liked unusual pens.

"I'd better get back to work," I said. "Thanks for this."

He waved me off with a flourish.

As I reached the end of the row, my cell phone buzzed.

"Security issue," Janelle said. "I'm tied up for the moment, but they need management at the aisle-fourteen door."

"On my way." I quickly dropped flyers onto display tables at the remaining booths and hustled to the entrance.

The temporary security people who manned the doors and kept the curious public from wandering in had stopped a woman with a dog. They were trying to explain to her that pets weren't allowed on the show floor.

The official show pass in its plastic holder said she was a buyer from Greenwich, Connecticut. She was maybe fifty and fighting it with every weapon at her disposal, but either long-term smoking or sun worship or both had worked on her skin to the point where even the recent face-lift hadn't removed all the damage. A small white, fuzzy dog with a pink bow in its hair nestled in her arms, close to her heart.

I spent a few minutes explaining to her why pets weren't allowed on the trade-show floor unless they were official assist animals.

She had tears in her eyes. "But Spiffy goes everywhere with me. I don't know what I'd do without him. He's practically an employee at the store. Our official greeter. He loves people and he's very well trained."

Spiffy? "That's wonderful," I said. "And he does seem like a real sweetie. In fact, he seems well trained enough to qualify for this wonderful pet-sitting service I know. They're just around the corner, but they're very exclusive and careful about which babies they'll take. If I tell them how sweet he is, they might be willing to take care of him for you while you're at the show. Would you like me to call and see if they would consider him? I can't guarantee it, you understand. They're very picky and they usually like to check pets out before they'll accept any of the very special babies they care for, but I think if I asked them, they'd be willing to make an exception for Spiffy."

The woman's expression smoothed out and she smiled. "It does sound like they would take good care of Spiffy."

"Oh, they would," I assured her. "I can guarantee it. Let me give them a call."

Because we ran up against this problem often enough to provide them considerable business, I'd become friendly with the owner of the pet-sitting service a block away. As expected, the owner said she'd be more than happy to take the animal and would even send someone to pick him up. I told her where to find us and ended the call.

As I did so, the phone buzzed again.

"Heather? I hate to keep you running around, but could

you come up here for a couple of minutes? Someone wants to talk to you." Janelle sounded frazzled.

"Be right there," I told her. I gave one of my cards to Spiffy's owner. "Wait here and someone will come to take care of Spiffy for you. If you have any doubts or questions, give me a call. But I know these people very well, and you can trust that he'll get the best of care. In fact, you'll be lucky if they don't spoil him rotten."

"Oh, he already is," she admitted as I headed for the elevator.

Janelle looked almost as frazzled as she'd sounded, but there was something else in her expression, too. A tiny gleam of something else I couldn't quite put my finger on. Some sort of excitement?

A man rose from one of the chairs facing her desk. I hadn't been able to see him until I got a couple of steps into the office.

"Heather, you remember Detective Gilmont? You talked to him yesterday."

I nodded. In truth I remembered that I'd talked to him, but not much more than that. I'd still been too deep in shock to take in details, so I'd missed a few things worth noting. Although he had to be in his forties, he was still good-looking. A bit above medium height and lean. Dark hair with a smattering of gray at the temples. Some lines on his face, but they didn't look mean. He had an air of toughness without the harshness.

He stuck his hand out and I shook it. "Miss McNeil? You seem a bit more composed this morning. Yesterday was a terrible shock for you, but you've recovered well."

I wished. "With the Gift Show going on, I don't have time to come unglued. I'm saving the nervous breakdown for when it's all over."

He laughed and it sat nicely on his face.

Janelle grinned and added, "We all get to indulge in a round of hysterics if we survive until Monday."

Detective Gilmont's brow creased as he looked at me again. "Miss McNeil, if you wouldn't mind, I'd like to ask you a few more questions."

It wasn't really a request, but I appreciated the way he couched it so politely.

"You can use the office," Janelle said. "I've got to double-check the press releases."

As she left, I saw Detective Gilmont's gaze follow her. Then he turned to me again.

"Sorry to take up your time," he said, "but there are a couple of things I need you to clear up for me."

"Not at all. I'm glad for the opportunity to sit down and take a deep breath."

A small smile curved his lips. "Janelle told me about how huge this show is and how it keeps you all hopping. I know that a murder investigation is the last thing you need right now."

"Actually, the last thing we needed was a murder. Since we've had one, we definitely need the investigation. In fact, the faster you can figure out who did it and make an arrest, the happier it will make everyone."

"I understand that. But people aren't going to enjoy the process of the investigation."

I sighed, thinking about the complaints I was going to endure. "No."

"But it's necessary."

I nodded.

"I'd like to go back to yesterday for a few minutes," he said. "I apologize that this will bring back memories you'd rather not think about, but there are a couple of points I need to clear up."

"Okay."

"Again, what did you see when you went into the shipping-and-receiving area?"

I told him about the mess, the cardboard everywhere, the gobs of tape and bubble wrap.

He jotted a few lines in a small notebook. "Did you happen to see a crowbar?"

"Crowbar? Oh! I forgot about that. I didn't exactly see it. I nearly tripped over it."

"Nearly?"

"I hit it with my foot and almost fell, but I caught myself at the last minute."

"Did you touch it or pick it up?"

I thought back. "No."

"You said Mark Templeton and Sam Boresi helped you clean up. Did you see either of them touch the crowbar?"

"No, but one of them must have. I remember looking out for it when I walked back to see what Mark was doing, but it wasn't there."

He scribbled more notes.

I thought about his questions. "Was it the murder weapon? How many sets of fingerprints did you find on it?"

Gilmont stared at me for a moment, his expression hardening. "Sorry, but I can't confirm or tell you anything."

I shivered. Had I said his expression didn't look harsh? For a moment it did—just long enough to make me glad I wasn't a criminal.

"You're not getting ideas about playing detective, are you?" he asked.

"Me? I wouldn't have the time, even if I had the inclination. It's just I can't help thinking about things and trying to make sense of them."

His expression lightened again, but not to where it had been at the start of the conversation. "Don't think too much about it," he advised. "Leave that to us."

"Be more than happy to."

"Good." He smiled. "Janelle said I should cultivate you. That you could help us."

"She did? How could I help?"

"She said people talk to you. They tell you things."

I wasn't sure what to say to that. "People seem to dump all their stuff on me. I guess I'm a good listener."

"If you hear anything you think would help us, like who hated Tim Bethel, would you please let me know?" He pulled out a business card and wrote another number on it. "This is my cell-phone number. Call me if anything comes up that might shed some light."

I took the card from him and promised I would.

"Thank you," he said. "Now, do you have a way to get hold of Mark Templeton?"

I pulled out the phone and pressed the speed-dial number for Mark. He answered on the second buzz and said he'd be right there. While we waited, Detective Gilmont—the card indicated his first name was Peter—questioned me about the show and trade shows in general. I found myself repeating much of what I'd told Scott Brandon earlier about how they worked and the differences between trade-only and public shows.

Mark appeared a few minutes later, and I excused myself. Then I stopped by my desk to check voice and email messages. I made notes about a few things, left a couple of messages myself, and walked down to the show floor.

My first stop was Triple V Designs and their espresso maker. I needed a caffeine refill. As I took the first sip, someone called, "Heather!" I turned.

"Lisa." I didn't have to fake my enthusiasm at seeing her. Lisa Willamont was a rep with Poncy, one of the bigger agencies. She was also one of the nicest people I'd met at any trade show. "I didn't realize Triple V was a Poncy client."

"One of our newest," Lisa said. "I'm still learning the product lines. Just between us, trying to keep the permanent botanicals straight is driving me crazy. I'm so not into gardening."

"You'll get it." She would, too. Nature or fate or God had blessed Lisa abundantly. Not only was she tall, blond, slender, and gorgeous, she was one of the sharpest tacks on the wall. I could have hated her if she weren't so damned nice. Still, I sometimes had to work to fend off the tweaks of jealousy, even though we were good friends.

She sighed. "Eventually I'll learn the petunias from the pansies." She glanced around, but the booth was quiet, except for a pair of buyers who discussed pots of faux freesias with a Triple V employee. Lisa gestured toward a table at the side. "I need to pump you."

We took our coffee to the plastic table. Lisa sighed as she sat. "Ten-thirty and already my feet are killing me. I don't know how I'm going to make it through the day. You were smart." She glanced at my shoes. I'd gone for comfort today. My low-heeled shoes were well cushioned, as well as decently attractive, but they looked pedestrian next to her designer slingbacks. I didn't envy her the three-inch heels, though.

"Survival," I said. "I'll be on my feet all day and into the night."

"Me, too." She sighed. "But anyway, fill me in. The rumors are running wild. I know Tim Bethel is dead and the Center is saying causes unknown, but the cops are interviewing people, so it's probably not an accident. Was he murdered? That's the favorite theory, but the motives are, like, all over the place."

I considered what I had a right to say. "I don't know.

He's dead, and it was ugly, but the police aren't saying if it was an accident or murder yet."

"Not too many people are going to mourn his passing," Lisa said. "He didn't much care who he trampled."

"I never met him. Don't know anything about the man other than what I'm hearing. So dish the dirt and give me the picture."

Lisa grinned and raised light eyebrows expertly filled in with perfectly matched color. "Whoa, how about your dirt? You spill what you know and I'll dish what I've got. That work for you?"

"Deal."

Lisa took a sip of her coffee, smiled, and closed her eyes. "Good coffee compensates for a lot." She opened her eyes and sighed. "You first."

I told her what I could about cleaning up the receiving area and Mark's finding the body in the trash bin. I didn't say anything about the crowbar, since I had a feeling Detective Gilmont wouldn't appreciate it. I didn't mention the watch, either, though I did tell her about seeing his shoes, the blood, and the pale stretch of ankle. She understood how that sight of actual human flesh had gotten to me, making it way too real, somehow.

"I'm so sorry, Heather," she said when I finished. "That must have been horrible. Were you able to sleep at all last night?"

"I fell asleep but woke up at four-thirty, and that was it."

She eyed me. "Are you going to the Blaise Foundation party tonight?"

"Of course."

"Good. I'm buying you a couple of drinks and sending you home in a taxi."

"By then I'll be in no shape to object."

"I mean it. Guess it's my turn." She took another sip and twirled the cup gently.

I doubted she'd tell me all she knew or suspected about Tim Bethel, any more than I'd told her all I knew. Lisa knew how to respect trade secrets and confidential information.

"Tim Bethel is—sorry, was—an ambitious, chauvinistic, attractive, charming, traitorous son of a bitch. He'd promise you anything to your face, then turn around and stab you in the back. Always had his eye fixed firmly on the main chance. He tried to maneuver every attractive female he met into bed and everyone else into the short end of some deal. He could be so damned charming people would go along with him for a while. But just about everyone who dealt with him for more than a few days ended up hating him."

"His partner?"

"Grantwood? I don't know. There are rumors."

"Saying?"

Lisa shrugged. "Stan Grantwood and Tim didn't agree on everything, and Tim ended up winning every argument. That had to irk Stan, wouldn't you think?"

"It would bug the heck out of me."

"Me, too."

"Rumor has it they're going to announce a merger of some kind Saturday night. Have you heard anything about who they're marrying?"

"There seem to be two main candidates. Everyone thinks Gaviscelli would be a good fit because the product lines would be complementary. Gaviscelli would love to get their hands on G & B's collectible lines, especially the Angaro and Roberta Harrison collections. I think those two lines have been keeping G & B afloat. And Gaviscelli has the Far East production facilities already in place, while G & B has just begun to take their stuff overseas. Only fly in the ointment is that Dave Powell of Gaviscelli wouldn't want to relinquish control in a merger, and he's probably in a better position than either Tim or Stan to maintain power. Stan could likely handle it but not Tim."

She stopped for another sip of coffee. "The other possibility is Kirshorn's."

"Isn't that the outfit that does those glass plaques and bottles?"

"And lots of ceramic figurines and some designer jewelry. Word is the company's shaky and needs the boost G & B's lines would give them. Kirshorn's has become a bit stodgy. But that outfit is Irv Kirshorn's baby and he'd be reluctant to share or let go control, so who knows how they'd bring it off."

She shrugged. "Or it could end up being someone else entirely."

A trio of well-dressed women in their early forties stopped to discuss the tabletop fountains on a corner display of the Triple V booth, and Lisa went on alert. We both stood up. Time for her to get back to work.

"I'll see you later," I said.

She nodded, but her attention was already focused on the potential customers.

I got stopped twice before I reached the end of the aisle and had to explain over and over that the police weren't sure about the means of Tim Bethel's death and whether or not it had been an accident. No one wanted to believe it might have been an accident. They preferred to speculate on who might have killed him and why. There seemed no lack of possibilities, confirming what Lisa had said about Tim Bethel's popularity.

Near the end of that row of booths, a nasty smell assailed my nose. Burnt popcorn. No doubt coming from the Blue Hills booth just ahead, which featured a movie theater–sized machine dispensing buttered popcorn into paper containers. Yeeks. I hurried to get past as quickly as I could.

No such luck.

Two people stepped out of booths opposite Blue Hills and moved into the aisle, blocking my passage. Their angry, determined expressions told me they had more than polite pleasantries on their minds. I stifled a sigh. I had a bad feeling this had something to do with the nauseating aroma permeating the area. What could I tell them? We tolerated a lot here at the Center in the interests of letting our exhibitors sell their products in whatever way they preferred. But still, this was going a bit far, and I sympathized with the people who had to live with it.

I sympathized but couldn't actually do much about it.

For a moment I indulged in a fantasy of walking off the floor and taking a job as a kayak guide, my favorite summer job during college. Just because it paid squat and only operated four months a year didn't mean it was a bad job for anyone other than a student. You never got complaints about the carpet being dirty or the power out or a neighbor's lights shining the wrong way on merchandise.

The man who'd stopped me said, "Miss McNeil? You're Ms. Addison's assistant, right?"

Before I could confirm it, he launched into his tirade. "I can't believe you allow this nuisance on the show floor." He flailed an arm in the direction of the popcorn machine. "It would be bad enough if it worked right and we had to put up with the smell of popcorn all day long. But the damn thing must not be right since it smells burnt all the time. It's disgusting. In fact, it's damned sickening and it's driving traffic away. Well, hell, would you want to stand here for more than a second or two if you didn't have to?

Even my salespeople have to take breaks to get away from it for a while."

He stopped for air, and the woman beside him took up the cause. "It's driving all our customers away. They can't stand to be here and I don't blame them! Surely there's some rule about having a nuisance like this. Can't you do something about it?"

I drew a deep breath. Mistake. I got a snootful of burnt-popcorn smell, which made my stomach start to roil. "I sympathize," I told them. "I really do. Let me see what I can do. If they're not willing to cooperate, I'll consult with Janelle and see what steps we can take."

The man who'd stopped me stared at me for a couple of long moments, making me worry that he'd demand more immediate action.

"It's all I can do right now," I said.

The man drew a long breath and sighed. "All right."

The woman behind him frowned.

Neither was mollified. Nothing short of me going over there and pulling the plug would make them really happy.

I sympathized, but I couldn't do that—yet. Though I really wanted to be out of there, I turned and headed for the Blue Hills booth.

I asked for the person in charge, and in a moment I was introduced to the company president, a petite red-headed woman with an expression like dynamite set to explode.

"We're getting complaints about the smell of your popcorn machine," I told her, after we'd done the polite niceties. "It appears the machine needs servicing since it definitely smells like it's burning the product. It's becoming a nuisance. If you can't get it fixed, you'll have to turn it off."

Spots of color showed in the woman's cheeks. "The

man who brought it and set it up assured us it was working perfectly. I don't see any problem."

"You can't smell that problem?"

She drew a sharp breath. "I don't smell anything."

"Your nose is probably too used—" My phone buzzed. The caller ID said it was Janelle. I sighed and speared the other woman with the sternest look I could manage. "It's driving everyone around you crazy. Get someone to check the machine. Today. Or we'll have to unplug it." I turned and walked away so I could take the call.

"Sorry to keep yanking you around," Janelle said. "But I'm up here with Carl Roper, who got in a few minutes ago. There's something going on at Grantwood & Bethel again. Can you go see what it's about? I'm guessing it has to do with funeral arrangements, but I'm not sure."

"I'm on my way," I said. I couldn't tell her how little I wanted to go there. *Kayaks. Drifting along on the rushing current of a cool, deep mountain river.*

Education debt, the more rational half of my brain countered. *A car, soon. A nice house in the suburbs someday.*

Ellen Spencer grabbed me the moment I came into sight of their booth and took me right to the private area in back. Stan Grantwood sat at the folding table, working on papers, but he looked up when we came in.

Annoyance crossed his face, followed by resignation. "I told you it was nothing, Ellen. Not something we need to worry about. I never should have said anything about it."

I stared at Stan, then Ellen. "About what?"

"Stan got a threatening phone call," she said.

FOUR

"WHEN?" THE WORD came out sharper than I intended. "How?"

Grantwood looked at Spencer again. "By phone. This morning."

"Cell phone? Did you recognize the number?"

He shook his head. "The booth phone. It doesn't have caller ID."

Each booth had a phone hookup. Though nearly everyone carried a cell phone these days, service could be iffy inside the building. The booth units provided a backup and were useful for some contacts, especially for checking with home offices and manufacturing facilities and for letting potential customers find them.

"Voice? Man or woman? Young or old?"

Grantwood shrugged. "I think someone was deliberately disguising his or her voice. It was kind of high and shrill. I couldn't even tell if it was a man or a woman."

"What did he or she say?"

"Can't remember the exact words, but the upshot was that it wouldn't be a good idea to go forward with the announcement we plan on Saturday."

"Anything specific about what he or she would do?"

Grantwood shook his head.

I considered the implications. "Ms. Spencer is right to be concerned. It would scare me, too. You'll need to tell the police, of course. And think about this. How many people actually know the details of the merger?"

He stopped and drew a breath. "I hadn't thought—"

"You'll have to now," I warned him.

"I don't have time to deal with the police and all their questions again right now. It was probably just a crank call."

I watched him. Grantwood was worried, more worried than he wanted anyone to know. I looked at Ellen Spencer. Her rigid stance and rapid breathing showed her concern and the work she put into controlling her emotions. She probably didn't even realize her hands had clenched into fists.

"Under ordinary circumstances, you could write it off as a prank call," I said. "But these aren't ordinary circumstances." I let that hang for a moment. "I have the number for the detective in charge of Mr. Bethel's case. Do you want me to call him for you?"

Grantwood and Spencer looked at each other before he turned his glazed stare back at me. "No, thank you. Give me the number and I'll make the call."

I doubted he'd do it, but I couldn't force him. I pulled out Detective Gilmont's card and copied the number onto a piece of paper Spencer handed me.

He took it, folded it, put it in the breast pocket of his shirt, and stood up. "Thank you for coming so quickly," he said. "I appreciate it."

His awkward, jerky movements betrayed his state of nerves. At the same time, his squared shoulders and tensed mouth indicated his resolve to go ahead and do exactly what he planned. *The show must go on.*

"I'll talk to our head of security about getting someone to keep an eye on your booth," I suggested. "Without being obvious about it, of course."

A faint wash of relief crossed his face. "That would be an excellent idea."

"I'll see what we can do."

Ellen Spencer walked with me from the curtained-off area to the edge of the booth. "He's a lot more rattled than he wants to admit," she said.

"Understandably. Please try to get him to call the police. They need to know about that threat."

"I'll try, but you know...men!"

I nodded and took my leave. While struggling down the aisle, ignoring a couple of people who tried to snag my attention, I texted Janelle a message that I needed to talk to her as soon as she was free. I ducked into a ladies' room, then headed to the snack shop downstairs. I needed food.

The place was a madhouse, with a line that snaked out into the table area, but I joined it. Fortunately, they'd hired extra help for the show, and it didn't take all that long to reach the counter, where I ordered a turkey roll and shake. Even better, I found an open table at one corner.

My luck ran out moments later when Sue Savotsky sat down, asking, "Mind if I join you?" By then she'd already planted herself in the chair.

I managed to hold in a groan as I considered how many complaints she could work in while I finished my lunch. "I'm only going to be here a few more minutes," I told her, trying to be polite and not too obvious about gobbling down my food.

"Oh, that's all right. I know you're busy." She began to pick at the salad on her plate, pushing aside the olives and peppers. "With the murder and all, you're probably run off your feet, trying to keep everyone calm and reassured."

"The police aren't officially saying it was murder."

Sue looked up, her blue eyes sparkling. She could do good humor well enough when it suited her, but something hard and cold and ambitious always lurked beneath any lighter expression on her face. "Oh, I heard, but—come on. We all know Tim's body was found in the trash bin. What kind of accident was that?"

I tried to keep the surprise off my face. I didn't realize word had gotten around about the body's location. Then again, people had undoubtedly seen the police combing through the container and had drawn the logical conclusion.

"I haven't heard anything official," I told Sue.

"The cops have been going around questioning people about where they were last night and when they last saw Tim and stuff like that. I had the cutest detective asking me what I knew about him."

"You knew Tim Bethel?"

"Honey, every presentable woman in the industry knew Tim. Some of us *knew* him very well, in fact."

"You—"

"Had an affair with him. Why try to hide it? Everyone knew. I'll bet half the women on the floor have slept with him."

"His wife was coming to join him. She's probably here now, though I haven't seen her. I wonder if she knows."

"She'd have to be blind, deaf, and dumb—and not in the 'can't talk' sense—to not know. But they've been married for a while, so I suppose she's figured out how to live with it."

"I guess," I admitted.

"I wonder if some woman finally got so fed up with him she killed him. I know I felt like it once or twice." Sue let out a self-conscious, tittering laugh. "I suppose I shouldn't say things like that, should I? Might give the cops ideas."

"I imagine they'll be looking for something more substantial than that, assuming it wasn't an accident."

"I suppose. Not to change the subject, but have you

talked to Kavanell about their music? They're still playing it too loud."

"I asked them to turn it down, but I'll do it again," I told her. It was a small lie. I'd forgotten about it. But I'd see them that afternoon. I finished the last of the turkey roll and crumpled up the paper.

"Stanaker-Wells is poaching my business, too," she said. "I've watched them all but reach out and grab people coming toward my booth. They see people eyeing my merchandise and distract them."

I sighed. "I'll try to take a look and see what's going on." I stood up before she could think of anything more to gripe about. "Got to get back to work."

"Good talking to you," she said. "Enjoyed the lunch."

I said goodbye politely. I swear I did.

I needed to get off the floor for a bit so I headed upstairs to the office. A well-groomed blond woman in her early forties stepped on the elevator behind me. Her beautifully cut and fitted suit probably cost more than my last month's salary. There were other offices in the building, but she didn't press the button for another floor. I smiled at her as the doors whooshed closed and she gave me a small, sad nod in return. She held herself very straight, very tight, and controlled, as though it would take only a wrong word or a small push to make her come apart. I guessed who she was.

I didn't say anything, though. She got out ahead of me on the third floor but stopped after a few steps, looking lost. As I went around her, I paused and turned back. "Can I help you find something?"

Her rueful smile was charming and heart-breaking at the same time. "I'm here to see the Center's director—Mrs. Addison, I believe?"

"Janelle Addison. I'm her assistant, Heather McNeil.

Come with me and I'll see if she's in her office." I extended a hand, which she took and shook.

She held my hand with more firmness and warmth than I expected. "Thank you. I'm Chloe Bethel, Tim's wife... widow."

"I'm very sorry about your husband. It must have been a terrible shock."

"It was. Tim was so alive, so vibrant. It's impossible to imagine him gone. He was one of a kind. I can't fathom what it's going to be like without him."

"I can't imagine how hard this must be for you." I led the way into the Center's offices.

For once Tina was at her post at the reception desk. "Is Janelle in her office?" I asked.

"Yeah, but she's got someone in there with her. The honcho from MCEI, I think."

"Buzz her and tell her Mrs. Bethel is here to see her."

She did as I asked and a moment later reported, "Janelle says she'll be out in a moment."

I thanked Tina and asked Chloe Bethel if she'd like some coffee or a soft drink.

"A soda would be nice. Any kind."

When I returned, I led Chloe Bethel to a group of chairs at the side of the room and sat down with her there.

She drank and said, "Thank you. I needed that. I spent all morning with the police, answering questions, and I got very thirsty. I swear if I have to answer another question about packing for Tim and his itinerary, I'll scream." She sighed, hunched her shoulders, and closed her eyes. "I wish I could have seen him once more. Before he left for Seattle, we had a rip-roaring argument and we really hadn't settled things. If I could have it to do all over again..." She looked at me. "Are you married?"

"No, ma'am. There's a guy I see, but neither of us is very serious right now."

A smile barely curved her lips. "When you do get serious with someone, never leave a disagreement unresolved. Don't walk away from each other angry. You could regret it."

The sadness around her eyes made my heart break for her. Her hands shook as she lifted her glass to take a sip.

"I'm sure he realized that you loved him, even if you did argue."

"I like to think so. But then I wonder. We said some really ugly things to each other. I accused him—" Her face started to crumple before she managed to get her expression under control. "I wish I hadn't been so stupid and petty. You can't imagine how much I wish it."

From what I'd learned of her husband, I'd guess she was neither stupid nor petty, but if I were in her place, I might well feel the same way.

We both looked around at the sound of footsteps approaching. I turned to see Janelle and another man coming toward us.

Her companion was fiftyish and losing the battle of the waistline as well as the war with age, despite the hair dye, comb-over, and what looked like a face-lift.

I introduced Chloe Bethel, and Janelle introduced Carl Roper. Roper's handshake was firm to the point of aggression but mercifully brief. He offered Chloe condolences on behalf of the Center and the company.

I managed to get Janelle aside for a moment while he continued to commiserate with the widow.

"Someone called and threatened Grantwood this morning," I told her, keeping my voice low. "He didn't remember the exact words. Something to the effect that it might not be a good idea to go through with the merger they're going to announce Saturday."

Janelle's eyebrows rose. "What did you tell him?"

"I urged him to report it to the police. I gave him Detective Gilmont's number."

"Good thinking."

"I doubt he'll report it. He tried to brush it off."

"We can't force him."

"I know, but we could tell Gilmont ourselves."

"Next time we talk to him, we mention it," Janelle said.

"I have a bad feeling about this. Grantwood was playing it down, but I could tell he was more rattled than he wanted to admit. Ellen Spencer thought so, too. However, they're both scared of rocking the business boat. I think it would be a good idea to have someone keeping watch on the booth."

"Good idea, but Craig's going to have a cow if we ask him to dedicate one of his people to that."

"Can we bring someone in from outside?"

"Hire a detective?" She thought about it and sighed. "Security is still Craig's thing, and I don't want to go around or over him. Can you talk to him about it? Tell him we'll fund it if he can get someone in right away."

"Maybe someone could pose as a rep at one of the booths across the aisle."

"Excellent idea, Heather. Will you set it up?"

"Sure. One other thing. It sounds ridiculous, but it's really driving people nuts. Blue Hills has a popcorn machine in their booth, and it's burning popcorn and spreading a really nasty smell. I nearly got sick on it myself. A couple of people complained to me this morning. I warned Blue Hills they'd have to get it serviced or turn it off, but I don't think they will. The company president was extremely defensive. Said the company that rented it to her swore it worked perfectly."

Janelle rolled her eyes. "Give them one more chance. If you have to warn them again and they still don't do anything, pull the plug. Get Security to remove it, if necessary."

"Will do. Thanks."

"No. Thank *you*. I don't know what I'd do without you, Heather."

"Hire some other eager business-school grad to do your dirty work?"

"I was lucky to get a business-school grad who hasn't had all the common sense educated out of her. I can't tell you how rare that is."

"In that case, when's my next performance review?"

She laughed, but before she could reply, Roper beckoned.

"Gotta go," she said. "Hope to get down to the floor in an hour or so. I'll stop by Grantwood & Bethel."

I nodded and went on to my desk, where I checked messages, responded to a few things that needed quick answers, and called Craig Vincelli.

"We've got a potential problem," I told him and listened to him sigh.

"Another one?"

"Bad one, possibly. Someone telephoned a threat to Stan Grantwood. He's the business partner of Tim Bethel, the guy we found in the trash bin yesterday. I want someone to keep watch on his booth as long as the show is open." Before he could even get the first syllable of protest out, I added, "Janelle said she'd fund hiring someone."

"It'll take us a few days to get someone in unless we get another temp, but—"

"But what?"

"Another temp isn't what you need for this."

"I know. Can you get what we do need?"

"By when?"

I considered. I wanted someone right now, but I knew that wasn't realistic. "Tomorrow morning?"

Craig snorted. "You're not serious."

"I'm very serious. A man's been killed and now someone's threatening his partner. I think that's about as serious as it gets."

"You're right. Hold on a moment. I have an idea. How do you want to handle the surveillance?"

"I thought we could plant someone at a booth across the way. Dress him or her as a rep. I'll work it out with one of the exhibitors. Can one of your people do it?"

"I'll make a couple of calls and get back to you."

I thanked him and hung up. My watch said two-thirty. I knew I should get back to the floor, but instead I went to the break room for a ten-minute power nap.

I conked out in seconds and dreamed about kayaking down a peaceful river on a gorgeous summer day. I heard the call of birds in the trees, the gentle lapping of the water, the buzzing of frogs. *Buzzing?* I roused abruptly, yanked out of my dream world by the cell phone.

Craig Vincelli said, "I've got what you want. Our new guy, Scott Brandon, is going to play rep. He'll wear a suit and meet you first thing tomorrow morning. I'll let you tell him what he needs to know."

"Are you sure he can handle it?"

"Yes, I'm sure. The guy's an ex-cop."

"A cop?" I was tempted to ask Craig why Scott had applied for a security position, but decided it was none of my business. "Okay. And thanks. I appreciate it."

The fact that I hadn't questioned Craig didn't stop me from being curious. Why was an ex-cop working here? A fairly young ex-cop. Police officers didn't get paid what they were worth, but even so, it had to be better than what our security guys earned. And most of ours were cop wannabes who couldn't pass the police-force exams.

Scott Brandon had passed the exams, and I was willing to bet he'd done very well on them. But something had gone way wrong, somewhere.

I retreated to the ladies' room to run a comb through my hair and renew my makeup. Then I walked down to the show floor again.

My first stop was Kavanall and Company. Sue Savostky might be cranky, but she was right about this. Their music was so loud it made conversation difficult in the surrounding booths. I found the person in charge and asked him to tone it down. The man looked shocked that others had complained and sent one of his salespeople to lower the volume. Within moments the sound sank to a more tolerable level.

I felt good about how well that had gone, but as I turned away, a rep from a neighboring booth wanted to know about Tim Bethel's death and what the Center was doing to protect everyone against murderers and other hazards. I told him about our extra security measures and how the police were present, but he mostly wanted to vent his fear and annoyance.

While he yammered, I listened with half of my brain. The other half watched buyers and others approaching Sue Savotsky's booth. I wanted to check out her complaint that her neighbors intercepted potential customers. After ten minutes' observation, I couldn't eliminate the possibility it was happening, but I certainly couldn't prove it was. I didn't see anything that looked like an attempt to waylay a customer heading for Sue's booth.

I assured the man, once again, that we were doing everything we could to ensure the safety of everyone. Then I escaped.

Someone called my name, and I turned to see Mark weaving his way through the crowd toward me. He dragged a dolly with three cartons piled on it.

"Problem?" I asked.

He rolled his eyes. "Not really," he said, pointing to the cartons, whose labels indicated they held bottles of rum. "I'm helping Charleston and Crick set up for their cocktail hour."

"Yikes, is it that time already?" I looked at my watch. Quarter to four. "Time flies when you're having fun."

"Or busier than a one-armed hangman."

I grimaced at his metaphor.

"The police grill you about finding the body?" he asked.

"I wouldn't call it grilling. But the detective asked me some questions."

"Did it worry you?"

It hadn't occurred to me that it should. "No. Why would it?"

"I just wondered if they thought we might have had something to do with it."

"Because we found the body? I don't know about you, but I barely knew Tim Bethel existed before yesterday. Why would I want to kill him?"

"I didn't know him, either," Mark said. "But it makes me uneasy when they start asking questions. I don't like the way they look at me. Like they're sure they'll find out I did something wrong if they keep digging long enough."

"Look, Mark, you didn't have anything to do with this, so don't worry about it."

"Okay. Where you headed now?"

"The Grantwood & Bethel booth."

"Later," he said.

As I walked away, I wondered why Mark felt uneasy. Guilty conscience? But not over Tim Bethel. It wouldn't surprise me to learn that Mark skirted the law on other issues.

I mentally worked on the wording for my request as I threaded my way toward G & B's booth, avoiding eye contact, hoping no one would tackle me for information about the murder.

At the same time, I tried to decide on the best angle for someone to keep an eye on the G & B booth. No matter where he was positioned, one corner would be out of sight. But I wanted him to watch the entrance to the private area in back, which limited the choices.

I finally settled on the place that gave what I considered the best view, then turned to introduce myself to the lone person manning the nearest booth, which proved to be Chang & Fitch Associates. I couldn't blame the man for the brief flash of disappointment that crossed his face when he learned I wasn't a potential customer. To his credit, he didn't let it linger, and he greeted me with considerable warmth.

"Martin Chang," he said, reaching out to shake my hand. His accent was pure New York when he said, "Nice to meet you, Ms. McNeil." He was probably in his mid-forties but had the sort of lean, slender build that tended to age gracefully.

His booth featured a variety of pottery vases, candleholders and tableware, gracefully shaped and glazed with subtle but beautifully blended shades. A range of candles in unique shapes and sizes accented the ceramics in a lovely way. They were some of the most tasteful and attractive products I'd seen anywhere in the show, but buyers weren't beating a path to it. He looked pleased when I complimented him on the merchandise.

"We acquire from a few select craftsmen," he said. "Nothing is machine-made and each piece is unique."

If he cooperated, I was going to have to find some way to steer some business toward him.

I explained what I needed and he said, "I heard that Tim Bethel was found dead, possibly murdered. It's kind of frightening."

"We're trying to add extra security. Of course, it's better if they're not all in uniform and obvious about it."

"So, if I understand you correctly, you want to station one of your security people here, posing as a sales rep for my company?"

"Exactly. His primary task will be to keep watch over the Grantwood & Bethel booth. We're concerned about them for obvious reasons, but he'll also be alert for anything suspicious happening."

Chang looked dubious. "And he would remain in my booth? I don't know about that. He might be in the way or discourage customers."

"I don't think he'd be a problem. He'll try to fit in and help you out as much as he can while he keeps watch."

"Would he be able to cover the booth for me while I take a break? I'm here by myself, and it's hard to find time to take care of personal matters."

"I suppose he could," I said. "But the man we'd like to put here isn't a salesman. He's trained in security and law enforcement, not—"

"I can teach him all he needs to know in just a few minutes. I wouldn't expect him to do more than get a name and contact information." Chang smiled. "It would also look good to have another person in the booth."

Maybe Martin Chang didn't need me steering business his way, after all. But then his expression changed again. "Business has been slow so far. I'm new to the industry and we don't have a big name, but the product is top-of-the-line. The best." He shrugged one shoulder in an odd, rotating motion. "Of course, we only need a few large orders to make it worth our effort. We couldn't handle too many. We don't mass-produce with machines and cheap, unskilled labor. We've already gotten one nice order, so I guess I shouldn't complain too much. A couple more and we'll be set up."

"I hope you get them. And thank you for helping us out. Our security man's name is Scott Brandon and I'll bring him to your booth first thing tomorrow morning."

"It should work out," Chang said. "I'll help him, and he can help me."

It was nearly five. A couple of the larger booths were serving cocktails and canapés. The aroma of meatballs in barbecue sauce and peach-flavored liqueurs teased and tempted, but I resisted. I needed to save space for the banquet this evening, and anyway, I was still on the clock.

I breathed through my mouth in order to resist the lure. Time to head upstairs, collect my things and go home so I could change clothes for the banquet. The Center was paying for a taxi. Thank heaven for small perks.

The Blaise Foundation/HDA benefit party was tonight's main event. I suspected everyone would go, if only to get the latest gossip. Center staff below the executive level weren't required to attend, but Janelle liked me to. It wasn't just that she needed my help. We both understood that she was grooming me to move up into her job.

Normally, I liked the banquets and parties. I reveled in the incredible food, the entertainment, the high-powered people in their expensive clothes and glad-handing facades—the sheer glamour. It was kind of nice to have an excuse to dress up in gorgeous clothes and socialize. Today, though, I dreaded it. It meant several more hours of being pumped for information.

I headed for the exit from the show floor but stopped at the sound of raised voices nearby.

A fight? One that hadn't come to blows but might not be far from it?

As I pushed through the group of people who'd already gathered, I pressed my speed-dial button for Craig.

"I need security on sixteen hundred," I said. "There's an argument in progress that could escalate."

FIVE

I PUSHED PAST a couple more people to get closer and halted a few feet away. Two men stood almost nose to nose, exchanging words in loud voices.

A tall red-headed man in a beautifully cut suit appeared to be defending himself from an onslaught of verbal abuse from a shorter, dark-haired man in shirtsleeves and loosened tie. Both vibrated with tension.

The shorter man reached out to grab the lapel of the other man's suit. Several people from the booth pressed forward, trying to calm the men down. The tall redhead signaled them to move back. It only seemed to further inflame the attacker. His body shook with fury barely held in check. I could hear his harsh breathing from several feet away.

"You cheating son of a bitch," the attacker yelled. "I'm an artist! You made my design into a cheap, pathetic knick-knack." He spat the last word as though it were the worst curse he could think of. "You turned my art into *trinkets*. How dare you?" His face was so red, I was afraid he'd burst a blood vessel.

The red-haired man tried to jerk back but couldn't pull free of the hold the other man had on his jacket. "You signed the agreement. Didn't you read the damn thing before you signed? It said right there in the contract we had the right to use the design in whatever way we wanted."

The artist took a deep breath. "I knew you'd gone with cheap production, so I was prepared for that, but I didn't imagine you'd do this to my work, that you'd produce this travesty." He held up something, but I wasn't close enough to get a good look at it. "I thought you had more sense. More integrity!" By the time he got to the last few words, he was shouting at the top of his lungs.

"We elected to do what we thought best for the business. You should be pleased. They're selling very well."

"Pleased! Pleased? I should be thrilled that you've turned my masterpieces into—" His hand closed into a fist.

I stepped forward. "Gentlemen," I said, "please. Calm down."

They paid no attention, probably didn't hear me. In truth, I could barely hear myself over the racket.

"You've made a mockery of me and my designs," Artist proclaimed.

"Take your hands off me, or I'll have you arrested," Redhead threatened. His people began pushing forward again, maneuvering their way between the two men until Artist had to let go.

A couple of our security people showed up at the same time. One of them was Howie Harper, a heavyset man in his early sixties. I hoped he wouldn't have to do anything too strenuous. He had heart problems. We rarely had this kind of trouble, so Janelle hadn't wanted to make him retire.

Fortunately, Scott Brandon accompanied him.

Brandon sized up the situation, met my eyes for a moment, long enough for me to give him a nod, and then he moved between the two men. He had to elbow and shoulder a few other well-meaning souls out of the way.

"That's enough," he said. "Step back, both of you."

The way he said it—loud enough to be heard, forceful enough that no one would ignore it—left no doubt in my mind he'd once been a cop. No one questioned his authority. Everyone backed away from him.

"Which one of you started this?" he asked.

Both men spoke at once, and a couple of bystanders added their opinions. Scott looked around and settled his gaze on mine, asking for help.

I stepped forward. "I don't know who started it, and it doesn't matter. I'm Heather McNeil, assistant to the director of the Center," I said for the benefit of the crowd. "This has to stop right now."

I faced the aggressive artist. "You. Come with me and we can discuss your options. This isn't helping anything." I took the man's arm and towed him away. I signaled for Scott to accompany me. When the artist tried to resist my pull, Scott took hold of his other arm. Together we moved him away from the booth.

Howie might not be much use in controlling physically violent incidents, but he'd worked here a long time and knew how to handle verbal stuff. I left him to warn Redhead and his group about creating scenes on the show floor.

Scott Brandon and I flanked the artist and escorted him off the show floor. I led them to a small, private conference room down the hall. By the time we got there, the man had calmed down and chagrin had started to set in.

Water service was set up in a corner of the room, so I poured out a cup and brought it to him. The man sat in one of the chairs at the conference table, accepted the drink with thanks, and swallowed it all in one gulp. I read the name on his name tag: Tom Rupika. I'd heard the name before but couldn't remember where.

"I'm sorry," he said when he'd drained the cup and set it down again. "That was stupid of me." He pulled off the tie that hung loose around his neck and stuffed it in his pocket. "I shouldn't have lost my head that way. I was so angry when I saw what they'd done with my designs…" He swallowed hard. "They had no right."

I sat down facing him while Scott stood near the door. "Are you sure?" I asked.

Rupika blinked and looked confused. "What?"

"Are you sure they don't have the right? Did you read the contract?"

"No, not really. But I had a lawyer draw it up. I told him what I wanted, and that included the right to review the design before it was marketed."

"And you're sure the lawyer wrote that in?"

"I think so."

"Get on the phone to him right now. Tell him what's happened, find out the exact terms of the contract, and see if he thinks there's a violation. You might have some legal redress. Think of how satisfying that could be."

A ray of hope broke through Rupika's frustrated, despairing expression. "Good idea! The contract is set to run out next month anyway, but I hate the thought they could take my designs and create this!"

He held up the porcelain figure he'd been clutching all through the melee. The shape was that of a woman in an ankle-length flowing gown of ice blue. The wings might have suggested an angel, but the pointed ears, the full breasts and a clever, coy twist of the hips said fairy—an alluring one at that. There was a subtle, graceful eroticism about the figure. Or would have been, except the facial features were muddied and blurred by poor-quality reproduction. The real travesty, though, was the way the top of the woman's head had been flattened and hollowed out to create a well for a candle. Rupika was right. It was practically sacrilege.

I looked it over and felt stirrings of anger. "Contact your

lawyer and see if he can't do some kind of cease-and-desist order or whatever the appropriate action is."

Rupika jumped up and pulled a cell phone out of his pocket, flipped it open, then stopped. "I didn't program my lawyer's number in. I'll have to get my briefcase."

"Where is it?"

"Back in my hotel room."

"Good. Make that call in your room. Then have a nice dinner somewhere. Have a drink or two. Calm down. But don't come back to the show floor today or attend any of the functions tonight where you might run into…" I realized I had no idea of the tall redhead's name.

"Chase Peterson." Rupika made the name sound as if it belonged to a particularly nasty bug.

"Peterson," I repeated. "Stay away from him. Okay?"

"Are you going to ban me from the show floor?"

I thought about it. He hadn't done anything more than argue with another exhibitor. It wasn't like that hadn't happened before. The exchange might well have advanced to physical violence without intervention, but then again, it might not have. One or the other or both might have come to their senses. I wasn't naïve enough to actually believe that, but I had to allow for the possibility.

"Just for the rest of today," I said. "You can come back tomorrow. But you're on notice. Another incident and you're out. Understand?"

He nodded, stood, and gave me a wry, lopsided smile. "Understood. I'll be on my best behavior for the rest of the show."

As he left the room, he stopped and took my hand. "Thanks for saving me from myself. I'd be even more embarrassed if I'd hit him. Not that he didn't deserve it. But it wouldn't have accomplished much and might have gotten me into worse trouble." He grinned a full smile. "Would've been real satisfying, though." He shook his head, eyes still alight. "Don't worry. I'm over it now. In the long run it's going to be much more fun to sic my attorney on him. And word will get out among artists and designers about what he's done with my work. He'll have a heck of a hard time signing anyone again, and it'll cost him if he does."

Rupika left, throwing another "Thanks" over his shoulder.

I sighed. I'd started out feeling sorry for him, but now I felt leery. Once he stopped being mad and started getting even, he sounded kind of scary.

"Nicely done."

I jumped, having forgotten Scott was there. "All in a day's work, sir."

"Please tell me this hasn't been a normal day. It's been a madhouse."

Now that it was just the two of us, he let stress sound in his voice and show in his demeanor.

"The shows are normally chaotic, but this is the biggest one we have. And of course the murder has made everyone more on edge than usual." I looked at him, hoping what I heard in his voice was just tiredness and the stress of coping with something new. "You're not going to walk out on us, are you?"

I'd be in such deep stuff if he did. We already had more problems than current security could cope with.

Anger tightened his mouth and narrowed his eyes. "What kind of bastard do you think I am? No, I'm not walking just because the job got a bit more colorful than I expected."

His expression changed abruptly, the anger melting into amusement. "This job is fascinating. I had no idea it would be such a study in human interaction and the layers of civilization. It's intriguing. And the most fun I've had in quite a while."

The grin changed to a full smile that carved an alarmingly attractive dimple in his cheek and made his gray-green eyes blaze. My pulse started thumping out a message of interest.

I shoved down the reaction. "It can be pretty fascinating and fun. But it's a job and I've still got work to do." I looked at my watch and my pulse jumped. "Yikes, it's after six."

"Quitting time for most people," Scott said. "What have you still got to do?"

"Party tonight. I have to go home, change, and get back to the Shelton by eight."

He quirked an eyebrow. "Will that happen tomorrow and the next night, too?"

"Afraid so."

"How do you survive?"

"Duct tape and hair spray. By Sunday we'll all be frayed. But we get time off next week to recover. A day and a half of comp time for each weekend day worked. Didn't Craig explain the schedule to you?"

"There was something about working weekends and getting comp time, but it was kind of muddled. He kept getting phone calls and his train of thought ran off the rails each time."

His expression changed. The amusement faded and a hard, shuttered look took its place. It was almost like watching a mask come down over his face.

We headed out to the lobby elevators. "Maybe next week he can find time to tell you more about the job," I said.

"Maybe. Tell me what I'm doing tomorrow."

"You're pretending to be a sales rep while keeping an eye on the Grantwood & Bethel booth."

"Your murdered exec was Tim Bethel, right?"

"Right," I said as we stepped into the elevator. Fortunately, no one else got on with us. "This morning, his partner, Stan Grantwood, received a threatening phone call."

"What did it threaten?"

Scott leaned back against the elevator wall, feigning a casual pose. In fact, he was totally alert and on guard. I couldn't help but notice that his stance never got completely relaxed. There was always some tension in the way he held himself. Nor could I fail to notice that the khaki uniform shirt and pants looked good on him. Really good.

I jerked my gaze back up to his face. "Nothing specific. Just said that it wouldn't be a good idea for him to go ahead with the merger they plan to announce Saturday night."

"Who are they merging with?"

"I don't know."

"Did he report the threat to the cops?"

"I don't know that, either. Janelle was supposed to stop by this afternoon and make sure he did, but I don't know if she had time. I'll ask her tonight."

"Make sure he does report it."

"We can try, but we can't force him." Maybe I was more tired than I realized. I don't know why I argued with him.

"You can report it yourself," he suggested.

"That's kind of a gray area. We'd be breaking a confidence."

"It's for his own good."

"Who are we to decide that? Maybe we don't know what's good for him. Maybe he knows something about this we don't."

"And maybe he's not the best judge of what's good for him. Maybe he's got his priorities screwed up and thinks his business is more important than a threat that could escalate to something worse."

"Again, who are we to judge that? Doesn't he have the right to decide for himself?"

"Maybe you—" He drew a deep breath. "Okay, I admit I don't know all the rules of this game. But it still seems to me that if there's any kind of threat, it should be reported to the police."

"I'm not arguing with that!"

He gave me a sharp look. "Damn, I'm sorry. You've had a hellacious day and I'm making it worse. I don't know what got into me."

"You're probably tired, too."

"That's no excuse."

A line had formed outside for cabs. It was close to full dark, but the plaza in front of the Center was well lit. Scott said goodbye, promising he'd see me first thing in the morning. For a moment he stared at me with an odd, hungry look. I had the notion that if we'd been alone, he might have kissed me. The expression vanished quickly, replaced by something almost angry. Strange. He wheeled around and walked away without glancing back. I joined the string of people waiting at the cabstand.

What would it have felt like to be kissed by Scott Brandon?

"Gotta love a guy in uniform," a voice beside me said. "And that one's really hot."

I didn't recognize the young woman admiring Scott as he moved away. "He's a co-worker," I said.

"I should be so lucky," she responded.

The line moved forward as several taxis arrived at once. A few minutes later I was inside one, trying to relax while the driver navigated the traffic. By the time I reached home, it was nearly seven.

I indulged in a bath anyway before changing into a knee-length black silk dress with a sprinkle of subtle beading along the throat and waist. It was from a well-known designer, but I'd bought it at a consignment store for a fraction of what its original owner had paid. I used more makeup than normal and twisted my dark hair into a French braid. It took three tries to get it right.

I studied my face in the mirror. Kind of okay. On a one to ten scale I was probably a seven. Makeup helped. A bit more mascara? Nah, just that much more to smudge.

The taxi returned on the dot of seven-forty. Traffic had abated some, so the driver got me back into town and to the hotel in less than twenty minutes.

People already flooded the lobby and hotel ballroom. Groups crowded around the bars to get drinks. I stopped just inside the entrance to survey the area. The tickets had table numbers on them and my table was reserved for staff, so I knew I'd meet Janelle at dinner. In the meantime, my job was to circulate and be nice. I collected the one glass of wine I allowed myself.

I expected this part of the evening to be a trial and it was. I had to keep repeating what I knew about Tim Bethel's death, and I must've said "I don't know" a hundred or more times to questions about details and suspects.

After ten minutes or so of scanning the crowd, I spotted Stan Grantwood, so I tried to keep my gaze on him from then on. He didn't act like a man worried about a threat. The way he circulated, shook hands with people, and talked, all laughing and smiling, suggested a man with nothing more on his mind than having a profitable show. So, maybe it was true. Or maybe he had some acting talent.

It wasn't easy to split my attention between Grantwood and the person in front of me at any given moment. The people I met and spoke to began to merge into

a hazy collection of faces I might remember and names
I surely wouldn't.

Until I got to one name that made figurative bells go
off in my head.

Irv Kirshorn was a distinguished-looking man in his
late forties or early fifties. Full, curly dark hair showed
a smattering of gray at the temples. The neatly clipped
black beard didn't disguise strong cheekbones. His dark
eyes missed little and gave the impression of a sharp mind.

He smiled when we were introduced, an expression
that held a subtle combination of warmth and calculation.
I got the impression he was hoping, maybe even expecting, I could be useful to him in some way and waiting to
see how that would work out.

It took me a moment to remember that his company was
one of the two mentioned as potential merger prospects for
Grantwood & Bethel. The one that maybe needed it more.

My mind roared out of sluggish mode and into full alert.

I asked him about his business, a topic that rarely fails
to draw people out and get them talking.

"Kirshorn's produces proprietary glass and ceramic
accents that have the look and feel of hand-created art-
work," Irv Kirshorn told me. It sounded like a well-
practiced sales pitch, but an underlying passion for his
product came through. "We've created a process that lets
us retain that hand-worked look even while we produce
the item at a faster rate. Our retail buyers love it and tell
us their customers get very excited about our merchandise. We have some new holiday and fall items that we're
sure will be big sellers this year. We also have a nice line
of exclusive designer jewelry and some fabulous crystal
ornaments, plus…"

I kind of tuned him out during the sales spiel, but I
wasn't the only one struggling to keep up the conversation

with only partial attention. I followed Kirshorn's gaze during one of its frequent trips from my face to a place off to my right. Oddly—or maybe not so oddly—the rest of his awareness was focused in the same place as mine. With an unreadable expression, he watched Stan Grantwood.

Grantwood still showed no sign of worrying over any threats. In truth, Ellen Spencer, who stood beside him, looked far more concerned.

I said, "How do you manage to retain the individual look when you're mass-producing?"

"What?" It took him a moment to drag his attention back to me, consider the question, and gather an answer. "Oh. Some of the process is secret, of course. But part of it came from moving most of our production overseas, where we can get skilled craftsmen to add those individual touches at reasonable cost."

"How long have you worked in the industry?"

"All my life. My father started the company. I went to work there as soon as I graduated from college. Started out as a clerk in the shipping department. My dad wanted me to know the business from the ground up."

"Is the rest of your family still involved in the company?"

He looked uncomfortable for a moment. "My father retired a few years ago. There isn't anyone else. My only brother is a stunt actor in Hollywood and wants nothing to do with the business. I have no sons or daughters."

I wasn't sure where to go with the conversation from there. "What do you like to do with your time when you're not working?"

He gave me a very odd look that I couldn't decipher, almost like he didn't understand the question or didn't want to understand it. Finally, he said, "I don't really have time for anything else. I'm always working." His glance flicked off to the right again.

"Surely you—" I realized I was about to dig myself into a hole and stopped. Just then a tap on the microphone on the stage preceded a request that we all take our places so that the waitstaff could begin serving meals. *Saved by the dinner bell.* I tried to make sure no one else saw my sigh of relief as I told Kirshorn it was a pleasure to meet him and I hoped I'd see him around the show.

I went over to the assigned table in the corner and found Janelle had kept a seat for me next to her.

"You look gorgeous," Janelle said, surveying me from top to bottom.

"And you're stunning." I returned the compliment and meant it. My boss had a great figure for a woman of her age, and the navy sheath with its red trim looked terrific on her.

Janelle said, "I heard there was a fight on the floor this afternoon."

"That got around quick." I'm not sure why it still surprises me how fast scandal spreads.

"You know the vine," she said. "Actually, Howie buzzed me to let me know about it. And to tell me what a great job you did in handling it."

"Howie and Scott Brandon, the new guy, did most of the handling. They managed to defuse things quickly."

"Howie was impressed by Scott."

"So was I. Craig said he was an ex-cop. He acted like it this afternoon. But it made me wonder—" I paused while a server laid a plate of mixed greens in front of me.

"What he's doing working for us?"

"Exactly."

"Who knows? I'm sure he has his reasons."

I picked at the stringy green stuff on the plate. I knew

it was supposed to be edible, probably even some sort of gourmet salad ingredient, and certainly good for me, but I couldn't work up any enthusiasm. Instead, I took a sip from the glass of wine I'd been nursing for the past half hour. "Janelle, do you know Irv Kirshorn?"

Janelle had dug into the salad with enthusiasm. After chewing and swallowing, she said, "I've met him a couple of times. Why?"

"I'm not sure. I just tried to talk to him and he seemed like a really odd individual."

"He's not much of a talker, though I've heard some people say he can go on and on about his company and products."

"I did get the quick overview. He was kind of distracted, though. And I asked about his family, too, but he doesn't seem to have one."

"I believe his wife left him a couple of years ago."

The man on the other side of Janelle leaned over to say something to her. Since I had an empty place next to me, I sat quietly, thinking, until the waiter removed the salad and replaced it with a dinner plate. A few artfully arranged green beans rested beside what I hoped was meat smothered by a delicious-looking sauce. I had a sudden, silly urge to turn the beans into a tic-tac-toe board. Long day, definitely.

I found a chicken breast buried under a sauce that tasted of wine, butter, and tangy cheese. I dug in with enthusiasm.

My long day wasn't over yet, I realized, when a man sat down in the empty seat beside me. Janelle's boss, Carl Roper, introduced himself again, then grinned and shrugged as he remembered we'd met earlier.

"You're Heather McNeil," he added before I could say anything. "Janelle's assistant. She raves about you."

I have to admit I'm never sure how to respond to a compliment like that. If I go all blushing and demure, murmuring about how sweet Janelle is to say such things, I'm going to sound like a spineless idiot. But if I accept it as my due, I look arrogant. So what's the middle ground?

I tried for calm acceptance and a self-confident but not too arrogant demeanor. "I'm glad she thinks so. I'm fortunate to be working with her. She's a great teacher and role model. I've learned a lot from her."

"She says you're an invaluable help."

Another compliment. Fortunately, Janelle came to the rescue, turning our way and saying, "I heard my name mentioned."

"We're talking about how great you think I am," I told her.

"Uh-oh. Do we have to go on swellhead alert?"

"After today, I don't think so."

"Both of you seem to be doing a good job of minimizing the damage to the show and the Center's reputation," Roper said. "You've made me confident you'll continue to do whatever's necessary to make everyone feel comfortable and secure."

I met Janelle's gaze. We read each other's thoughts, but we made sure our expressions showed nothing more than polite agreement.

"We'll do everything we can," Janelle said. I wondered if she'd mention anything about Grantwood and the extra precautions we were taking, but she didn't.

Mercifully, waiters brought our dessert and coffee, and then the entertainment began. The stand-up comic had everyone huffing and rolling with laughter within a few moments. I was so tired, I felt sort of detached and floaty, but I chuckled with everyone else at the funnier jokes.

The routine ended with an appeal for support for the charitable endeavors of the Blaise Foundation.

Afterward, a live band provided music for those who still had the energy to spend on the dance floor, but a lot of people headed for the exits.

Roper excused himself, pleading exhaustion from the long trip that day. Janelle left to talk to an old acquaintance. I started toward the exit, but my friend Lisa Willamont waylaid me.

"I bet you forgot I promised to buy you a drink tonight," she said, nodding toward the cash bar.

"I guess I did," I admitted.

"Never mind. I keep my promises. You're going to sleep soundly tonight." I followed her, sort of on automatic pilot. As we waited for the bartender to pour a couple more glasses of wine, I turned and surveyed the crowd.

Some twenty feet away, Ellen Spencer and Stan Grantwood appeared to be engaged in a serious discussion. Their tense stances and tight expressions suggested a disagreement as they shot words at each other. Grantwood was only a couple of inches taller, but he took up more space with his broader shoulders and large build. He had his arms folded across his chest and his head cocked at an angle. After a moment, Ellen shook her head, making her chestnut hair wave. Her chest heaved in a deep sigh. She looked around, scanning the crowd. Her gaze swept over me without recognition.

It landed on a man somewhere off to my left, and her expression changed. Annoyance gave way to something else. Something that looked like fear.

I followed her line of sight to Irv Kirshorn. My stomach knotted with a vague dread. Presumably, Spencer knew whom G & B would be merging with. Her look suggested she knew who would be losing out, too, and was afraid of the results. Or maybe she knew he would win and had reason not to like that outcome.

My brain wasn't functioning on all cylinders, and I couldn't work out all the possible permutations.

Lisa collected our two glasses and led me to a grouping of armchairs in a quiet corner of the lobby. "You look totaled," she said. "Drink up."

"You can't be feeling much fresher yourself."

She shrugged, raising one shoulder in its beautiful royal-blue-silk suit jacket. "I didn't find a body yesterday. I didn't have to deal with a million complaining, worried exhibitors today." Her wry smile humanized her beautiful model-like face. "Just a few picky buyers vying for the deal of a lifetime."

"You eat those for breakfast."

She laughed. "Mmm. Tasty, too." Her expression grew more serious. "I've been hearing lots of rumors about Tim Bethel. You can imagine he's on everyone's mind. And lots of tongues, too. You want to hear the choicest?"

"I'd like to hear the ones you think most likely to be true."

"Booooorrrring," she said, dragging out the word. "Those can mostly be summed up by reciting a list of who he seems to have slept with."

"I've already heard of a couple. Sue Savotsky of Trim-states admits to it."

"Wow! I wonder if that isn't wishful thinking on her part. Tim was a tomcat, but he was a smart one, and she's a quagmire he should have had sense enough to avoid. But who knows? I'm pretty sure about some others." She rattled off names. I recognized a few but not all.

I could feel my eyes getting wider as the list went on. "He did get around," I said when she trailed off. I watched her steadily.

"No, not me," she added. "Not because he didn't try. He's just not my type."

"I'm betting that didn't make him happy."

"Ask me if I care."

"What about within Grantwood & Bethel? Any rumors about him sleeping with co-workers?"

"You know, it's odd, but nobody has said anything about that. I wonder if he only fools around at shows and affairs like this one. I know a few—men and women both—who regularly meet someone at these things for a bit of sex on the side. I've even heard of a few long-term relationships where the participants only meet at shows. At home they walk the straight and narrow. He might have been like that. Have you met Tim's wife?"

"Yes. She was in our office yesterday. She seemed pretty broken up about his death." I almost told her about the argument Chloe Bethel had said she'd had with her husband, but I thought that might be breaking a confidence. It also veered too close to venal gossip. Not that I was opposed to venal gossip in some instances. It just didn't seem right in this case.

"What is she like?" Lisa asked. "I've never met her, but I hear she's a classy lady. I seem to recall hearing her family had money and some of it helped fund Grantwood & Bethel for a while."

"She did seem like a classy lady. I liked her." I tried to stifle a huge yawn.

Lisa grinned. "Okay, Sleeping Beauty. Time to put you in the pumpkin coach and send you home." Escorting me to the door, she stayed with me until a cab showed up.

Once I had entered my apartment and collapsed into bed, I took a few brief moments to set the alarm and consider that, while I hoped for a better day tomorrow, I expected it to be worse.

SIX

THE ALARM JERKED me awake. A shower got my sluggish body moving, but it took those first few sips of the venti quad-shot cappuccino to rouse my mind into something resembling consciousness. As I stood on the Metro platform with all the other Friday-morning commuters, I harbored a sneaky hope the trains would stop running for a while to give me an excuse to go back home and back to bed. Not that fate ever managed anything so convenient.

The train arrived with disgusting promptness, and I squished into the nearest car with the rest of the waiting crowd. At least tonight I could look forward to another cab ride home. Small thrills.

The building was already open when I got there at seven-thirty, though the show floor remained locked up tight. Exhibitors weren't allowed in until eight and it opened for everyone else at nine. As usual, I was the first person in the office. I liked having a few quiet minutes to myself, to catch up on paperwork and messages, before the madness of the day started.

I'd only gotten halfway through the new email messages when I heard the elevator ping and the sound of footsteps in the lobby.

I looked up and, after a disorienting moment, recognized Scott Brandon. A suit and tie made such a difference. Or maybe it wasn't the suit and tie. There was something else different about the way he carried himself. It was almost as if he'd lowered his own level of alertness so it was closer to normal, allowing himself to blend in with the rest of the sales-obsessed business people who populated the show.

"How do you do that?" I asked him.

He looked confused. "Do what?"

"Change yourself so much. It's more than just the clothes and the way you've combed your hair. It's like you've changed your attitude, your expression, even the way you walk. How do you do it?"

Instead of answering, he frowned. "You worry me, Heather McNeil."

"Why?"

"You're too smart, too observant, and too curious for your own good."

"Is this the cop warning the civilian to stay out of the way?"

A flash of something that looked like pain crossed his face so quickly I barely saw it. "I'm not a cop. I just act like one for fun and profit."

That second sentence cost him something. I remembered what Craig had said about it not being a good idea to get interested in him. Deep waters here and probably nothing I wanted to dip my toes in. Except there was that curiosity Scott had mentioned. And the fact that I didn't like the thought of him being in pain.

I did the only thing I could think of that might help. I took it the way he wanted. "When you find either fun or profit around here, would you let me know? I'm looking for some myself."

"But do we define either one the same way?"

He had me there and his laugh said he knew it. "One of these days," he continued, "we'll have to compare notes on what fun and profit mean to us. But for now, we have work to do."

I wondered if we would ever do that comparison. It would be interesting to know how Scott defined those things.

When Scott and I went down to the show floor, I have to confess that I gave him more than a once-over in the elevator. The suit looked good on him. The blue shirt and navy striped tie brought out the blue in his oddly colored eyes.

He noted my examination. "Coffee stains on my tie already?"

I felt a flash of heat in my face. "You look fine."

"So I pass the inspection. You think I'll blend in?"

"Well enough." I didn't mention that every woman on the floor would be taking a second and third look at him. The bell pinged and the elevator doors opened, sparing me the need to say more.

Exhibitors had begun to open booths and set up for the day.

"Do you have a cell phone?" I asked Scott as we crossed the lobby.

He pulled one out of his pocket. "Craig gave me this one."

"Good." I programmed its number into my phone.

Scott checked out each exhibition booth we passed, raking his gaze over shelves of vases, figurines, plates, bowls, dolls, stuffed animals, candles, and other doodads. Mirrors in every shape and size imaginable covered the walls of another booth, while the one next to it had jewelry hanging from rafts of display boards. Lace-edged linens and generous swathes of curtains in silks, satins, and velvets, combined with rafts of crystal and ribbon-bedecked pillows to make the booth beyond it into a sybaritic boudoir worthy of some Eastern sheik.

We turned the corner onto the twenty-two hundred aisle and headed for the Grantwood & Bethel booth.

I almost ran into Lisa, who was coming the other way.

"Hey, girl," she said, "You're looking much better this morning." She noticed Scott, who had stopped to wait for me, so I introduced them. I didn't say what his job was. As they shook hands, Lisa gave Scott a comprehensive and appreciative look. Then she turned to me and cocked an eyebrow. "Gotta go now. Catch up with you later."

Her look said much more. She wanted to know about my companion. She would indeed catch up with me and she'd have more than a few questions about Scott. I'd have to decide what to tell her.

"I'll bet she sells a hell of a lot of whatever it is she sells," Scott said. He sounded less dazzled than I expected.

"She's an independent sales rep, so she sells a lot of different things and helps out at different booths. Need I say she's in high demand?"

"I think we can take that as a given." Again, Scott's tone was surprisingly dry. Most men on the receiving end of a Lisa Willamont once-over ended up with their tongues hanging out.

At the Grantwood & Bethel booth, only one young woman stood out front, leafing through sell sheets. When I introduced myself and asked for Stan Grantwood, she nodded toward the curtained-off area. I knocked on the metal frame that formed part of the side wall of the booth.

"Yes?" Grantwood's voice came back to me.

"Heather McNeil. May I come in?"

"Of course."

He stood beside a pile of boxes at the far end, but came over to us. I introduced Scott and the men shook hands. Grantwood was a couple of inches shorter but broader and heavier.

"Scott is part of our security team," I said. "Have you received any more threats?"

Grantwood shook his head, irritation obvious in the abrupt gesture. "No. It's a tempest in a teapot."

"Any threat should be taken seriously," Scott said. "Have you reported it to the police?"

"I told the detective about it yesterday. I also told him I didn't think it amounted to anything."

"Let them decide," Scott advised.

"I will. I've got way too many other things on my mind. The police can handle a meaningless threat."

"You don't think there's a connection with your partner's murder?" I asked.

Grantwood looked up at me, and his eyes narrowed. Something shadowy and almost dangerous lurked in his stare. "The threats are nothing. Just someone with a grudge and too much time on his hands. It's not something I dwell on, and nothing you should worry about, either."

His expression smoothed out into pleasant blandness as he went all salesman on me. "However, I do appreciate the way the Center is taking it seriously and doing so much to help and look out for me." A glance down at paperwork suggested dismissal.

"That's a worried man," Scott said when we'd moved away from the G & B booth.

"I know. He's trying to hide it and pretend nothing's going on, but it's not very convincing."

"The question is, why is he trying so hard to convince everyone it's nothing?"

"He wants a merger to go through very badly and is afraid this might create problems?"

"Or he knows who's behind it."

"Why'd he say anything about the phone threat, then?" I thought back. "Wait a minute. It was Ellen Spencer who mentioned it. Maybe he wouldn't have said anything if she hadn't found out about it."

"Maybe."

We crossed the aisle to Martin Chang's booth. When I introduced Scott, Chang greeted him like an old friend, or maybe the cavalry coming to the rescue. I reiterated my warning that Scott was there to keep watch rather than sell pottery. Still, Scott had to learn to talk the talk, so I left him and Chang discussing various types of candles.

My next destination was what I'd come to think of as the Popcorn Aisle. I wanted to find out if Blue Hills had had the machine serviced. But as I passed by the G & B booth, I ran into Ellen Spencer. Literally.

She rounded a corner in a wide arc, digging for something in her purse. I'd let my thoughts drift. By the time either of us saw the collision coming, it was too late to avoid it completely. We snagged arms and bumped shoulders as we each tried to lean out of the way. My small shoulder purse remained safely in place even as I teetered, but Spencer's handbag had been hanging on her wrist and it flew off when we collided. A sturdy table beside us helped us both right ourselves without damage to life or limb.

The purse, however, was on the fast track to destruction. It slid along the tiled floor until it smashed against the base of a curtained table. A life-sized ceramic statue of a blue-and-red parrot sitting on a tree branch rested on the table, which shook and rattled, making bird and perch waver precariously. Several people converged, reaching to brace the display, but it stabilized on its own, thank heaven. I had horrible visions of the whole thing crashing to the floor, splattering plaster bird remains over the entire exhibit and a couple of neighboring ones.

The pocketbook didn't fare as well. It had sprayed its innards along the aisle. Spencer and I both scrambled after the contents, assisted by a few other helpful souls. I retrieved a lipstick, a couple of coins, the empty wrapper from one of those sanitizing hand wipes, and a lovely pin in the shape of a dragonfly, set with blue sapphires in various shades. I wondered why she wasn't wearing it, then realized that, as pretty as it was, it wouldn't go well with her burgundy suit.

I returned the items and apologized for not looking where I was going.

"I wasn't, either," she admitted, while stuffing everything into her purse. She handled the pin carefully, wrapping it in a handkerchief before settling it back inside the bag.

"Thanks for all your help and concern," she said. "I wish Stan would take the threats more seriously, but he's determined to act like nothing's changed. He can be so stubborn. I guess it's a man thing, but he feels like once he's made up his mind about something, nothing and no one's going to change it."

"If it makes you feel better, I've got a security person assigned to keep an eye on your booth,"

"Thank you. That helps. I guess I'd better get going. We'll be opening in a few minutes."

I made it to the Popcorn Aisle without further mishap. I checked at the Blue Hills booth where the same fierce woman I'd talked to yesterday coldly informed me that the service people had looked at the machine last night and found nothing wrong with it.

"They didn't say why it was burning the popcorn?" I asked.

"They suggested perhaps the person running it wasn't paying close attention. I've had a talk with her, and she's promised to watch it very closely today."

"All right, but I don't want to get any more complaints."

"I plan to keep an eye on it myself," she said, and I pitied the poor operator under the supervision of the Blue Hills dragon lady.

Janelle had given me a list of other things to check on, but as I was leaving, an odd banging sounded from the next aisle over. Three booths from the end of that passage, I found a young couple trying to repair a metal support that held up one corner of their backdrop. Their booth featured stationery, plaques, keychains, fobs, and other items decorated with line drawings of big-eyed animals in a style so distinctive I figured one of the pair had to be the artist. Theirs wasn't the most sophisticated display, but it was attractively put together.

I introduced myself and said, "What's the problem?"

The young man, who was attacking the metal with hammer, pliers, and no idea what to do, looked up at me. "I think we've lost a bolt here." He wiped at a damp spot on his forehead. "I guess I'll have to find a hardware store. Maybe you can give me directions to one close by?"

"I can do better than that." I pulled out the cell phone and pressed the speed-dial button for Mark.

He answered on the third buzz. "What's up?"

I explained.

"Sounds like a job for Super-Mark," he said. "I'll be there in five minutes."

I chatted with the couple while we waited. It took almost fifteen minutes, but the time passed quickly. As I'd guessed, the wife was the artist, the husband the accountant, and the two of them were trying to build a business based on her skill and clever product ideas. They had a firm grasp on the realities of the industry—how difficult it would be to succeed and how high the odds against them stood. I was happy to take one small burden off their plates.

Mark arrived carrying an enormous toolbox. He muttered to himself as he clattered around in the metal box for a minute. Ten minutes later he'd screwed a bolt into place.

The couple thanked both of us profusely and handed us packets of note cards. We're not supposed to accept gifts unless they're very small, but this seemed like it would qualify as small. It would have been churlish to refuse, so I thanked them in return.

The artist must have seen me eyeing the cupful of pens, too, because she pulled one out and handed it to me. It was a really nice one, made of sleek metal, jewel-toned aqua for the body with a silver-tone top. An oval on the side bore a miniature version of one of her drawings of a cat. I'm not much of a pet person, but this one was just too cute, and besides, I definitely *am* a pen person.

Over the next hour, I ticked off several items on Janelle's checklist.

Then I got cornered again by people wanting the latest news on the murder investigation, which amounted to repeating "I don't know" a couple of dozen more times.

It was nearly eleven by the time I got to the last stop on the list, Gaviscelli. I was curious about their product line since Lisa had said it would be a good fit with G & B's, which seemed to be mostly collectible knick-knacks. I was even more curious about their CEO, Dave Powell, but wasn't sure if I could manage a credible way to meet him.

Gaviscelli had one of the largest and most elaborate booths at the show. They had managed to encompass an entire half of an aisle by renting all the booths on either side, and they showed a wide-ranging assortment of home-décor products. Mirrors and wall art took up about a quarter of the space, with lamps comprising another quarter. The other side of the booth featured a series of alcoves formed by shelves standing perpendicular to the back walls of the booth. Those held an extensive collection of vases, small picture frames, candleholders, trays, bowls, and other accessories.

At the back of that side was an enclosed space that looked like a tent with translucent white fiberglass panels for sides.

I needed to pick up a press release they wanted copied and distributed, but several people came over to grill me about Tim Bethel's demise and what was being done about it.

The reps and other salespeople made way, though, when a tall, lean, dark-haired man in his late forties came through and approached me. He stuck out a hand and said, "Dave Powell. I understand you're Miss McNeil, assistant director of the Center."

I took his hand and said, "Actually, I'm assistant to the director, Janelle Addison. Heather McNeil. Please call me Heather."

The handshake was neither too firm nor too limp, not too enthusiastic but not too wimpy, either. Just right. I wondered how long he'd practiced to get it so perfect.

"Glad to meet you, Heather," he said. "And I'm Dave. I'd like to talk to you if you have a few minutes?"

Wow. I hadn't even had to work any subterfuge to get an introduction. Was I living right or what? Then it occurred to me to wonder what was on *his* agenda.

"Of course," I said.

"Let's go back here, if you don't mind." He nodded toward the enclosure at the far end of the booth. I followed him there and he ushered me inside. The interior looked much like the back area at G & B. Boxes stacked against a far wall held sell sheets and promotional booklets. Order forms and clipboards occupied a folding table at the side, with a couple of cases of bottled water beneath it. A small refrigerator hummed in a corner. Boxes of assorted soft drinks had been stacked next to it.

The panels let in some light and a couple of lamps added to the illumination. Powell pulled out a folding metal chair and set it down next to one already there so that when we sat, we faced each other, with a couple of inches separating our knees. His eyes were dark, an attractive warm brown, his gaze direct, sharp, and assessing, but in a comfortably interested way.

He offered drinks and snacks, which I declined. Then he said, "You're the young lady who found Tim Bethel's body, aren't you?"

"Yes."

"That must have been tough for you. Dumped in a trash can. What an inglorious end for Tim."

He said it with an odd, unreadable inflection. I honestly couldn't decide whether the news dismayed him or gave him a weird satisfaction. His reaction creeped me out. I'd instinctively liked him on first glance, but now I wondered if I should revise that.

"A detective talked to me about it for quite a while yesterday," he added. "Not that I had much to tell him. I saw Tim on Wednesday, late afternoon, so I couldn't tell them anything about what he'd done later. Did they say anything to you about it?"

This wasn't random conversation, so what was he digging for? "'Fraid not. They asked me about what I knew, of course, but I hadn't even met Mr. Bethel before I found his body. Did he seem like he had anything on his mind when you talked to him?"

Powell's dark eyebrows rose. He thought about it for a minute before he said, "He seemed like the same old Tim to me. Excited about the show and G & B's plans, but always on the lookout for new opportunities." Something flickered in Powell's eyes, and his gaze flashed to the floor for a moment. He wasn't telling the truth, or at least not the whole truth. He didn't give me time to think about it though, before he asked, "You'd never met him at all?"

"I guess I might have last year, but I don't think so. I don't think I would have forgotten him."

"Probably not." A bit of amusement flittered across his face and disappeared. "The one thing you have to understand about Tim, he approached everything with enthusiasm and a competitive spirit. Everything—everyone, in truth—was a challenge to him. Every interaction was a contest, and he had to win. No matter what it cost."

Powell described Tim Bethel with what sounded like a mixture of admiration and loathing. I wondered which aspects he'd hated and which he'd wanted to emulate.

"Rumor has it that he was a highly driven person," I said, "and that he alienated a lot of people."

"Understatements, both. He was aggressive to the max and a lot of people here hated his guts. Which is why the cops might have a tough time figuring out who killed him." He saw my frown. "I know the police haven't said it was murder, but we both know it was. And there are plenty of candidates for killer. What is it they look for…motivation? I'll bet more than half the people on the floor might have wanted to kill him."

"Then I suppose the police will have to look at other things to try to figure it out. Like who was around to do it or what kind of evidence there is."

Something moved in his expression on the word "evidence."

"Do you know if there is any?" he asked.

So this was what he wanted from me. Or maybe one of the things he wanted.

"The police haven't told us much about their investigation. If they found anything, they haven't mentioned it. It may hinge on who was around that night."

Again, something made his expression tighten ever so slightly, but he smoothed it out within moments. "I heard Ellen Spencer saw him about seven, and then someone saw his wife here around seven-thirty."

I still didn't get where this was leading, but that last fact was news to me. "Really? I thought his wife didn't arrive until yesterday."

"That's what everyone thought, but people saw her on Wednesday. Someone even overheard her arguing with Tim."

A tinge of anxiety laced Powell's words, along with something else. He was testing me, probing to find out what I knew.

Well, well. This *was* getting interesting. "That's all news to me," I said. "Do you think she might have done it?"

"Killed Tim?" He sounded genuinely shocked. "Good Lord, no. But I'm afraid the police might suspect it."

"I imagine it's fairly likely they will, if they find out she lied about when she arrived."

"I know." He let out his breath on a sigh.

"You obviously know Chloe Bethel," I ventured.

"I've known her for a long time. She couldn't have killed him. She might have wanted to at times, even though she adored Tim. She might have had reason to. But she wouldn't do it. It isn't in her."

"I'm not sure we ever know what's in people until they're pushed to the wall. Then sometimes they surprise us."

He looked at me with a combination of shock and suspicion. "*You* think she might have killed him."

"I have no idea. I met Mrs. Bethel yesterday, for a few minutes. How could I judge from that?"

My cell phone beeped, announcing a new text message, but I ignored it for the moment.

He shook his head. "You're right. I'm sorry. It's just I've known Chloe for years. She's one of the nicest, most genuine people I've ever met, and it's a damned miracle, considering her family."

Interesting. He was probably just a few years older than Chloe Bethel. A good-looking man with a lean, gym-honed body and spray-on tan. Had there been something between him and Tim Bethel's wife?

"I liked her, too," I said, "and I don't think she killed her husband. I was just pointing out that it's hard to know everything about a person."

"Who do you think did it, then?"

Why was he asking me? "I really have no idea. And it's not my job to try to find out."

"No, of course. I just wish I knew."

"I think most of us do." I studied him. The salesman was trying to figure an angle, a way to get something he wanted from me. But he couldn't come right out and ask and he was having a hard time finding a handle on whatever this was. I suspected it might have something to do with finding out exactly what the police knew, but he wasn't going to voice that directly.

"Is the Center doing anything to increase security?" he asked.

"We've brought in additional people, and we're keeping a close eye on things. We've got someone assigned full-time to watch Stan Grantwood."

His surprise looked genuine to me. "You do? Why?"

"His partner might have been murdered. He could be in danger, too."

"You think so?"

"Let me ask you this: Can you think of any reason

why someone would want to stop a merger of Grantwood & Bethel and some other company—say, yours, for
instance?"

I could sense the wheels turning in his head, and I
knew before he opened his mouth he wasn't going to say
anything useful.

"Right offhand, no," he said, and that was an out-and-
out lie.

"May I ask you a question?" I made it sound all innocent.

"I can't promise an answer," he said.

"I understand. You've told me about Tim Bethel. What
about Stan Grantwood? Is he as aggressive and ambitious
as Tim?"

A flare of relief crossed his face, but then his expression
went remote while he considered the question. It shouldn't
have required that much thought, but I already knew there
was more going on in this conversation than showed on
the surface. I just wish I knew what I was stepping on in
the depths I couldn't see.

"No. Stan's driven, in his own way, but it's not the same
way. If Tim was a laser pistol, Stan's more like a batter-
ing ram. Tim was the outside guy, the one with the charm,
wit, and intelligence to handle relations with suppliers and
customers. Stan's the inside man, the organizer, the one
who keeps the company running."

A tentative knock sounded on the frame and then a
young woman stuck her head in. "Sorry to interrupt," she
said, "but the editor from *Luxury Home* is here. I thought
you'd want to talk to her."

"I'll be there in a moment." Powell turned back to me.
"Can I ask a favor? If you hear anything about the murder,
would you let me know? I have a couple of good reasons
for my interest, even if I can't talk about them right now."

That pretty much answered the question about the merger. I told him I'd share what I could with him but warned it wasn't likely to be much.

As I took my leave, he handed me a piece of paper, the press release he wanted copied.

I left the Gaviscelli booth and ducked into the nearest door marked "Authorized Personnel Only." It proved to be a closet for storing cleaning supplies, but it also provided the commodities I most needed at the moment: privacy and quiet.

I had a text message and two voice mails on my phone. The text message read: Up 4 lunch? Hannahs 1.15? L. I texted her back a one-word reply: On.

I was just pressing the button to retrieve my voice mails when the phone buzzed, startling me so badly I almost dropped it.

"Heather? Where are you?" Janelle asked. The background noise nearly drowned out her words, so she had to be on the floor.

"I just got the press release from Gaviscelli. I was planning to take it upstairs. Anything urgent I need to do down here first?"

"Yes! I got a camera-phone report on twenty-eight-oh-six and need help with crowd control at eleven forty-two. Poston Brothers has a decorating guru signing copies of her newest book and it's turning into a mob scene. Take your pick."

"Camera phone."

"Good choice," Janelle said, very dryly. "Except I can't spare any extra security. They're all trying to keep the book signing from turning into a riot. You'd think they were handing out gold bars or lottery tickets. Oh, wait. Pull Scott Brandon off G & B for a few minutes if camera-guy gives you any trouble. You have his cell?"

"Got it. I'll use it if necessary."

I left my nice, quiet closet for the chaos of the show floor again. It took a few minutes to get there, especially since people still tried to stop me to ask about Tim Bethel. I shook most of them off with a minimum of rudeness.

The person who'd reported the camera incident described a woman in her mid-thirties wearing a flouncy, multi-colored skirt and a blue shirt. He wasn't one-hundred-percent sure she'd been taking pictures, he said.

"But something about the way she was acting made me suspicious. She seemed just a little too casual when she pulled out the phone, and then she was turning this way and that. People don't move like that when they're really talking on the phone. And I think I saw a flash coming from it a couple of times." He shrugged. "I guess that's not much help."

"It's enough to start with," I assured him. And a good description. Her clothes were distinctive enough to make her easy to spot, especially in this crowd, where most of the women wore conservative clothes—business suits in neutrals or dark slacks.

I walked the length of the aisle but didn't see anyone resembling the description, so I turned at the end and went back up the next aisle. I didn't spot her until I was three aisles away. She stood a third of the way up the passage, cell phone in her hand.

Instead of lifting it to her ear, she fiddled with buttons, holding it out as if she was reading a text message. But she kept moving it into different angles. It was subtly done and would fool someone not suspecting anything else. But I could see the occasional wink of the flash as she took pictures of some of the merchandise offered at a booth displaying luxury pillows and bedroom décor.

I didn't recognize the woman and was pretty sure we'd

never met. But when she turned and saw me watching, her eyes widened, her stance straightened, and a challenging expression crossed her face. Busted, and she knew it. She clamped the phone shut, dropped it in her purse, turned, and began to walk quickly away.

I pulled my own phone out, pushed Craig's speed dial, and asked him to alert all the entrance guards to stop a woman in a long, multi-colored skirt and blue top from leaving the show floor. He promised to pass it on right away. I then dialed Scott Brandon and asked for help.

The woman reached the back end of the aisle and turned left. I kept the phone line open with Scott as I tracked her. I described the woman and then we worked on positioning to intercept her. I was currently at the middle of aisle twenty-five hundred. He was coming from twenty-two hundred, off to my left. With a bit of maneuvering, we should be able to keep her from getting past us.

"Head toward the back," I suggested to him. "I'll stay in the middle and we should be able to box her in."

"I see her," Scott said moments later. "She just turned into twenty-six."

"I'm heading that way."

I got to the intersection of twenty-six hundred and the center cross-aisle about three steps ahead of the picture-taking woman. She stopped short when she saw me move into her path. Her eyes met mine. The determination in her face made me wonder if she would barrel past and try to bowl me over. But she turned to go back the way she came and discovered Scott stood right behind her.

She whirled toward me again. "What's going on?" she demanded. She did a good imitation of outraged innocence. "Why are you guys chasing me?"

I introduced myself and said, "May I see your cell phone, please?"

She looked aghast. "Why?" She clutched at her purse, but too late. Scott had already reached in and pulled out the phone. Over her outstretched and grasping hand, he passed it off to me.

The woman reached to grab it, but I turned away from her, flipped the phone open, took a moment to study the controls, then pressed the biggest button, hoping to get a menu. Bingo. The photo option was there along with a way to review pictures. I started paging through them. There were a lot of them. More than I would have thought the phone could hold. I checked, and, sure enough, there was a card slot in the back.

I turned back to her. "You've been busy. How long have you been here?"

She didn't say a word, but if looks were razor blades, I'd be lying on the floor in shreds. I began pressing the delete button on each picture. "Did you read the notices about no photography?" I asked her. "They're posted in several places."

Again she remained quiet, but her eyes narrowed as she watched me destroy her work. I wondered if she would try to reach out and grab the phone away from me. She wanted to. Her body all but vibrated with anger held in check. I suspected that if Scott hadn't been present, I'd be stretched out on the floor while she fled the scene. Or maybe we'd be rolling around, wrestling for possession of the phone.

I deleted pictures and we escorted her to the nearest exit.

"I'll trade the phone for your badge," I told her. She yanked the lanyard holding the badge over her head and slapped the cord over my right arm. I grabbed for it with my left hand and snagged it. As I handed the phone back, I added, "On our way out, you faced the security camera and it got a good look at you. That image will be shared with all of our entrance guards, so don't try to re-register and get back in. If we catch you trying, we'll call the police and prosecute for trespassing."

She glared at me. "Your employers will be hearing about this, young lady. Your rude treatment is inexcusable. You'll hear from my lawyers, too. I promise you that." Then she marched off in a huff, out the doors to the street.

"Sweetheart," Scott commented, watching her exit.

"No joke." I let out my breath in a long sigh. "Well, my inner bitch is now satisfied for a while."

Scott stared at me. "Remind me to stay on your good side. What was that all about?"

"We don't allow photography on the show floor. She obviously knew that and was trying to sneak pictures with the camera phone."

"I gathered that. Why?"

"Why don't we allow pictures? In a word: knockoffs. Cheap replicas of expensive products. Usually mass-produced overseas and delivered to market, sometimes even before the original producers get theirs out. It's been a problem for ages, but in the last few years some of the Far East sites can take an image of a product and be churning out knockoffs on an assembly line a week later. We ban photography in an effort to protect our exhibitors. It's a losing battle, but at least we look like we're trying."

"Learn something new every half hour or so here. I'd better get back to Chang's. By the way, I sold fifteen cases of candles this morning." His grin showed a bit of ironic pride. "I think Chang might offer me a job."

A flare of panic curled in my stomach. "Would you take it?" His smile broadened, almost as if he could see my reaction. "No. I'd go nuts having to extol the extraordinary properties of candles and vases for very long." His expression darkened. "Besides it's…not quite— No. Never mind."

"Not quite what?"

"Truth?" He gave me a funny look.

"Truth."

"It's not quite real, somehow. It's like a carnival. Or a circus. Loud, glitzy, dizzying, kind of fun but not real."

"I can see how it looks that way. And in some senses—and some cases—it's true. But there's more to it. Think about how many peoples' livelihood depends on the outcome of this show."

"But it's about—gewgaws. Sorry, decorative accessories and gift items. Keychains, statues, mirrors, candles, pillows, stuff no one really needs."

"Are you sure? I don't think it's that easy to dismiss, but it's a philosophical discussion we don't really have time for right now."

"Right. Maybe tonight. By the way, did Janelle tell you that I'm your date tonight?"

"What?"

"The boss lady wants me to be your escort tonight, so I can keep an eye on Stan Grantwood. She said your ticket would cover a date."

"Yeah, it will. But isn't that above and beyond? Do you get overtime pay for it?"

"I don't know. Doesn't matter. Heck, I get a date with you out of it. Even if it is a kind of a faux date. Don't you think that's its own reward?"

The words were said lightly, but what was in his eyes wasn't light at all. It made me uncomfortable. And excited. And uncomfortable that I was excited. "You don't have to resort to that to get a date, and I don't have that high an opinion of myself."

He laughed. It lit his oddly colored eyes with sparkling glitters of blue and gray. "I'm not touching the truth of either of those statements. I expect being your escort tonight to be the most pleasant business assignment I've had in a long time. Why don't I drive you home this evening? That way I'll know where to come to pick you up."

"You don't have to take it that far. I can meet you at the hotel."

"Will it make any difference if I say that I'd *like* to drive you home?"

"In that case, how can I refuse?"

"You can't. That was part of my nasty, nefarious plan."

"Sounds interesting. I can't wait to hear the rest of it."

"You'll have to wait until later," he said. "I need to get back to work."

I looked at my watch and yelped. "So do I." I had exactly twelve minutes to get the Gaviscelli press release upstairs, hope Tina was at her desk, tell her what to do with it, and get back down and across the street to Hannah's to meet Lisa for lunch.

When I charged into the office upstairs, I found Tina buffing her nails and talking on the phone. She moved her mouth away from the phone long enough to say, "Janelle wants to see you."

I handed Tina the press release and explained what I needed.

Janelle was also on the phone. She gestured toward a chair and said, into the handset, "I know someone I can recommend." After a short pause, she added, "I'm sure you're upset. Anyone would be. But it'll work out. I'll talk to you again in a few minutes."

She hung up the phone, drew a deep breath, and let it out on a long sigh. "The police have detained Chloe Bethel for questioning. She thinks they're going to arrest her."

SEVEN

"THEY FOUND OUT she arrived here a day earlier than she said?" I asked.

Janelle's eyebrows rose. "So that's why. But who told you?"

"Dave Powell of Gaviscelli's. He's known her for some time."

"I wonder how he knew she was here when no one else did."

"He says she was seen by others. He also said she'd argued with her husband the day he was killed."

"Interesting," Janelle said. "But beside the point right now. I just wanted to let you know I'm getting a lawyer for her."

"Okay. I'm headed out to lunch. I'll check with you when I get back." I started to leave but stopped at the doorway. "Oh, and nice maneuvering with Scott Brandon. Escort, my foot! When did you decide to become Mama Matchmaker?" I turned to look at her.

She wore one of *those* grins. "He's hot, isn't he?"

"Yeah, but I suspect he's bad news, too. There's something going on with him. That man doesn't belong working here as a security guard, and I don't like any of the reasons I can come up with for why he's reduced to it."

"Would you rather not have him go with you? I can get him in some other way."

"Don't you dare. I'm looking forward to it. Just don't make a habit of this."

"Oh, please," she said. "Me? Ms. Relationship Success herself?"

"I feel better. Gotta run."

I was ten minutes late getting to Hannah's, which was across the street and a block down from the Center. Lisa waited at a table for two near the back. She wasn't looking at me, and something about her demeanor struck me. Depression? Sorrow?

She jumped, startled, when I apologized for my tardiness and sat down, but she recovered quickly and had her usual perky smile back in place. I picked up a menu, but put it back moments later. "What's wrong?" I asked. "Bad day? Sales rotten?"

Lisa never got down or looked discouraged. At least not during the time I'd known her. Which wasn't all that long, in truth, since I saw her maybe five or six times a year, for an hour or so each time.

"No," she said. "I'm a bit tired, I think. You hanging in?"

"So far."

The waiter came and took our orders. When he departed Lisa said, "Tell me about Mr. Tall, Blond, and Scrumptious, the guy you were with this morning."

"He's a sales rep for Chang." I laughed at her raised eyebrow. "Cute, isn't he?"

She chuckled. "Girlfriend, cute is for teddy bears. That one is no teddy bear. He's flat-out gorgeous. Not pretty-boy pretty, but better."

"You interested?"

She let out a sigh. "I would be, but there's someone else. You remember I mentioned Jim Forrester last year?"

"I've got a vague memory, but I didn't realize it was serious. Isn't he in the army or something?"

"He's a Ranger."

"I'm impressed."

"I was, too. And he's a good guy. Really good. And he's got a killer smile. Dimples, lights in the eyes, the whole package."

"So what's the problem?"

"He's off doing intelligence in some Asian hot spot you couldn't find on a map with a magnifying glass. And I haven't heard from him in almost a month."

"Ouch. That bites." Now I knew why she'd looked so down.

"You're telling me." She picked up her tea and took a long drink. Her hand shook enough to set the ice cubes rattling as she put down the glass.

"Does he do that often?"

She waited while the server slid plates in front of us. "A couple of weeks, sometimes. Never this long without a word."

"I don't know what to say. It's terrible for you."

"I keep asking myself if he's worth it. All the agony and uncertainty. Unfortunately for me, he is."

"Talk about your seriously mixed blessings."

"Yeah. But, hey, I can't get all gloomy and teary-eyed. I've still got to sell a bunch of lamps this afternoon. At least I'm off the hook for any dinners tonight. I plan to go back to the hotel, get a drink at the bar, order room service, have a nice long, hot bath and then a nice, long sleep. I suppose you're stuck going to the Design Achievement Awards dinner."

"Yeah, but it might not be that bad."

"Oh?" She gave me a sharp look over a forkful of salad. "Come on, girl. Spill it."

"Scott Brandon is going with me."

"Mr. Tall, Blond, and Scrumptious himself? When did

all this happen, and how come you haven't mentioned him before?"

"It's new," I admitted. "I haven't known him long, but he seems interesting."

"Interesting?" Her eyebrows went all the way up. "Interesting is meatloaf for dinner with vanilla ice cream for dessert. He's steak and crème brûlée. Solid and filling first, then smooth and delicious to cap it off."

"Too many calories; dangerous to my health."

"Live dangerously for once. Was he in the military? He has that look about him. Reminds me a bit of my guy. Or maybe law enforcement." Her eyes widened. "He's security, isn't he? An undercover detective? Chang's booth! He's keeping watch on G & B, right?"

"Dammit, will you quit being so smart? You're not supposed to know. Yeah, he is, but do *not* tell anyone else."

"My lips are sealed. Seriously. I won't tell a soul. It'll hurt because you know how I love gossip, but I'll refrain, I promise. So, is he married or committed?"

"I don't think so. I haven't actually asked him, but he doesn't act like someone who is."

"Then go for it."

"I can't even think about luxuries like having a personal life until the show's over."

"By the way, speaking of G & B, I've heard some juicy stuff. You interested?"

"Heck, yes."

"There's a rumor that the cops are questioning Chloe Bethel because she was here a day earlier than she was supposed to be." She watched my reaction. "You already knew that. True?"

"I knew about the cops questioning her. I've heard the same rumor that she was here a day earlier."

"Well, drat. I thought I had a good one for you. But

that's not all. One of the reps I worked with yesterday was at G & B for a while. She was happy to spill all the dirt she knew about Tim Bethel and the company. This is all third- and fourth-hand gossip, you understand, and you didn't hear any of it from me, right?"

"Right."

"Not all was well in G & B land. They may need this merger more than anyone is letting on. G & B's product line is mostly collectibles, or at least that's where the bulk of their profits have come from, and it's been really profitable for them. But the buzz says the collectible craze is pretty much over. It seems that for the past couple of years, G & B has been working to make the bottom line look better by cutting expenses to the bone. They've laid off people and cut back everywhere possible. It may not be common knowledge since they're private and don't have to file the same reports a publicly held company would, but rumors say they're in trouble. I've even heard they may lose one of their design licenses. One of the big ones. That would really bite them."

She chewed a bit of food and sipped her iced tea. "The rumor also says that Stan Grantwood and Tim Bethel have not been seeing eye-to-eye about the direction of the company and how to reverse the downward trend. In fact, there was one very loud knock-down drag-out that was overheard by half the employees."

"Given what I've heard about Tim Bethel's temperament, I guess it can't be too surprising."

"I think I mentioned he manages to alienate people regularly."

"I wonder if one of the partners wanted to sell the company and the other didn't."

Lisa shrugged. "My source didn't say."

"Of the two, Stan Grantwood would be more amenable to selling out. Or would he?"

"Couldn't tell you," Lisa said. "I can see it going either way, depending on the terms of the deal. So this is news to you?"

"Yup. Good gossip. Thanks."

"Welcome. Got one more. It's not relevant to your problem, but it's kind of interesting."

"All right, I'm shallow. I want to know, even if it has no bearing."

"Rumor has it Ellen Spencer's one of those people who's having a show affair."

"Show affair? One where she only meets her lover at the trade shows?"

"Yes. She's still a pretty good-looking woman for her age."

"Could it have been with Tim Bethel?"

"I doubt it. I think that would have been too complicated for him. He liked one-offs."

"True. Grantwood? Nah. She's worried about him, but I don't see any sign she's in love with him."

"Smart people don't have show affairs with co-workers, competitors, or strategic partners," Lisa said. "Too much opportunity for problems."

"Ellen Spencer didn't get to be vice president of sales for G & B by being stupid."

"Right. That's it. All I know."

For the rest of the meal we talked about TV shows, movies, clothes, and fashions. We said goodbye in the Center's lobby and I went upstairs.

Janelle was still in her office, looking even more frazzled than earlier. "What's up?" I asked her.

"It looks like they're going to arrest Chloe Bethel for killing Tim."

"Do you know why?"

"I don't know all of it," Janelle said. "But apparently what you heard about her and Tim arguing was on the money."

"Doesn't seem like much to build a case on. They must have more than that."

"There was something about a note they found on Tim's body, but I don't know any details."

"Do you believe that she killed him?"

"Not really. But the police must have pretty good reason to think she did. Anyway, I can't spend too much time worrying about it. I've got my hands full with the show." She glanced at the stack of papers on her desk. "And I've got the detective and a lawyer coming in a few minutes to talk to me. My boss has decided to hang around, too."

"What do you need me to do?"

She handed me a couple of scraps of paper with scribbled notes. "This stuff is mostly hand-holding. A couple of maintenance issues. A complaint about a neighboring booth. You know the drill." She sighed. "I feel guilty sloughing so much of this off onto you, but you bring it on yourself."

"How's that?"

"You're so darn good at it. Everyone tells me how wonderful you are. Even when you don't actually do anything, venting to you seems to make people feel better. You have a way of soothing nerves and calming frayed tempers. Think you can bottle it so I can give it to some others?"

"I have no idea what it is. I mostly listen."

"That's the thing. You listen so well. You let people talk; you don't interrupt; you don't try to cut them short. You sympathize nicely. People eat it up."

"It's not something I practice or try to do."

"I know. It wouldn't work as well if you did."

Janelle's phone rang and I took that as my cue to start earning my salary. The first couple of items were routine stuff. All easy to handle.

Dave Powell at Gaviscelli called, asking me to talk to him again, but I still had the last item from Janelle to finish first.

At booth eight sixty-four, Stanaker-Wells, Inc., I stopped and asked for the person in charge.

A young woman at the booth who identified herself as Joanne said he'd gone for a moment but would be right back. She asked if I could wait. When she offered a bottle of water, I accepted gratefully. We talked about their business—wind chimes and other outdoor and garden accessories—and how the show was going for them.

"We've done really well," she told me with genuine enthusiasm and a bit of surprise. "This is our first time so we didn't know what to expect. We haven't had a really huge amount of traffic, but we've written several good orders, so we're happy. Plus we have promises from a couple of buyers to come back, including one from—get this!—Halson's."

Joanne's excitement and enthusiasm lifted my spirits with a reminder of the kinds of good things that could happen at these shows. I agreed it would be awesome to sell their products into Halson's, a large chain of home-décor specialty stores. I started to add that I needed to be going and would stop back later, when she looked up the aisle and said, "Wait, please. Here comes Dan now."

A large, heavyset man in his early thirties approached. His eyes and expression redeemed the plainness of his features. The good humor and infectious enthusiasm on his face made it attractive, though more for its warmth than its beauty. I'm as shallow as the next person when it comes to good looks—witness my reaction to Scott Brandon—

but working here has taught me to value other things, too. Things like honesty, integrity, and a pleasant personality. If I'd learned anything, it was that outer and inner beauty didn't correlate all that often. I treasured the exceptions, wherever I found them. I think that's why I like Lisa so much. I really hoped what I read on this man's face accurately conveyed what was beneath.

When I introduced myself, his mobile features showed both gratitude and a hint of relief. His handshake was nice. A little too firm, but I forgive that. Men are trained to do it.

"Thank you for coming by, Heather," he said. He drew a deep breath and did a funny little eye roll. "I hope you can help. That woman's going to drive me crazy." He ran his fingers over a decorative porcelain stepping stone. "I'm a pretty low-key guy, but she's going to push me into doing something we'll both regret if she keeps it up."

"She who?"

"That woman with Trimstates. Sue…" He looked at his female assistant for help.

"Savotsky." She and I said it at the same time.

"Yeah. Her."

My turn to sigh. "What's she doing now?"

"Now?" he said. "So I'm not the only one she's tormenting?"

"Hardly. What's she been doing to you?"

"She keeps coming by and accusing us of stealing her customers. She says we're luring buyers away from her booth. Bad-mouthing her products, her company, her… person, even." He shook his head. "That's not how we do business. I wouldn't do any of those thing normally, but in her case, I'm getting tempted," he said.

Joanne added, "She sort of accused us of stealing a couple of designs, too. Even though we had them first. This is the first time we've come to the show, so I don't know how she thinks we could even have seen her stuff before."

Dan took up the tale again. "I've talked to a couple of the others around here, and she's been doing the same thing to them. Not about stealing designs, but accusing them of luring her business away. She's gotten kind of loud and aggressive about it a couple of times, too. It's driving us all crazy."

"I can imagine."

"The weird thing is I hear she'll do that to buyers, too, if they're not from big chains or large stores." He shook his head. "She accuses us of stealing her business, but then she drives away people who do stop at her booth. The woman's gotta be a bit nutso."

Urgh. Another talk with Sue Savotsky was in my near future and I was so not looking forward to it. I let them vent for a bit longer, but when they wound down, I promised Dan and Joanne I'd have a talk with the woman. That seemed to satisfy them, thank heavens. They smiled and thanked me when I left their booth.

It would take some mental girding of my loins to face that woman, and I wasn't quite ready for it yet.

Dave Powell seemed like the lesser irritation at the moment, so I headed for Gaviscelli next. People crowded into his booth, but most of them hovered around a table in the nearest corner where they served delicious-smelling canapés. I sniffed crabmeat and cheese. My stomach growled. I'd already had one filling meal at lunch and would have another big dinner, so I told my stomach to shut up as I walked on by. I could've sworn I heard a bit of crabmeat calling my name, but I resisted.

Powell stood in front of a wall full of mirrors, with several other people crowding around him. He saw me approaching and made eye contact. After a moment he walked toward me. He didn't speak, merely angled toward the enclosed area and gestured for me to follow.

No one else occupied the tent with its translucent fiberglass sides. Powell retrieved a bottle of diet soda from the small refrigerator. I declined when he asked if I wanted one.

"They arrested Chloe," he said with his back turned to me, as he closed the refrigerator door.

"That's what I've heard."

His shoulders moved up and down with his deep breathing. He twisted the cap off the bottle, then sat on one of the metal chairs. I took the other seat. Powell's muscles seemed tight. He held himself carefully, as though keeping some urge or desire in check. He took a long pull on the drink.

"Do you know why?" he asked. "Being here early and having an argument with Tim seems too circumstantial for an arrest."

"The police don't share their information with outsiders. Janelle has arranged for a lawyer, and if I know Janelle, he'll be good. The police might tell the attorney what they've got."

He squeezed the bottle hard enough to make the plastic crinkle and pop. He breathed in and out loudly, several times without saying anything. Obviously, some kind of internal debate raged.

"I want to ask a favor of you," he said finally. "It's not a small thing, either."

"What is it?"

"I want you to help me figure out who did kill Tim Bethel."

EIGHT

I THINK MY MOUTH hung open for a second or two. "What does that mean?"

"You've met Chloe. Do you really think she could have killed Tim?"

"We had this discussion earlier."

"I know. But I'll tell you the answer this time. Chloe wouldn't kill anyone. Or even try to harm anyone. She's almost too upstanding for her own good. I take that back. Chloe is too upstanding for her own good." He squeezed the drink bottle again. "I've known her for a long time."

I wanted so badly to ask what was between them, but I had a feeling it wouldn't be a good idea. "Why are you asking me to do this? I'm no detective. You need to hire a real one."

"Under ordinary circumstances, I would. But these aren't ordinary circumstances. Time's too pressing. It will take too long to bring someone in from outside and get them up to speed. Don't you get the feeling it's got to be someone here at the show?"

I did feel that way. But, still. "What makes me your best second choice?"

"I considered asking your boss, but she's a bit too tied to the bureaucracy. You're younger and more open. Plus, you know everyone. They talk to you. You have a way about you that puts people at ease."

I sighed as I considered what might happen if I did as

he asked. "My boss wouldn't be happy about it. Neither would the cops."

"Do they have to know?"

"They'll find out. I'll have to ask questions people don't want me asking, and they'll complain about it. I'm great at listening and getting people to talk, but I'm not good at lying about it."

"You can tell them I asked you to get the information. That I thought it very important, in fact."

"They'd only buy it up to a point. Not far enough. I might lose my job."

His body language shifted suddenly, shoulders slumping, head dipping, eyes lowered. The salesman was about to adjust his approach.

The thing is, it sort of worked, even though I knew what he was doing. When he shook his head sadly and said, "Chloe deserves better than this," I agreed with him.

"If the show breaks up without the real killer being found, her life will be ruined. They probably don't have enough to convict her of murder, but I could be wrong. What if they do?" He straightened up, bracing himself. "I guess I'd better hire that detective. Do you know anyone you can recommend?"

He was conning me with the not-quite-real dejection, and yet a very real desperation lay beneath it. He couldn't admit to the genuine emotion, so he had to use a faked one instead. Very bizarre. Was this a guy thing? It was okay to show fake emotion as long as people realized it was fake, but you had to hide the real thing?

I had no way to sort out that conundrum and it was irrelevant anyway. My own dilemma gave me enough to consider. I didn't think I'd exaggerated when I told him the risk to my job status. Janelle would give me a lot of leeway, but she had Carl Roper breathing down her neck.

She was going to get a few complaints about me anyway, especially if photo-woman followed through on her threats, but she could deal with those. However, if she started getting complaints about my asking too many prying questions, it would put her in a tough position.

"I don't know," I said at last, answering more than one of his questions. "I'll ask about a detective, and I'll think about asking a few questions myself. I can't promise anything." Anger stirred inside me. This was not anything I needed right now.

Powell reached inside his jacket and groped for a moment. Finally, he held out a business card. "My cell-phone number's here. I don't give it out to many people."

I took the card and stood up. Rising emotion nearly choked me.

He'd pressed on a weak spot, a chord he could strum.

I'd read my share of Nancy Drew stories while growing up. Part of me found the idea of playing detective intriguing and kind of cool.

A more serious part was also concerned about Chloe Bethel, convinced she was innocent but worried that she might be tried and found guilty anyway. Was my job more important than her life, her freedom?

I wandered down to the end of the aisle in a haze of deep thought until the buzz of my cell phone jerked me out of it.

"Clean-up on aisle ten," Janelle said, mimicking a supermarket announcement. Then she added, "Only barely kidding. It seems to involve popcorn, too, so I suspect it's your friends with the malfunctioning machine. I've already dispatched maintenance, but you probably need to have another talk with them."

"Crap. Can I have a whine?"

"Sure, go ahead."

"Thanks. I'm getting dangerously close to my limit on

the shit-meter. I want to go take a kayak trip down a nice quiet river where no one will complain about anyone else or refuse to use common sense with a damned popcorn machine that doesn't work right. I need a vacation. One where I won't find a body in a trash bin. Where the body's wife won't get arrested for killing him and I won't be worried about that because I don't think she did it. This show is the worst ever. I wish it was over." I took a couple of deep breaths. Janelle remained quiet. We'd done this routine a few times before, and she knew she didn't need to say anything. Just letting me blow off steam worked.

One more deep breath later, I said, "There. I feel a little better now. I'm on my way to the popcorn disaster."

"Thanks, hon."

I stopped, aghast, when I got close enough to see the Blue Hills booth. Their machine hadn't melted down as I'd feared. It had exploded.

Big, fluffy balls of popcorn littered everything in the Blue Hills booth, as well as the booths closest to it. A thin layer coated the carpet and a lot of the aisle in front. It looked like a blowout in a packing-peanut factory. But the kernels also decorated the display tables, tops of pictures, mugs, figurines, and all the other paraphernalia Blue Hills sold. A lot of it was faux movie memorabilia, and the popcorn coating looked sadly appropriate.

Worse, though, it was buttered popcorn. Each kernel had deposited little splotches of grease where it first struck and where it landed. Most of the Blue Hills products looked as though they'd been left out in the rain, but they weren't going to be easy to clean. Neither was the carpet.

Maintenance was on the scene, sweeping up the kernels from the aisle and mopping up the slick spots. They had their priorities right.

The same wasn't true for the company president,

the Blue Hills dragon lady. She stood in the middle of her booth, scrunching popcorn kernels every time she moved and loudly berating a much younger woman. Tears streamed down the unfortunate girl's face.

Magda Crane, the dragon lady, yelled, "Who's going to pay for cleaning up all this mess? It's going to cost us a fortune! I'll have to call the temp company and tell them what you've done."

The girl's dismayed expression told me she expected the company to fire her and maybe to dock her pay. Which was probably already meager. It wasn't fair.

The dragon lady broke off her diatribe when she saw me coming. If I expected chagrin or remorse, I should have known better.

"I can't believe this idiot filled the machine so full it blew up," she said to me. "Look at this mess. What are we going to do?"

"You told me to," the girl muttered.

It took a huge effort to contain my fury. "First, we're going to calm down and lower our voices." I realized I was unconsciously imitating the authoritative voice Scott Brandon had used during the fight yesterday.

It seemed to work. At least the dragon lady's voice wasn't as loud when she turned to the girl and said, "Get out of here. Tell the temp company I don't need any more of *their* kind of help."

A sob broke up her words as the girl said, "I'll get my purse."

"I'll go with you," I offered. The dragon lady would presume I was making sure she didn't steal or vandalize anything, but in truth I wanted a word with the young woman. Once we were out of earshot I said, "I know it wasn't your fault. I talked to her yesterday about that machine not working right. I'd like to talk to you, but I need a few minutes here. Would you wait for me in the lobby? Sit on one of the couches and I'll join you as soon as I can."

She gave me a watery nod, pulled her purse out from behind one of the display cases, and said, "She told me to put it all in."

The maintenance crew had cleared the aisles and were sweeping up the kernels that had dropped into the neighboring booths.

The dragon lady said, "Why are they working over there? The worst of the mess is here. Why aren't they sweeping up this mess?"

"Because, ma'am, it was your machine that caused the problem. Out of courtesy to your neighbors, we're going to try to repair the damage to their displays first."

"But it wasn't my fault," she protested, sounding like a two-year-old. "It was that fool girl. She overloaded the machine."

I counted to three—in my head. "Ma'am, your company brought the machine here. It was in your booth, at your request. It was your responsibility to ensure it functioned correctly and any staff you brought in was properly trained in using it."

Two maintenance men had paused to watch the exchange. I couldn't tell if it was curiosity or concern that spurred their interest.

"By the way," I added, "I'm pulling the plug on that machine, if it hasn't already been pulled. I don't want to find it running again. I'd like you to get it out of here as soon as possible."

"You can't! I have a major promo event tomorrow tied to that machine. We're hosting a movie-nostalgia party. I need the machine. How can we have a movie tie-in event without popcorn?"

"I'm sorry, but I can't let you run that machine again.

If we had a fire inspector come in and look at it, I suspect he'd conclude it was a hazard and order it off the premises."

I bent over to the bottom of the machine, found the cord, and traced it back to the outlet. The woman followed me, sputtering and yelling. "You can't do this, young lady! Who are you? You don't have the authority!"

I ignored her, reached the floor outlet, and yanked the plug from the machine out of the socket. I'm sure I pulled harder than necessary, but it felt good to disconnect that monster.

"Your boss is going to hear about this," the woman threatened. "Center management is going to hear. This is a ridiculous way to run a show. Where's the respect for your clients? We pay to be here. We have a right to set up our displays however we want."

I knew arguing with her was a bad idea but I couldn't resist. "I'm doing this out of respect for your neighbors, who've been damaged enough already by that machine. Did you read the rental contract for your booth? It specifically says the Center reserves the right to remove or request removal of any item or display Center personnel feel is inappropriate or represents a hazard. This machine represents a hazard."

"It's had a few mishaps, but only because the stupid people operating it didn't know how to do it right."

My temper pressed at the boundaries my will imposed on it and threatened to blow at any moment. "Feel free to complain to the Center's director. Her name is Janelle Addison." I turned and marched to the lobby, still fuming.

The girl had waited. When I found her in the lobby and asked what happened, she said, "That bitch! I can't believe she'd try to blame me for her stupidity. She *told* me to put in all that popcorn. She kept telling me she didn't want it to burn, to put in some more. And I was like, this isn't a good idea, lady. Did she listen? Uh-uh. She didn't want to hear it. And now she blames *me* for the mess!" Her face fell and some of the spirit drained from her. "The temp company will probably blame me anyway after she complains."

"No, they won't. It wasn't your fault. Give me the name and phone number of the company."

I called and explained why I was calling and what had happened. A woman said she'd make a note in the records. I thanked her and asked if she had any other assignments for the girl.

"Do I ever," she said. "I've got a couple of requests from people at your show for help."

I escorted the young woman to another booth. The crew greeted her like a long-lost family member and put her to work helping distribute sales literature, logo keychains, and small boxes of candy. I picked up a stick pen in a holographic rainbow of colors.

I made a mental note to check on Blue Hills tomorrow during that event the dragon lady had mentioned. I wouldn't put it past her to turn on the machine again despite my warnings.

Sue Savotsky was next on the to-do list, but I had to calm down a bit before I got to her, so I walked a couple of aisles, just glancing at the merchandise. I got hooked by a booth showing large, lavishly framed reproduction art and stopped to study the pictures. A couple of lovely, peaceful landscapes caught my eye, especially one that showed a river meandering through a quiet forest. It reminded me of my favorite daydream and I let myself sink into it for a moment.

I started checking other pictures, but I didn't get far before my cell phone buzzed again.

I expected Janelle, but it wasn't. "G & B Booth. Right now," Scott Brandon said and hung up.

NINE

I SEARCHED FOR SCOTT as I approached the G & B booth but didn't see him. One of the young reps I'd seen there before noticed me and waved me toward the back area.

I interrupted an argument. Raised voices, the sounds mostly indistinguishable, spilled from inside the enclosure, but it all stopped abruptly at my entrance. The last words, in Grantwood's voice, hung in the air. "Dammit, I don't need that!"

The space seemed crowded at first, until I realized there were only four people already there. The small area made it seem fuller.

Stan Grantwood stood in the middle of the room, glaring at Scott Brandon. Bits of Grantwood's hair stood on end as though he'd run a hand through it, making the gray strands shine more prominently. A flush colored his face and his stance was tense, too tightly controlled. His hands clenched into tight fists and his breath heaved in and out in harsh pants. He looked furious.

Ellen Spencer, on the other hand, appeared almost sick. The blood had fled her face, leaving it grayish beneath the tanning-bed color. She swayed. Without looking at the others, I moved a folding chair behind her and pushed her gently into it. "Put your head down," I told her. She nodded and complied. I grabbed a bottle of water from a case nearby, screwed off the cap, and handed it to her. She took a long gulp that seemed to steady her. Her color improved.

The other person in the room was a young man I didn't recognize but who was probably one of G & B's sales-people.

I looked over at Scott.

"What happened?" I asked.

Everyone started to answer at once.

"Nothing," Grantwood growled. "An accident."

"I just found it," Spencer said.

"Another threat," Scott answered. He nodded toward the box but added, "Don't touch it. Just look."

The box was maybe four inches square and two inches deep, plain white, with no markings. The lid sat beside it, also unmarked. Beside that was a piece of white copy paper. It had been folded several times, leaving wrinkles in the paper, so that even open, it didn't lie quite flat on the table.

Written in pencil, in large, careful block letters, the message on it said: DO NOT GO THROUGH WITH THIS MERGER!

At first glance the block letters looked like the work of a first grader. But the precision of the curves, the sym-metry, and the neat spacing of each character indicated a more adult control in the creation.

I looked into the box. Shards of porcelain, maybe two good handfuls of them, made a layer an inch thick on the bottom. Bright paint colored many of the pieces. They al-most glowed amid the snowy dust of broken china and all the raw edges. Whatever it had been wasn't just broken. Someone had thoroughly smashed it. None of the shards were larger than a quarter and some had been reduced to powder or grains the size of coarse sand. It took me sev-eral long moments to recognize what I was seeing, and it set off an odd twist in my stomach when I did.

"It was one of those little angel figurines," I said. I

didn't particularly like them, most certainly wouldn't buy one for myself or anyone else, but it seemed almost a sacrilege to see the broken pieces delivered this way, like a tiny, smashed body in a square white coffin.

"The latest Vittorio Angaro," Spencer said, the words so devoid of expression they just hung there. No one quite knew how to react.

"You have an exclusive license?" I asked.

"For the last fifteen years." Grantwood stared at the box and color rose in his face again. "Someone has a sick sense of humor."

"Really?" A new voice intruded as a man pushed aside the curtain and entered. "Someone want to explain what's going on?" Detective Gilmont looked at each of us in turn. His eyes narrowed when his gaze landed on Scott Brandon and remained there for a second too long. Scott stared back with a look almost as aggressively cold, but he didn't say anything.

Grantwood shook his head and breathed out another angry sigh while Spencer looked frightened again. The young salesman just stared, perplexed but intrigued.

Scott said, "On the table. I believe it's self-explanatory."

The detective walked over and studied the box, lid, and note for a moment. "Have you got a carton or something I can put these in?" he asked.

"Jason?" Grantwood said.

The salesman nodded and walked away.

"Who found it?" Gilmont asked.

"Ms. Spencer," Scott answered.

Gilmont pulled a notepad and pen from his pocket. "When and where?"

Spencer had regained control. Her voice sounded steady when she said, "I found the box sitting on a corner of the Bissanguet display. It's on the far corner." She pointed off to her right. "A couple of the figures had been moved and the box was stuffed in between them. I thought someone had set it down there and forgotten it, so I brought it in here, thinking I'd see if there was something inside to identify who'd left it or if it was something of ours that hadn't been unpacked. But then I was putting my purse away and someone asked me a question and I forgot all about it." She looked at Grantwood. "I'm sorry, Stan. I wish I'd remembered it or looked at it before you found it. I'd have tossed it in the trash."

"Just as well you didn't," Gilmont said. "What time did you find it?"

"I was coming back from lunch, so I guess it was about one-fifteen."

"And you left it here?"

She nodded. "On the table."

The detective looked at Grantwood. "You just opened it?"

"About fifteen minutes ago," he said. Irritation edged his words as though he begrudged the time or effort all this had taken up. "I saw it there and wondered what it was and why someone had left it. You see what I found when I opened it."

Jason came back with a cardboard box, but the detective ignored it for the moment.

"What did you do then?" he asked Grantwood.

"I asked a few people about it," he said. Color flooded his face again. "Rather loudly, I admit. It startled me."

"The note or the damaged figurine?"

"Both."

"Did anyone know anything about it?"

"No one said so."

Gilmont continued to scribble notes on a pad. "So you

touched the box and the note." He looked at Ellen Spencer. "You didn't open the box?"

"No. I just picked it up and put it down."

"Anyone else touch it?"

Scott and I shook our heads when he looked at us. Jason said, "No."

The detective wrote a bit more then turned to Scott. "What are *you* doing here?"

Scott looked at him steadily. "Working. I heard the fuss and came over to see what was going on."

"What's your job?"

"Security."

Gilmont's eyebrows rose just a fraction and the two men stared at each other a few seconds too long. Gilmont turned and looked at me. "Why are you here?"

"Scott asked me to come. He thought Center authorities should know about this."

Gilmont's nod didn't give anything away. He watched as I met Scott's eyes for a moment. Then he turned to Scott again and said, "I want to talk to you later. Where can I find you?"

Scott told him where he'd be. The detective pulled on a pair of latex gloves and loaded the box, lid, and note into the carton Jason had brought.

"Show me where you found this," he said to Spencer. She looked much more together when she stood up and led the way out of the enclosure. Gilmont followed without a backward glance at the rest of us.

Stan Grantwood took a deep breath and glanced pointedly at Scott, myself, and Jason when he said, "We have work to do."

Nonetheless, I said, "Mr. Grantwood, could I have a minute to talk to you?"

He gave me an impatient look. "Not right now."

I gave up and followed Scott out of the enclosure.

"What do you make of that?" I asked him.

He shrugged. "Not enough information yet." But I could see him mentally chewing it over. A moment later he said, "I'll meet you upstairs at six-fifteen?"

"Okay. You can go on if I'm late. Just leave a note. I sometimes get stuck and can't get away."

"I hear you," he said.

I watched him walk back to Chang's booth. All my female hormones did a little happy dance at the thought of a date with the guy. Even if was a faux date. Even if being interested in Scott Brandon wasn't really a good idea. What do hormones know or care about stuff like that?

I ducked into the restroom and spent a few minutes sitting and thinking. Once I ejected Scott Brandon from my brain— and that wasn't as easy as it sounds—my thoughts whirled around Stan Grantwood, Tim Bethel, and Chloe Bethel. How could Detective Gilmont know about the threats to Stan Grantwood and still believe Chloe Bethel had killed her husband? He surely didn't believe the two things were unrelated?

Or *was* it possible that the two weren't related? Maybe the cops had some other reason to think Chloe had killed her husband. I found it hard to swallow Chloe as a murderer. Or maybe not so much that she couldn't do it as that she would conceal it afterward. She might actually kill him. But she'd tell the world about it and take her chances with the law. Dave Powell had said she was too upstanding for her own good. In our brief encounter, that had been my impression, as well.

But I'd met her only once and talked to her for maybe fifteen minutes. That made me such an expert?

Still, my gut kept insisting Chloe Bethel hadn't killed

her husband, overruling everything my brain had to say on the subject.

I redid my makeup before I left to take on the next chore. One that required all the armor available.

On my way to the Trimstates booth, I dialed the number Detective Gilmont had given me. When he answered with a gruff "Gilmont," I asked if he could give me a few minutes before he left the Center.

His disinclination made itself clear in the momentary pause, the sigh, and finally his tone of resignation when he agreed to meet me. "At the front in thirty minutes. It'll have to be brief," he warned. "And I won't have time to wait around for you."

"Understood," I agreed, making note of the time. It would have to be a fast conversation with Sue Savotsky. How likely was that?

One person tried to waylay me on the way to the Trimstates booth, but I avoided him, saying I couldn't talk and promising to stop by later.

Part of me hoped Savotsky wouldn't be there or she'd have a customer with her. No such luck. The woman paced the confines of the small space, her head swinging back and forth to follow the traffic down her aisle. Her expression changed the moment she saw me. I wondered what she had on her mind. I couldn't afford to let her go on for long, but it might help if she could unload something before I had to tackle my warning.

"Heather, thank goodness," she said. "You've got to do something. They're stealing all my business."

"Who?"

"These people." She swung an arm out to encompass the other booths along the aisle. "They waylay customers trying to come to my booth and keep them for as long as they can, and then they steer them away."

I drew a deep breath. "You really think they're deliberately steering business away from you? Why would they do that?"

"They're jealous. They know my products are better. They're afraid once people see mine they won't want to buy any of theirs."

"You do have some nice things." That, at least, was true. She did. Some of her yard art was attractive. Some of it looked absurd to me. Still, what did I know about the whims of consumers around the country?

"Sue, listen," I continued. "I've been getting some complaints about you, as well. You've got to stop going around and confronting everyone. I understand you're upset about the problems and what they seem to be doing to you, but you can't argue with them. You're going to create problems for yourself."

"But they're screwing around with me," she protested. "What am I supposed to do? Put up with it? You know I'm not that kind of person."

I snuck a glance at my watch as she rumbled on. I still had eighteen minutes, but Sue could chew up that much time and more with her endless laments.

"Look!" I had to say it loudly and firmly to interrupt her. "I'm trying to help you. Janelle is already getting complaints. If you keep it up and she gets too many, you know what will happen, don't you?"

A flash of alarm drove away the aggression from Sue's features. "What?"

"If you create too much trouble, they won't let you rent space at the show anymore."

"They can't do that."

"Yes, they can," I insisted. "This is private property and a private event. There's no law that obligates us to rent to anyone who asks."

Actually, I had no idea if that was true, but Janelle would find a way to make it true if Sue's shenanigans continued to create problems.

"So I should just let them steal all my business and not say anything? It's not worth my coming here for that. Why should I bother?"

I knew what I had to do, and I so hated the idea. I should get extra Brownie points from Janelle for taking one for the Center. "I have a suggestion. Instead of complaining to your neighbors or whoever when you see a problem, write it down. Do you have a notebook or pad or something you can use? I'll come by each morning and pick it up, and I'll talk to whoever has caused problems. I can't promise it will fix your problems with them, but it will keep you from having worse problems with the Center."

"You promise you'll talk to everyone who causes trouble?"

I checked my watch. Six minutes. I was going to regret this, but it was only for a couple more days. "I promise I will."

She nodded. "I'll have a list for you tomorrow morning."

"I'll come and get it. I've got to run now."

I said a rushed, barely polite goodbye and went off to meet Detective Gilmont. I actually beat him to the main exit and waited for him for almost five minutes before he appeared.

"What can I do for you?" he asked, making no apologies for being late.

"I hear you've arrested Chloe Bethel for her husband's murder."

He gave a quick nod, while simultaneously setting down the cardboard box he still carried, pulling out his phone, and glancing at it for messages.

"I take it you don't think the threats to Stan Grantwood are related, then?"

Gilmont took his eyes off the phone to stare at me for a moment before he answered with a nonanswer. "We're considering all possibilities."

"But arresting Chloe Bethel indicates you don't think they're related."

"It might, or it might not. Why are you asking?"

"People who know Chloe Bethel don't believe she killed him."

"People who knew Ted Bundy didn't believe he'd killed a bunch of people, either."

"Not the same thing."

His expression turned harsh. "Leave it alone and let us do our job, Miss McNeil. I appreciate that you have to do as much damage control with your exhibitors as you can, but don't interfere with our work." His tone made it a warning.

"What are you doing to protect Stan Grantwood?" I asked. He couldn't claim that wasn't my business.

"What can we do? He says there's no threat. He doesn't want our protection or help. In any case, you've already got a man on guard and he's a good choice for the job."

"You know Scott Brandon?"

"We've met."

If he got any more terse we'd be sending signals in Morse code. I gave it up. Since I pretty much had my answers, I thanked him and said goodbye. He picked up the box again and headed for a side door out of the Center.

I spent more time trolling the aisles, trying to sort out my thoughts and make a couple of decisions. One name grabbed my attention as I passed: Kirshorn's. The other potential groom in the wedding negotiations with G & B.

Their booth wasn't as large as G & B's but it encompassed six spaces. A quick glance showed why their prod-

uct lines might mesh well. Although there were large
sections that held glass plaques—some showing nature
scenes, some with inspirational quotes, some just geomet-
ric designs—and a bunch of glass vases, there were also a
lot of shelves with items that looked quite a bit like some of
the statuettes and figurines I'd seen at G & B. Not exactly
the same things, of course. But similar. Lots of porcelain
birds, butterflies, flowers, fruit, human figures, and especially lots of bedraggled, pouting children.

I like kids as well as the next unmarried, childless,
mid-twenties woman who hopes to raise a few of her own
someday, but I failed to see the appeal in these. They just
looked sad.

Funny thing about all the Kirshorn products, somehow they weren't quite as nice as G & B's. I couldn't put
my finger on the difference, but the ones I looked at most
closely didn't seem as finely detailed or carefully painted.
The quality wasn't as good.

Off to my left, another set of rustic wood shelves sup-
ported vases filled with faux greenery and larger statuary. On the right, pegboards with hooks held a display of
jewelry. Lots of pendants, pins, bracelets, and earrings,
crusted or embedded with sparkling crystals in a rainbow
of colors. They were packed together so tightly and shined
so brightly that to approach meant risking blindness. There
might be some nice stuff there, but I valued my eyesight
enough to stay away.

I looked around for Irv Kirshorn. As long as I was here,
I hoped to ask him a couple of questions. He stood at the
far end of the display, near the boards of jewelry, but hov-
ering over stacked wooden crates displaying autumn and
Halloween decorations. Most of the pumpkins, gourds,
haunted houses, black cats, spiders, scarecrows, and
candleholders in orange and black were either glass or

ceramic. A group of two men and a woman surrounded him and watched as he pointed from one item to another, apparently extolling their virtues or sales potential.

Lit by his obvious enthusiasm for his products, his face became much more lively and attractive than it had been last night when I talked to him. It made him almost handsome, at least for a guy his age. He didn't look like someone who'd kill a rival or send him veiled threats. Well, okay, maybe I could see him doing the threats, though that was a stretch. I couldn't picture him bashing Tim Bethel over the head with a crowbar and dragging his body to the Dumpster. Still, what did I know about what a murderer looked like? Gilmont had reminded me they didn't wear warning labels.

Kirshorn flipped a switch, and a light came on inside one of the porcelain haunted houses, highlighting ghostly figures and skeletons that hadn't been visible before. Cute. I might actually like one of those for decorating my apartment.

A saleswoman approached and asked if she could help me. I introduced myself and said, "I was hoping to speak to Mr. Kirshorn, but I can see he's occupied." One of the sacred rules for Center employees: you didn't disturb an exhibitor when they were with a client.

"Would you like a drink while you wait?" she asked.

I thanked her but declined. "I can't really wait around. I'll catch him later."

So much for distraction. As I walked away, my mind reeled right back to the main problem at hand and the decision I needed to make. Could Kirshorn be a killer? If Chloe Bethel hadn't done it, someone else had. Almost undoubtedly someone right here at the show. Someone I'd very likely talked to in the past couple of days. Someone who might kill again if he didn't get his way. That thought sent chills rushing up and down my spine.

Finally, I drew a deep breath and forced myself to pull out the card Dave Powell had given me. I rang his number. He answered on the second buzz. When I said I wanted to talk to him, he told me to come right over.

It only took a couple of minutes to get there. I walked fast and refused to think about it any more until I arrived. Otherwise, I'd lose my nerve.

He waited for me outside the private area and gestured for me to follow him in. He went through the polite ritual of offering a drink, and this time I accepted a diet soda. Once we were both seated and our thirst slaked, he said, "You've decided to do it?"

"On the condition that you tell me everything I want to know. Everything. No holding back. No talking around the answers, no bits and pieces. Everything."

"You're angry."

"Yes. I'm getting ready to do something incredibly stupid. I'm going to risk my job, one I love and really don't want to lose, for a man and woman I barely know and another man who'd rather I didn't. For some obscure sense of obligation I don't even understand. I really *don't* want to do this."

Powell let me vent for a second, his dark eyes sympathetic. "You may not believe it, but I understand where you're coming from. It's hell when your conscience starts to bite."

"There's no reason on earth why I should do this."

"Except you're probably the only one who can."

"It's the cops' job. And they might even be doing it. I just don't know."

"And you're not sure you can take the risk that they won't do it right."

I sighed and took another long drag on the soda he'd given me. "Yeah. So will you tell all?"

"I'm just as reluctant as you are."

"It's an all-or-nothing deal."

"I figured. You're just making the price higher than I expected."

"No, I'm not. You're a smart man. You knew if I were smart I'd ask for it all. And you wouldn't have asked in the first place if you didn't credit me with a reasonable quantity of brainpower."

He grinned. "Looks like I'll be getting what I pay for. The promise I made earlier stands. If you get in trouble, I'll do everything I can to help." He sucked in a big gulp of air. "I asked Chloe to come here a day early and not tell anyone."

TEN

IT ACTUALLY KNOCKED me speechless for a moment. "Why?"

He stared at me. "Before I answer, I want a promise from you that you'll keep what is said here confidential."

"As far as I can, I will. But I'm not going to perjure myself to protect you. Or risk a contempt of court or whatever it is they do to people who won't say who told them things. And it's possible I may have to confide in someone else. But I won't gossip about it or talk about it with anyone other than officials or people whose help I need and whose discretion I believe I can count on. That's the best I can offer. Bottom line? Whatever you tell me will stay with me unless there's some really pressing reason to share it. Will that do?"

"I guess it will have to," he said. "There are some things I can't talk about. It would be violating a legally binding contractual agreement. But I might be able to help you understand the general principles and you can extrapolate from there. Even that you have to keep to yourself."

There might be an idea for a board game in this somewhere. I'd call it "Negotiation."

"I like a good gossip as well as the next person," I answered, "but if I give you my word that I won't disclose what I know—or even what I guess that's relevant to this— unless I have to, you can count on that."

"All right. I asked Chloe to come early because I wanted her to persuade Tim to see reason."

"About what?"

"He wanted to back out of our deal."

"The merger?"

"More like a buyout," Powell said.

"So it *is* you that G & B's going to merge with?"

He nodded.

"Why'd he want to back out?"

"There were certain clauses in the agreement that would kick in if certain things happened. He'd just found out one of those things was likely to occur. At least that's my best guess."

"Really. Tell me about those clauses."

"In a general sense, most merger or buyout agreements provide for audits and financial reviews, and they spell out the consequences should the results of those be less than satisfactory or not match previously made claims. Or certain parts of the business are guaranteed to be intact, with no major changes made before the contract takes effect. Often the penalty action triggered is to void the contract and end the deal. However, if one party wants to continue with the deal despite an unexpected hitch, they can specify other events will happen. Those might include financial penalties or the removal of certain principal parties from positions within a merged firm."

"I see what you're saying. If Tim Bethel feared such an invoked clause might threaten his position, he might decide it made more sense to call off the deal. When did he first tell you about this?"

"Last Friday," Powell said.

"Tim flew to Seattle earlier this week to meet with a supplier. I guess we can find out if he was in the office the previous week and what he was doing there."

"There was another factor involved, and this is where it gets both interesting and a bit dicey. Put most simply and plainly, Tim needed the money. He might not like the terms of the deal, they might offend his pride, but I felt sure Chloe could convince him to swallow it for the sake of the payoff."

"What made you so sure of that?"

"You've met Chloe." He looked at me. "Okay, maybe it wouldn't work on another woman, but she's just about the last word in trophy wives, even if that was all she was. But she has a lot more going for her. Tim might be…might have been incapable of fidelity, but he still adored her. She could have convinced him. But there's something else going on, and I don't know what it means."

He stopped to take a drink. His brows lowered as his eyes narrowed in thought. "I ran into Tim Wednesday afternoon, not long after I got here. Maybe about four or four-thirty. I pressed him for a definite 'go' or 'no-go' on the deal. He wasn't ready to say, and he wouldn't give me a direct answer why. In fact, he seemed preoccupied with something else, which was odd, considering how big an effect this deal was going to have on him. But he said there were problems and he wasn't ready to sign.

"I tried to press him on whether it was the financial terms and even hinted there was still room for negotiation if he or the company had a problem."

Powell stopped to take a breath and scraped at the damp label on the soda bottle with a fingertip. He didn't wear a wedding ring or any kind of jewelry, not even a watch.

"I can't remember his exact words, but these are pretty close. He said, 'We've got financial issues, but that's the least of my problems right now. I just found out I've been stabbed in the back. Betrayed. Plain and simple. Stabbed in the back!' Of course I asked him who'd betrayed him and how, but he shook his head and wouldn't say anything more. In fact, he stomped off. He was angry, furious about something. And I think he just found it out because he's usually in better control of himself."

Oh, wow, this was getting really complicated. Tim Bethel had something on his mind that trumped even the biggest deal of his business career in importance? Then the little lightbulbs started popping in my head.

"How much of this did you tell the cops?"

His eyes narrowed again. "Most of it. Why? Oh." Those lightbulbs were firing up in his mind, too. His hand tightened around his drink so hard the plastic crackled loudly and the bottle imploded. Fortunately, there wasn't much in it, so instead of the fountain of soda we might have gotten, it just spluttered out a few sticky droplets. "Crap. Damn, damn." I felt sure he'd have used even worse language if I hadn't been there. "Why didn't I realize? No wonder they're suspicious of Chloe."

"Is it possible he saw her with you?"

"Not me," he said. "Couldn't have been me he saw her with. First, I didn't actually see her until later. And if it had been me, he'd have put his fist in my face the moment he saw me."

"Makes sense. In fact, I guess it could have been anyone. Just the fact that she was there and hadn't told him would be enough."

"Maybe, but he kept repeating he'd been stabbed in the back. Makes me think he must have seen her with someone he knew and it must have looked pretty compromising. Maybe a rival or a competitor or even his partner."

"Stan Grantwood? But would Tim automatically assume a betrayal if he saw Chloe with Stan? I'm not sure I'm buying that."

"To be honest, I'm not, either."

"But I'm learning to imagine a lot of things I couldn't have guessed at a week ago. There's another possibility with Grantwood. Maybe it had something to do with the deal, and Grantwood had done something Tim didn't know about. Depending on what it was, Tim might take it as a personal betrayal. And then Grantwood could be creating the threats himself to divert attention."

"I can't think of what Stan might have done to Tim that I wouldn't know about," Powell said. "What threats?"

I gave him a quick, condensed version.

"Interesting," he said. "With Tim out of the picture, who would still want to keep the merger from happening?"

"A competitor comes to mind."

He thought that over. "Possible, I suppose. But then, who? Since we're working on the assumption that Chloe didn't kill him, I guess we're back to those competitors."

"Competitors, plural?"

"There's more than one."

"One name keeps popping up as the most likely alternative for a merger with G & B."

"I know who you're talking about, and there's good reason why that name keeps coming up. They have the best product fit and probably the most to gain. But they're not the only possibilities."

"Who else?"

He rattled off three names, but only one of them rang a bell—Gruber's Exchange. I sighed, thinking I'd have to check them out.

A young man poked his head in to question Powell about the availability of some candleholders. I told him I needed to go but that I'd check back with him tomorrow.

As I left, though, one more question occurred to me. I stopped and turned back to him. "Why did you ask Chloe not to tell anyone she was coming early?"

He paused in the act of drinking down the remaining soda but took a moment to swallow before he answered. "I hoped it would catch Tim by surprise and make him more amenable. Plus, I didn't want word to get around. People might realize there were problems."

I met his eyes for a long moment without saying anything. A faint blush of pink washed across his face. I could have pushed it. He knew I could, but I decided to accept it for now and left for real.

In his place I probably wouldn't have admitted it, either. He'd probably told Chloe something like that to justify the request, but I'd bet large chunks of my salary he'd hoped she would, in fact, catch her husband in some compromising position. I wondered if Chloe herself had realized Powell's intent. Likely she did.

I made a mental note to find out if Dave Powell was married. He thought it would make me less inclined to help him, and not because it made him seem less sympathetic. It didn't really. I could understand the impulse behind it.

Perhaps that was what *had* happened, and Chloe had argued with her husband and somehow accidentally killed him. I didn't think so.

It left me with another possibility. Powell himself had a strong motive for getting rid of Tim Bethel. Was that what the cops suspected? Was Chloe Bethel's arrest an attempt to draw Dave Powell out? To wrest an admission from him? If he were guilty, it might work. But if he weren't, he'd be desperate to find out who *had* done it, hence his pulling me in. Or was I a blind, too?

Damn, this was getting deep.

I had a lot more information to digest, but I needed to go back upstairs and check with Janelle. As I walked up the aisle toward the front, I was astonished to see people closing down booths. I looked at my watch. Five forty-eight! Where had the afternoon gone? I'd had no sense of time passing at all, yet all at once I felt totally exhausted.

I dragged myself to the elevators and mercifully didn't have to wait long for one.

When I got to Janelle's office, Scott Brandon was already there, draped comfortably in one of the armchairs, talking to her. It appeared casual and friendly. They both looked up when I rapped on the doorframe and said, "Knock, knock."

"Come on in," Janelle said. "We were just talking about you. Scott was telling me about the threat to Stan Grantwood. And Mark told both of us about you dealing with the Blue Hills popcorn machine."

I groaned. "I'd almost forgotten that."

"Mark gave your performance a glowing review. You were pleasant but firm and refused to take any grief from her. He said you pulled the plug on that machine like Arthur pulling the sword out of the rock in that movie."

"Disney does Camelot? Is that how he saw it?" The mental image teased me, so I imitated the sonorous tones of a sports announcer. "She's got hold of the cord. She's pulling. It's resisting. But Heather McNeil is no quitter. She keeps pulling. It looks like it's jiggling. It's coming loose. With a huge effort, she tugs one last time. And the plug pops out of the outlet! What an effort. What a competitor. Not too graceful. Too bad she fell on her rear end."

Janelle laughed and Scott looked amused. He looked at Janelle. "Is she always like this?"

"She's punchy, I think."

"I'm on information overload. Maybe a bit tired, too."

Scott stood up. "I think that's my cue. Let's head out."

Janelle got up, too. "You know, you don't have to go to this thing tonight," she said to me. "If you'd rather just stay home and rest."

I thought about Stan Grantwood and Dave Powell, Irv Kirshorn, the late Tim Bethel and his wife. The other people Tim Bethel had alienated, some of whom might hate him enough to kill him. Sue Savotsky, who claimed she'd had an affair with him. A competitor who might be increasingly desperate to stop the merger. Someone who'd stabbed Tim in the back. Figuratively. And someone who'd attacked him with a crowbar. Literally.

I pictured myself at home, trying to watch TV or read, but unable to keep my mind off what might be happening at the dinner. "No," I said. "Better I go. And I get extra Brownie points for dealing with Sue Savotsky today. I agreed to follow up on her complaints—all of them—myself, just to keep her from driving everyone else in the vicinity nuts."

"Jiminy Christmas," Janelle said. "I didn't know you were such a masochist. You get Brownie points and a date with a shrink."

"I'm planning my nervous breakdown for next week," I told her. "Can we make my shrink date sometime around then?"

"Suit yourself."

"Let's go," Scott said, pulling a set of keys from his pocket. On the way down in the elevator, he said, "They're going to feed us at this thing tonight, right?"

"They call it a dinner."

"Are you hungry?"

"Yeah, but I'm holding out for the free food."

"Fine. Just making a note that you get grumpy when you get hungry."

"I do not."

He grinned at me. "Yes, you do. Although maybe it's just when you're hungry *and* tired."

"Okay, *that* might be true."

We got out of the elevator in the basement and took a back entrance to the employee parking lot. Scott's car was a five-year-old Honda Accord. He saw my reaction to it. "Disappointed?" he asked.

"Surprised. I expected a sports car. Or a pickup truck."

"It's what I could afford. And it's paid for."

"I'm not criticizing. It's nicer than what I've got."

"What's that?"

"A Metro SmarTrip card and two functioning legs."

"Where do you live?" he asked as he got behind the wheel and started the car.

"Bethesda."

"Good. That's on my way."

"To where?"

"Rockville."

"You have a house there?"

His mouth crooked as he pulled out of the parking lot. "Apartment. Tell me about yourself. Are you a native of the area?"

"Area in an extended sense. My family's in Richmond."

"How did you end up working for the Show Center?"

"I have a degree in business. When I graduated, I started answering want ads in the *Washington Post*. The Center hired me."

He negotiated a couple of cross streets and turned north. Traffic had thinned from what it would have been an hour ago but was still thick enough to slow us down. Scott showed no impatience as he waited at traffic lights or for a line of cars to move. The car hummed and handled smoothly. "Is this the only job you've had?"

"Other than part-time and summer jobs. Waitress, retail clerk, guide for rafting and kayaking trips."

"From kayaks to trade shows. Quite a leap."

"Yeah, and when things get really hairy during a show, I sometimes daydream about going back to kayaking. Too bad it pays squat and only lasts for four or five months of the year."

"Everything has a downside."

"Your turn," I said. "You from around here? I detect something more northern in your accent."

"Philadelphia. Born and raised."

"Family still there?"

"My mom and a sister. Father died a couple of years ago." He turned north again. "Directions?" He didn't really need them just yet, but I got the message. He'd said all he was going to about his own background.

He had to concentrate on traffic signals and lanes, or at least he gave a good imitation of it, so conversation veered into my telling him where and when to turn. We got to my apartment at six-thirty.

"I'll be back at seven forty-five," he promised as he let me out at the curb. That probably barely gave him time to get home, clean up, and change, but that wasn't my problem. He'd offered.

It didn't give me much time to shower and re-do my hair, either. If I hadn't been going with Scott, I probably wouldn't have bothered. I'd already admitted the attraction, so I felt no need to chide myself for it again. He was a good-looking, interesting guy. And my thing with Chris was so casual I felt no obligation there. I didn't plan to marry either of them, for heaven's sake. Why couldn't I have a bit of fun?

I put on a knee-length royal blue jacket dress with beading around the tiered hems and the bottom of the sleeves. It had cost nearly a week's salary on sale at Nordstrom's, but it was so worth it. With it, I wore high-heeled black sandals.

Scott knocked on the door at seven forty-five. On the dot. I wondered if he'd been sitting in the car outside, waiting for the exact moment. I was still transferring the essentials from my day purse to the evening bag, but I stopped to let him in.

The stunned look he gave me said it all, but he still added, "I didn't dress for a date with a goddess."

"Good thing. You're not getting one."

"It's a hell of an approximation."

"Whoever taught you the fine art of flattery did a damn good job."

His sandy eyebrows rose. "Someone forgot to teach you how to accept a compliment gracefully."

"You're right. It's a deficiency in my education."

He distracted me so much I couldn't follow my own train of thought. He looked good, too—freshly shaved, his blond hair shining clean and combed smooth, his lean body encased in a dark suit that emphasized long legs and broad shoulders. The burgundy shirt looked terrific against his light tan and set off a navy tie.

"So tell me what I should have said after your compliment." I turned to lock the door. "How do *you* respond when I say you look fabulous?"

"Geez, Heather. I knew you were trouble the first time I saw you. I just had no idea how much trouble."

"That's how you respond to a compliment?"

"No, it's how I respond to a woman who's making my head spin."

"Should I be letting you drive?"

"Yeah."

He seemed less dazed once we got in the car and he had to concentrate on the road. I let my thoughts drift back to who had killed Tim Bethel.

Scott made a few offhand comments about things we passed.

Then he said, "What did I do?"

"Do?"

"You've gone very quiet. Did I insult you?"

"Oh. No. I'm just thinking."

"About work?"

"Sort of."

"The murder," he said. "Do you flash back to finding the body?"

"Sometimes. How did you know?"

"It's fairly common when something so shocking and unexpected happens to you. I'd be surprised if you weren't having flashbacks."

"I spend more time wondering who killed him. And why."

"How much time are you spending trying to find out?"

"Like I have time in my schedule to go around questioning people?"

"Heather, I know— Drat. We're not finished with this." But we'd arrived at our destination.

Scott turned into the front entrance of the hotel, and a valet came out to get the car. As we joined the throng heading inside, his hand moved up my arm to help guide me, but it dropped off when we got to the door and he pulled it open for me.

Even before we arrived at the ballroom, people I recognized waved and said hello. I introduced Scott to a number of acquaintances, saying that he was helping out at Chang's, which was close enough to the truth. He stayed by my side for the entire cocktail hour, except for a brief foray to the cash bar to get my glass of wine. He drank Sprite.

Of course, people still wanted to ask me about finding Tim Bethel's body and what the police were doing about catching his killer. I defended the authorities as best I could and assured people we'd increased our own security force. Scott pointed out several times that the cops couldn't share most of their information with the public, at least not until after they'd made an arrest.

When he wasn't talking, Scott scanned the crowd until he found what he sought. During a lull in the conversation, I followed his line of sight to Stan Grantwood. The man's usual shadow, Ellen Spencer, wasn't with him. Instead he talked to a woman and two men I didn't recognize.

I looked around for Spencer. As ridiculous as it was to consider the woman any sort of protection, I didn't like the idea of Grantwood going around entirely on his own. But maybe those were some of his other salespeople with him. I hoped so.

At eight forty-five everyone began to drift into the ball-room where the dinner tables were set and waiting. Scott and I took our time, letting most of the crowd go ahead of us, until Grantwood and his companions sat down. Then Scott selected a couple of seats at a table in the corner nearest the door. At his guidance we took the two seats that backed against the wall. The location let us watch the entire room.

Grantwood remained with the group of companions I'd seen earlier. Apparently, Ellen Spencer had decided to take a pass on this. I tried to remember if G & B had been nominated for any awards. I kind of thought they had, which made it doubly surprising she wasn't there. Maybe she wasn't feeling well. She hadn't looked good earlier.

I scanned the crowd for other faces I knew. Dave Powell sat on the other side of the room. I recognized one of his tablemates as the young man who'd interrupted us this afternoon. Andy Tarantoro was three tables to his left.

That prickly feeling of being watched nagged at me, so I turned to my right. From four tables away, Sue Savotsky waved. I nodded her way. When she noticed my companion, her eyebrows rose, mouth curved in an approving smile, and she winked. Oh, damn.

"Are you all right?" Scott asked.

"Yes. Fine."

He responded to my tone rather than the words. "What is it?" He followed my line of sight. "Who's that?"

Fortunately, someone had said something to the woman and she turned away. "Sue Savotsky."

"The infamous Savotsky, for whom you famously martyred yourself?"

"The one. And now it's going to be worse. She'll be all over me tomorrow about you. I'm going to get grilled."

"I supposed that's better than being fried or barbecued. As long as she doesn't eat you."

"The look she gave you, you're more in danger of that than I am."

"I'll take my chances."

Our food arrived then, distracting us for a bit. At least it distracted me. I was ravenous by that point. I pushed the pea pods to one side and concentrated on the gorgeous medallion of steak in the middle of the plate. I didn't realize how much my enthusiasm showed until Scott leaned over and said, "I like a woman who enjoys good food."

"I'm starved and I'm working twice as hard as normal."

"Hey, that's my point. You don't have to make excuses. It's normal. It's healthy. I'm glad to see you've got a good appetite."

I put down my fork and looked at him. The lights were turned down low, making the room dim, but something sparkled in his grayish eyes. "There's a sexual innuendo in there somewhere," I said.

"I'm here on business." He managed to sound offended but not serious about it. "I'm saving the pleasure for later. Although the temptations are considerable. But it's about business for now. And speaking of business, what have you learned about the murder?"

He must have felt me jolt because he added, "Janelle said if anyone other than the cops would figure it out, you would. She said people tell you things because you're a good listener, and that you're both curious and bright. Of course, I already knew those last two."

I drew a deep breath, giving myself time to figure out how to answer.

"It's all right," he said. "I know you're expecting a lecture on letting the cops do their jobs and not interfering. I'm betting it doesn't make any difference because your approach would be totally different and not something you set out to do deliberately anyway."

I debated how much to tell him. "People do talk to me about it. And, yeah, I've learned a few things."

He didn't say anything, just waited for me to go on. "Hey," I said, "that's my technique."

"What?" He looked startled.

"Waiting quietly for people to talk. Not filling the verbal space for them. I do that."

"Works, doesn't it?"

"Yeah."

"Care to fill me in on what you've learned?"

I studied his face. He kept his features carefully passive and neutral, with just a hint of personal concern softening them. I drew another deep breath and braced myself. "What's your interest?"

"I work security for the Center. That means knowing about problems and trying to head off bad results from them. Also, since you seem determined to get involved in this, you need someone at your back."

"Someone who knows a bit about guarding backs.

You do, don't you? You may not be a cop now, but you've been one."

His face stiffened, the eyes going hard and cold, mouth tightening into a thin line. I thought for a moment he wouldn't answer, but I waited. At last he said, "Yeah. *Was.* Not now. That's all I have to say about it."

What had happened to him? It had left a wound that hadn't healed. The police force's loss was the Center's gain, but there was a potential for danger in him. A potential for violence that could get scary. And I wasn't about to confront it.

"Okay. At least you do know about protecting people. Here's the thing. The police arrested Chloe Bethel for killing her husband, but I don't believe she did it. Neither does someone else who knows her better than I do. I can't tell you everything because I gave my word, but here's what I know."

I told him most of it. Actually, I told him just about everything except for identifying Dave Powell. I called him the owner of a rival business. I had no doubt Scott would figure it out. When I was done, he sat quietly for several long minutes. I ate the rest of my dinner and let him meditate on it. He'd cleaned his plate while I'd been talking.

The waiter came and took away our dishes, and then another one replaced them with dessert plates. Scott ignored the chocolate mousse. I dug in. After a few spoonfuls had slaked my chocolate craving, I pushed it aside.

"So, what conclusions have you come to?" I asked.

He tapped his fingers on the table in syncopated rhythm for a moment, then stopped. "Probably nothing you haven't already thought of. This unnamed person who asked Chloe Bethel to come early strikes me as a prime candidate. Not the only one, though. Have you considered that Grantwood himself might have done it? And is creating the threats himself? We only have his word about the cell-phone call."

"It's occurred to me. He does seem to have an alibi, though, since he was in the hotel bar with the other sales reps at the time Bethel must have been killed."

"How are you pinpointing the time?"

"Some of the G & B people said they saw Bethel around seven at their booth. The building closes at eight, and security shuts all the doors, including the bay doors. Didn't Craig tell you the drill? They keep an eye out for any stragglers still inside. There's an alarm that goes off if anyone tries to get out after that. So you have to figure he was killed sometime before eight. I guess he could have been killed outside, but how would someone get him into the Dumpster like that?"

"Reasonable. Who else might have done it?"

"If not Grantwood, then several other possible competitors for merger partner become suspects. Irv Kirshorn of Kirshorn's is the most likely, but I found out yesterday there are a couple of others I need to check out."

"You're going to start actively questioning people about it?" Disapproval blended with skepticism.

"I sort of promised I would."

"Heather, that's not such a—"

The MC called for attention, interrupting Scott's warning. The awards ceremony took a couple of hours. Scott kept sweeping the room with his gaze, settling periodically on Grantwood and those at the table with him. For lack of anything better to do, I followed suit. Nothing happened, though. The evening would have been a drag if I hadn't been with Scott, but enough energy hummed in the air between us that it buzzed in the back of my mind all night long. Except when our hands or arms or shoulders or legs touched. Then it was more of a sizzle between us and definitely at the forefront of my awareness.

When the ceremony ended and the affair broke up, we went into the lobby, but I noticed that Scott kept his gaze on Grantwood from the time the man almost passed us on his way to the door until he got in the elevator to go up to his room. If the car hadn't been packed, we might have accompanied him there, as well.

"He should be okay for now," I said. "There are plenty of people around him."

"I expect you're right. You ready to head for home?"

With so many others leaving at the same time, it took fifteen minutes for the valet to show up with Scott's car. We drove in silence for a while until traffic thinned.

"How much are you planning to question people tomorrow?" he asked.

I sighed. "As much as I can and still do my job. The big announcement is tomorrow night, so there's not much time."

"You think someone's going to try to stop it?"

"Grantwood's gotten two threats that we know of."

"I hear you."

"So that gives me one day," I said.

"All right. I'll help you as much as I can."

"What?" Was he *humoring* me? "You'll do what?"

"Help. Not that I can do much since I'm on guard duty, but people stop by and talk."

"Why aren't you lecturing me about how stupid it is to stick my nose into this?"

"Would it do any good?" he asked.

"No. But it would make me less suspicious."

"Of me? You think I killed him?"

"No, of course not. You didn't know him. Did you?"

"Never met the guy."

"I meant suspicious of your motives," I said.

"Pure as the driven snow. Which, when you think about it, is one odd metaphor. Snow that falls in this town is a mess within moments after it hits the ground, especially if it's driven on."

"Interesting, but a bit off topic."

"I know. Just struck me."

"So, why are you offering to help?"

The silence that ensued was charged. When we passed a cluster of streetlights, I got a good look at his face. His lips were tight; in fact, all the muscles of his face looked tense. "Just call it an interest in seeing that justice is served."

He knew what it was like to want answers. Or to be sure someone was innocent and be unable to do anything about it. Or the other way around. I thought about the way he'd said he wasn't a cop. *Not now.* End of conversation. So maybe it was something more personal.

"Works for me," I said.

He pulled up to the curb near my apartment and found a parking place without having to go around the block even once. The evening had gotten cooler. A chilly March wind blew my skirt around my legs and my hair into my eyes. I brushed it back and put the key in the lock of the front door.

The key turned and I reached for the doorknob. "Would you like to come in?"

"I'd very much like to come in, but I better not. It'll be damned hard to leave again."

His hand on my arm turned me toward him. Then he leaned forward and his lips made contact with mine. I sort of lost track of things after that, other than the sharp little tingles running under my skin.

Finally, though, he pulled back. His expression was gentle, belying the glint in his eyes. His blond hair gleamed gold in the porch light.

"Heather, if I don't get out of here right now, I'm not going to get out at all."

I gave him a dazed grin as he dropped another gentle salute on my forehead, then turned and walked back to the car. I went inside and locked the door behind me.

As I got ready for bed, it occurred to me tomorrow was going to be one hell of a day. Fortunately, the thought crossed my mind only briefly before it disappeared into the fog of sleep.

ELEVEN

THE GOOD NEWS was the Metro wasn't terribly crowded on a Saturday morning. I even got a seat for a change. The bad news was that I was going to work on a Saturday, and I had approximately twelve hours to figure out who was threatening Stan Grantwood and to stop them. Oh, and I would be risking my job, asking unpleasant questions of people. Not to mention dealing with Sue Savotsky. I yanked a book out of my purse and did my best to concentrate on it for the next twenty minutes.

I didn't see Scott when I got to the Center, but Janelle was in her office. I spent a few minutes with her, reviewing what needed doing. We went down to the show floor together at eight-fifteen but split up once we were there.

I started with Sue Savotsky. Might as well get that over with.

She went and got her list when she saw me coming. I took it with some trepidation, but only four names were on the sheet of paper she passed to me. Doable, if not exactly pleasant. Still, I hadn't promised to spend much time with each of those people.

As soon as she'd handed over the list, though, she arched an eyebrow and asked, "Was that your boyfriend with you last night?"

"Just a friend. He's working at Chang's."

"I thought I'd seen him around. He's the kind you notice. But, really, Heather. Just a friend? No way. Not a guy who looks like that."

I shrugged. "I met him at the start of the show, so I've barely known him a couple of days."

"You two looked pretty cozy together. Think there might be a future in it?"

It was too early in the day for this, but I swallowed my irritation. "Who can tell after just a couple of days?"

"Does he live in this area? These show-only affairs can be hard on the nerves."

"Close enough," I said. "I'd better get going. I've got a lot to do today and I need to talk to these people." I waved the paper she'd handed me.

"Don't forget to remind them they've got to stop interfering with my customers."

"I won't forget." I turned and headed away.

She'd thoughtfully included booth numbers. All four were on this aisle, the first of them just three booths down on the other side. When I got there, I looked around and wondered how on earth Savotsky could think these people were drawing off her business. The product line was completely different. Cooper-Works specialized in those porcelain village scenes that pop up everywhere during the holidays, especially during Christmas. The displays showed charmingly arranged towns of miniature houses and public buildings, all lit up and placed on boards where cotton passed for snow. Little people marched along the main street, guided by small streetlights with tiny bulbs, passing churches, the train station, stores, and the town hall. Off to one side of the booth, the Halloween version made a display as dark and eerie as the Christmas one was light and soothing. I'd seen something similar at Kirshorn's, though I thought these a bit nicer.

"Can I help you?" a woman in her late forties asked, breaking into my momentary distraction.

I introduced myself and added, "I'm here because I

promised Sue Savotsky at Trimstates I'd talk to you." The woman's eyes narrowed and she drew in a breath.

"Wait," I said. "Give me a minute. I know she's a nuisance. I'm actually doing this to protect you from her. After numerous complaints, I told her yesterday that if she would refrain from confronting people herself and just make a list, I'd talk to everyone on her list. I didn't make any promises about what I'd say."

The woman stared at me for a moment before she got it and started to laugh. "You're a brave soul to volunteer to do that."

"My boss says I've got a martyr complex, but really I'm just an idiot. Anyway, consider yourself admonished." I sighed. "I've got to go repeat this to three other people."

"Thank you for making the effort," she told me. "It's got to be above and beyond."

"Definitely beyond," I said.

I repeated the spiel at the next booth on the list. A young man with limited English smiled and nodded and probably didn't understand more than one word in three I spoke. Since they didn't include either the words "buy" or "money," it didn't really matter to him.

When I introduced myself at the third booth, a man in his early thirties said, "Heather McNeil. You're the girl who found Tim Bethel's body, aren't you?"

I admitted it, bristling at being termed a "girl" and waiting for the inevitable questions. They came, but after I'd related what I did and didn't know about the murder, he drew me off to a back corner of the booth to tell me something he didn't want overheard.

"I've been debating whether I should tell this to the police or not," he said.

"What?"

"I knew Tim Bethel. Not real well, but I recognized his voice when I heard him arguing."

"On Wednesday?"

He nodded.

"With whom?"

"I didn't see her. I just heard. It was a woman, but I don't know who it was. I couldn't make out her voice as clearly, but she and Tim were arguing. I couldn't understand most of the words, but one thing I did hear clearly from him." The man blushed a bit. "Pardon my language, but this is what Tim said. 'You treacherous bitch.' He said it loudly."

"You didn't hear what the woman said back to him?"

He shook his head. "I heard a kind of hum like she was talking low, but I couldn't make out the words. I thought about going back there to see if everything was cool, but it seemed like it would be intruding."

"Back there?"

"The receiving area."

"What time was this?"

"A little after five. I'd finished setting up and was getting ready to leave. I'd just taken some stuff over to dump in the trash, but I decided not to interrupt them. Instead I came back here and stuck the bags in the back of the booth. I tossed them the next day." He stopped and drew a deep breath. "Now, I wonder—"

"He wasn't killed then, if that's what you're thinking. People saw him later. But if it will make you feel better, I've got the number for the detective in charge of the investigation." I pulled out the card and he copied down the number. It probably wouldn't do Chloe Bethel's case any good, though, since he couldn't prove she was the one arguing with Tim.

"Thanks," he said. "I doubt it will help them, but I'd be glad to get that off my mind."

I remembered why I'd come, gave him my spiel about Savotsky, and headed for the last booth on the list. It turned out to be Stanaker-Wells and the couple who'd complained to me about her the day before. They were serving coffee from an espresso maker, so it was definitely worth the stop. Besides, I liked them. I accepted a cup of java with enthusiasm. After I gave them the spiel, they told me to keep the nice mug showing a design from one of their garden tiles on one side and their logo on the other.

"You can have two or three of them if you want," Dan said. "An entire matched set. It's more than worth it to get that woman off our backs. Would you like a couple of garden tiles? We don't plan to take all the display items back with us."

"If I had a garden, I'd be happy to take you up on that," I told him. "But I'm in an apartment with no yard, just a tiny little balcony." I saluted him with the coffee mug. "I'm happy with this. Thank you."

"You're welcome."

I headed for the Grantwood & Bethel booth, stopping briefly to admire a display of gleaming silver tableware and serving dishes. Beautiful stuff but probably a pain to keep clean and free from tarnish. I took a long pull on the coffee and went on.

Two people were busy dusting shelves when I got there. Stan Grantwood stood nearby discussing something with a young woman I recognized as another of their salespersons. They both looked up as I approached.

"Mr. Grantwood? If you have a minute, could I have a word with you?" I asked.

He looked annoyed but nodded. We retreated to the curtained-off area again. The space showed less organization than it had a couple of days ago, with boxes and papers scattered around. Grantwood sat down in a metal chair on the far side of the folding table, leaving me to take the other one, facing him across the faux-wood surface. Though it was only nine-thirty, he looked tired and sort of ragged. He'd shaved and his hair was neatly combed, but the puffy bags under his eyes suggested he hadn't slept well. Strain had etched deep lines in his face. His usually ruddy complexion had a grayish cast. When I first met him I'd thought him in his late fifties. Now I thought sixties might be more accurate.

"You've had a rough time," I said. Finding sympathy was no strain at all. The man looked like he'd been run over by a semi. "Is there anything I or the Center can do to help?"

He drew a deep breath and let it out on a long sigh. "You're already doing what you can, keeping that young man over there on watch."

"Is it enough? Have you gotten any more threats?"

"No more threats."

"Have you considered postponing your announcement? Everyone will understand."

He barked a short, humorless laugh. "Did Ellen put you up to this?"

"No. Is she pushing for it, too? Maybe you should think about it. It's a good idea."

He shook his head. "I need to get this thing done."

There was something in the way he said the last words, almost like he wanted to say more but either knew he shouldn't or couldn't bring himself to do it. I waited. My heart went out to him. He looked beaten up, flattened, almost defeated.

After a moment or two of quiet, he added, "I haven't told this to the police, but I'm sure they know, if they're worth anything at all. I *need* to get this deal done. The company's in trouble and I'm in trouble with it."

I didn't have to feign looking sympathetic.

"Most of my net worth is tied up in this company. I have a lot of debt at home. My wife likes to shop. It wasn't a problem as long as we were doing well. In the last couple of years, it's become a problem. This deal will take care of things. And in truth I'm ready to get out."

"You're retiring?"

"Sort of. I'm ready to let go of Grantwood & Bethel and put my energies into something else."

"I see." I paused a moment. "Your partner wasn't as enthusiastic about that prospect."

"He was thrilled about the merger at first, when he thought we were going to get more out of it. But he wasn't accepting all the realities of the situation. I realized he wasn't going to be able to bend reality to suit him. He tried, though. Give him that. He tried."

"Is this about the designer you're going to lose?"

His eyebrows rose. "You know about that? No announcement has been made yet."

"The rumor's out there."

"I should have known." His head drooped forward a moment. Then he straightened back up. "It's a factor," he admitted. "A big one. But Tim was pretty sure he could sign another well-known designer. He knew one who was unhappy with his current situation. Tim said no one else knew about it, and he could sign him before word got out. He was going to get it sewn up on Wednesday. I guess it didn't get done, though."

"So Mr. Bethel wanted to stop the merger?"

He reared back as though I'd struck him, and his eyes narrowed. "Are you suggesting I had something to do with Tim's murder?" He nearly choked on the words.

"No, I'm not," I answered as calmly and forcefully as I could. "Not at all. I'm just trying to understand the situation. I'm sorry if I even implied any such thing." I sighed. "You know the police have arrested Chloe Bethel?"

"She's the last person who would have killed him. She adored him. Practically every other woman at the show would have been more likely than she."

"Apparently the police don't see it that way."

"They've been wrong before."

"Can I ask one more question?"

A grin cut across his serious expression. "Why stop now? You haven't been shy about it."

"No, but this one may be more touchy. Who do you think is behind the threats?"

"What makes you think—?"

"Please," said, cutting across his words. "Don't insult my intelligence."

He looked at me more closely, shook his head, and smiled a wry, almost sad grin. "I wouldn't. The odd thing is I really don't know. I have a good guess, but I can't prove anything."

"Is that why you're not particularly worried about it?"

"I'm worried about it. I just have a hard time taking it seriously, knowing who's likely to be behind it. I worry that he's so desperate."

"You do think it's Kirshorn, then."

"Damn it, I didn't say anything of the sort."

"You didn't have to."

His eyes narrowed and speared me with a hard look. "If you let that get out, I'll raise such a fuss with your employers you'll never work here again."

I didn't let any emotion get to my face. "You don't have to threaten me. I don't betray confidences. Besides, neither of us actually knows. We're just guessing."

He glanced pointedly at his watch. "I need to get back to work."

Taking the hint, I stood up. "One more thing, Mr. Grantwood. Since I'm assuming you're going on with tonight's announcement, please be careful today. A desperate person will sometimes do desperate things. Out-of-character things."

"I hear you," he said, standing and glancing at his watch again.

I thanked him and left.

Once outside the curtained area, I took a deep breath and let it out slowly, releasing some of my tension with it.

I still had errands to do for Janelle. I passed Chang's as I walked away. Scott stood there, his gaze flicking from the curtained part of G & B's booth to scan the crowd, then to look at me.

He didn't exactly smile but his expression brightened when he saw me. "Learn anything new?" he asked quietly as I got close.

"Not much." I gave him a quick recap, leaving out Grantwood's suspicions but adding, "Have you met Irv Kirshorn? Would you recognize him?"

"I think so. He spoke to Martin yesterday."

"Good. Keep an especially close watch on him if you see him around the G & B booth."

Scott's eyes narrowed and his expression hardened for a moment.

"I agreed not to repeat any guesses Grantwood made about who was behind the threats."

"Understood. This morning I talked to a kid named Taylor over there about Bethel. Mostly about when they last saw Bethel. Taylor said Bethel was at the booth from around three to four on Wednesday. He didn't see him after that at all. Oh, and he said it was damned tense there. Grantwood and Spencer have been arguing. Taylor thinks she's worried about those threats and she's been trying to convince Grantwood to put off the announcement."

I must have looked surprised because Scott said, "I've been getting friendly with some of their sales reps. It gets slow sometimes and there's nothing much to do, so we talk across the aisle or visit where we can keep an eye on our booths."

"That's cool. Anything you can find out is good."

"Be careful," he said. "You could be putting yourself in danger."

The biggest danger was to my employment status, but there were other possibilities, and I'd have to be a fool to ignore them completely. I hoped I wasn't a fool.

I took care of a few more assignments from Janelle, then I had a few free minutes, so I headed over to the twenty-eight-hundred aisle, the one closest to the loading-dock area. I talked to people at each booth along either side. I hoped to find someone who had seen Tim Bethel or heard something Wednesday evening. Unfortunately, at this far end the booths were mostly smaller companies. I found only three people who actually knew Tim Bethel well enough to recognize him on sight. None of them remembered seeing him on Wednesday.

Of the half dozen I spoke to who'd been around after four that day, only one remembered hearing anything. It wasn't especially helpful. He'd heard someone sliding a box across the floor at around five-thirty.

And that was all I could get, except for one cool pen, a gift from the man who'd reported the woman with the cell-phone camera. This one was sleek and silvery, with a pink cap. Lights flicked on inside it when you pressed down on the point.

By the time I finished canvassing those booths, it was nearly eleven. I rang Janelle to give her a status update.

I filled her in on what I'd done with her requests and she added another issue for me to check out.

Before she let me go, she hesitated for a moment and then said, "Heather, there's something I've got to bring up. I just got a call from Ellen Spencer. She said you'd been talking to Stan Grantwood and apparently asked some questions that upset him. She was quite unhappy about it." Janelle sighed. "I think I understand where you're coming from and why you're doing it, but you've got to be careful. Remember, Roper is here, so I don't have a lot of wriggle room. I don't want to get any more complaints."

"Okay, I'll try to be more careful."

"Good. Thanks. Let me know what the heck's going on at twenty-four twelve. The stories are sounding kind of wild."

I flipped my phone closed and held on to it for a moment. I had a sort of unreal, out-of-time-and-space, out-of-body feeling. I felt sort of floaty. What was I doing here? What was the point? What did I know? What did I think I could or should do?

I had no answer and gave up on the philosophical musings in favor of going to twenty-four twelve to check out the source of the complaints.

What I found was best described as "When Good Marketing Ideas Go Bad."

Sandorn & Ackles were promoting a brand-new and extensive line of angel-themed merchandise. They had shelves and racks of porcelain and metal angel figurines and images in felt and stiffened silk appliquéd on every conceivable home-decorating item.

Two women adorned with gold wire haloes and enormous, glitter-coated wings held trays of canapés they tried to pass out to the crowd. Their halter tops and low-slung white skirts were more temptress than angel. They certainly attracted a crowd, though, and that was adding to the problem.

Hanging from the pergola over the booth, amid the angels, were dozens of large, glittery sets of wings. Wispy streamers of shimmering fabric fluttered from them.

The designers of the display had neglected to take a few things into consideration. The fact that the wings were hanging over the aisle, a main traffic route, for one. And the pergola was only seven feet high, while the angel wings were almost three feet long and most people were somewhere above five feet tall. Put those three things together and you ended up with a de facto maze blocking the aisle. People struggled to maneuver among the hanging obstacles, slowing foot traffic through the area.

The designers hadn't planned for the ventilation system, either. Each time air blew from the ceiling vents, the wings fluttered. Wispy bits of cloth and clouds of glitter flew loose, blessing those nearby with showers of string-and-confetti glory.

As I maneuvered through the mess, pulling bits of shiny netting out of my hair, I searched for someone who looked as if he or she belonged to the mess. I also thought about what to do about it, beyond another summons to maintenance.

I finally located a salesman, who directed me to their vice president of sales, a harried-looking man with a cell phone against one ear and a contingent of unhappy neighbors surrounding him. The nearby booth-owners demanded he remove the wings and clean up the mess.

I had to push through the group to get near the man. When I identified myself as an employee of the Center, he looked at me like I'd just saved him from being tarred and feathered. Given the angry mutterings growling around us, that might not be too far from the truth.

"We…um…we seem to have miscalculated a bit on our party idea," he said to me. "I'm truly embarrassed and chagrined about this, but I'm not sure what to do about it. I just sent a couple of guys to see if they could find ladders or stools or something so we can take some of it down."

I pulled out my phone and hit the speed-dial button for maintenance. Once I had an assurance that someone would be there shortly to help with the clean-up, I relayed the word to the harried man in charge.

"Praise the Lord. And thank you, dear," he said. "It seemed like such a good concept, making this place into a sort of paradise."

"Yeah, a real hell of an idea." That came from a would-be wit standing to my right.

I gave the comic a hard look. The man colored, then turned and stalked off. Sam and the two Sandorn people appeared while I was still appeasing the throng. The men immediately set up the ladders and began to take down the angel wings. The process spread more bits of fabric and glitter all over the place. My navy suit ended up speckled with fine bits of silver, and I pulled at least one more piece of stringy fabric out of my hair.

Once the decorations began to come down, the hostile neighbors dispersed. I voted the situation under control enough to take my leave.

I looked at the messages on my cell phone and discovered the call that had come in while I tried to calm the hostile neighbors wasn't from Janelle. It was from Dave Powell. When I followed up, he asked if I could stop by and offered lunch as an inducement. They were serving Chinese food. I refused to think about what sweet-and-sour chicken drippings would do to the carpet and concentrated, instead, on how happy my stomach would feel.

Powell saw me coming and disengaged from a group of

people to meet me. "Let's get some food and take it to the back," he suggested, nodding toward the side of the booth where the caterer had set up tables with chafing dishes. The aromas of rice, noodles, egg rolls, sweet-and-sour chicken, something with shrimp and vegetables, and pork strips with peppers had already set my mouth watering and stomach growling. It didn't take much to convince me.

"Made any progress?" he asked after we'd settled down in the private area and had a few bites of food.

"I've learned some things, but nothing that really helps. I do know one person who overheard Tim Bethel arguing with a woman late Wednesday afternoon. Unfortunately he didn't actually see them or recognize the woman's voice, so it wasn't much help. No one in the booths nearest the loading dock saw Tim or heard anything unusual."

After another bite of egg roll, I added, "I talked to Grantwood, too. Learned a few things I can't spread around but nothing that really helped."

Powell had only taken an egg roll, which he ate in small bites, wiping his hands and mouth on a napkin between each nibble. "I've been asking around and digging out rumors myself," he said. "The only interesting thing I've come up with, you've probably already heard. We already knew that the G & B designer, Roberta Harrison, is ending her licensing deal with G & B. Word on the aisle is that Tim Bethel was frantically negotiating with someone clse to replace her."

"Any word on who?"

"A couple of names mentioned, but nothing firm. Tom Rupika. Kristian Grange. Both solid names, though neither has the following of Harrison. But they're the only two around who would be good enough to replace her."

"Any idea where Harrison's going?"

"Don't know how much faith to put in this, but the

rumor says Kirshorn's. They've called a press conference for this afternoon at four. Great timing if that's what it is, with G & B making their announcement tonight."

"Thumbing their noses at them."

"And us," Powell agreed.

"Interesting, but I don't see how it relates to Tim's murder."

"Yes, you do. You're just don't want to face the possibility."

"Grantwood murdered his partner? I've considered it. But the motivation bothers me. A business deal falling through doesn't strike me as good enough reason for a man to attack his partner and beat him to death. Even if the killer wanted the deal to go through very badly."

"You think I have a stronger motive, don't you? I haven't exactly tried to hide the way I feel about Chloe. Or Tim."

"Would you confess to it if it looked like she might be convicted?"

His face froze for a moment before an odd, wry grin curved his mouth. "You know, I hadn't thought about it. I suppose I might have, except I don't think I could. I don't know when the police think the murder happened, exactly, but I'm afraid that, like it or not, I've got an alibi for pretty much the entire day."

I wasn't sure how much the cops were letting out about the timing, so I thought I'd better keep what I knew about it to myself.

"From the questions the cops asked," Powell continued, "I figure it had to be sometime after I saw him that afternoon but before the Center closed. I had a meeting with a couple of buyers at five and then we had a dinner sales meeting for everyone at six. It didn't finish until almost eight."

That did seem to pretty much eliminate Powell as a candidate, if what Spencer had said about seeing Tim Bethel at seven was correct. But how sure was she of the timing? I needed to check on that. Which was going to be tricky, given Janelle's warning about asking questions.

"What are you going to do now?" Powell asked.

"I've still got questions to ask. And I'm already getting push-back from my employers."

"My promise stands," he said.

I thanked him, finished the last of my food, and said goodbye.

I wandered for a bit, my mind racing through possibilities and options. It was nearly one o'clock, half the day over, and I still had no idea who was behind Tim's murder and the threats to Grantwood.

Irv Kirshorn seemed like my best bet, so I headed for his booth. When I got there, the same woman I'd talked to the day before informed me that he was off somewhere.

"He's gone to meet with some people and sign some papers." Excitement sped up her words and made her voice rise. "We're going to have a press conference in a couple of hours and we've got a big announcement to make. Very big."

"I heard."

"Are you going to come?"

Heck, yes. "I'll be here. But could I first ask you a couple of questions? I'm just trying to gather some information for a report to the Center authorities on the murder of Tim Bethel." It was a lie, but only a little one. I did intend to put a report together when this was over. If I still worked for the Center by then.

"I'll tell you what I can."

"We're trying to establish who was present in the building this past Wednesday afternoon. Do you know who from your company was here?"

Her brow wrinkled as she thought. "I'm not sure." She rattled off a few names of the people she thought might have been present.

"I assume you were here yourself?"

"Oh, yeah. I helped set up the display."

"What time did you leave?"

"About six, I think."

"Was Mr. Kirshorn here?"

"He was here, at the Center, but not in the booth much. He had meetings with lots of people that day."

And that was the best I'd likely get on that subject. How to ask the other question, though? Then a nasty inspiration hit. I felt guilty about it, but not guilty enough to refrain.

"If we were to start a collection for a memorial fund for Mr. Bethel, do you think the company or Mr. Kirshorn would be interested in contributing?"

She looked surprised. "Well, I guess he might if everyone else was doing it."

"You don't sound like he'd be very enthusiastic."

"You must have heard the rumors. There were issues between them."

"They argued? Have you seen them do it?"

"No. I just know that a while back there were some negotiations between them for some kind of partnership or something and then it broke off and Mr. Kirshorn was mad about it. But he did say he wasn't going to let it get him down. In fact—"

I waited, saying nothing.

Human nature abhors a verbal vacuum. The young woman looked both ways. "You've got to keep this just between the two of us. I heard from someone else that he said he wasn't going to get mad. He'd get even. And he knew just how to do it. He'd found out how to get something Tim Bethel wanted very badly. Isn't that wild?" She shook her head. "But he wouldn't have killed him. I'm sure he wouldn't have done that."

"Unless his planned revenge hadn't worked out the way he wanted."

The woman grinned. "I think it did. Mr. Kirshorn has been very happy the last couple of days."

I gave her what I hoped was a co-conspirator-type look and whispered, "Do you know what made him so happy?"

"No," she answered. "But I think you'll find out if you come to the press conference. I'm pretty sure he's going to announce it."

"Okay, I'll be eager to come to the conference."

"Good." She grinned as though she'd sold me something. Maybe she had.

I kept an eye out for Kirshorn during our conversation but didn't see him. When a group of buyers strolled by and began eyeing the merchandise, I couldn't hold her any longer.

It was two-thirty by then and I was still far from having any kind of answer to who had it in for Stan Grantwood. I couldn't put together Kirshorn's satisfaction with the threats to Grantwood. Or could I?

Kirshorn might have the licensing agreement G & B was losing, but they'd still need cash to make it worth anything. It took capital to start up a new line. Did Kirshorn hope to induce Powell to call off the deal with G & B and look at him instead? Very possible. But would threatening Grantwood really help his cause that much? Couldn't he leverage the licensing agreement to raise more capital? Unless he was badly in debt—too deeply for others to risk any more on him. Also possible.

Lots of questions and no answers.

I headed for the Gruber's Exchange booth in the seventeen hundreds and found Andy Tarantoro free. He greeted me like an old friend. It made me comfortable enough to launch right into my reasons for coming.

When I told him his company had been mentioned as a potential merger candidate, he looked amused.

"Yeah, I've heard those rumors, too," he said. "But there's no fire to go with this smoke. We don't need a merger and we're not interested."

"Thanks, that's helpful. Have you heard anything about G & B's merger?"

"Gaviscelli. That's who I'm hearing. Makes sense. I hear G & B's on the skids. Got problems. Bethel was doing some kind of mad-rush damage control. That's all I know. Never liked the man myself. Avoided him as best I could, but I didn't care enough to go to the effort of killing him, if you're thinking that."

"No, I wasn't. I don't see you have any motive. But do you have any idea who might have?"

"About two-thirds of the people in this building hated him. But I don't know of any who hated him *that* much. Unless you've got some kind of psycho running around."

He meant it as a joke so I summoned a laugh, but the prospect he raised was enough to turn a nightmare into a vision of hell.

I said goodbye and went in search of another candidate Powell had mentioned.

Devlin Shea's reaction to my questions was impatient, terse, and definite. "Fine Design and Decorations isn't interested in a merger with anyone. We're doing very well on our own. Not interested in anything involving Tim Bethel, his partner, or his company. I don't wish anyone ill, but I can't say he'll be missed very much."

The man turned away to greet someone approaching, and that ended our conversation.

I guess it eliminated a couple of potential suspects. Maybe.

I cruised the aisles with all that stuff going round and round in my head. Because I was so distracted, it took a few minutes to penetrate, but at some point I began to notice a familiar fragrance in the air. Popcorn. My stomach tightened as I followed my nose toward it.

The faint aroma grew stronger as I headed toward the popcorn aisle and the Blue Hills booth. My blood pressure rose along with the smell assaulting my nose.

I stopped before I turned into the corridor. No question but someone was cooking popcorn close by. It didn't reek as much as before but it still had a faintly burnt tinge. Of course, the Blue Hills dragon lady might have figured out some other way to do it instead of using that infernal machine. In that case, I'd likely have no gripe with her, unless she was violating the fire code.

Hoping to check out the situation before she saw me, I leaned around the corner to peer up the aisle.

The popcorn machine had been moved back into position near the front of the booth, right by the aisle. It hummed gently, tossing around the fluffy white kernels of popcorn that filled its large belly.

My anger grew out of all proportion to the offense. I was going to overreact. I knew it. My head knew it. I drew three deep breaths, counted to ten, and said every swear word in my vocabulary under my breath. None of it helped. Fury pounded against the inside of my skull. I wanted so badly to go blast that woman out of the place, to pull the plug in front of all her customers, and throw her bodily out of the building. I wanted it *badly*. So badly I shook with it. I thought my head would explode.

I'm not sure what kept me from acting on the impulse. It felt like a war going on in my mind, one part trying to rush forward to pound on her, the other part holding back the rest and telling it to calm down. All the layers of education, discipline, and control instilled by my parents and teachers asserted themselves. The civilized part of me finally did triumph over the primitive, barbaric urge to do violence to someone who defied and challenged me.

I waited there several long minutes, letting my pulse calm down and my heartbeat and breathing return to normal. As the aggressive impulse wore off, my consternation grew. Where had that come from? I'd never guessed I had such a shockingly violent side to my personality.

When I had control of myself, I stepped out into the aisle and headed for the Blue Hills booth.

She saw me coming and drew herself up tall and straight, preparing for battle. A battle that wouldn't happen.

I stalked right up to her. She started to talk, but I cut right across, using that authoritative tone I'd learned from Scott. "We need to talk. Privately," I said.

She sputtered and objected that she had customers.

The only other person in the booth was a bored sales rep, watching us. "This is important. Very important," I insisted.

Our gazes met and clashed, but I think she realized that in this game of wills, I was entirely prepared to make a scene, while she wasn't. She gave way with poor grace, and we went off behind the main panel of her booth's backdrop for privacy.

I wasted no time. "You have ten minutes to produce

evidence that this machine has been repaired or to un-plug it. Those are the only two options. I'm going to walk away for ten minutes. When I come back you will either have in hand a dated piece of paper showing this thing has been inspected in the last forty-eight hours or it will be unplugged. If neither of those things has happened, I will summon security and they will remove the machine. You'll also be barred from participating in the show in the future. Is that clear enough?"

"You can't do this. You don't have the authority. You're just the director's assistant."

"You're right. I'm just the director's assistant. You're wrong about the authority, though. The director will back me. If you doubt it, here's her number." I pulled out my notebook, tore out a sheet, and scribbled on it. "Please give her a call. Right now, if you want. Ask her. Or ring her after I'm gone."

"You can be very sure I'll do that, young lady," she called after me as I walked away.

I gave her almost fifteen minutes, time I spent stalking up and down nearby aisles.

An ugly part of me, the part that still sort of itched for a fight, hoped she wouldn't do anything. I would really *enjoy* getting security in and watching them unplug that machine and roll it away, over her loud objections.

But the realistic piece of me that liked my job and liked peace knew it would be better for everyone if she either came up with the paperwork or quietly unplugged the machine.

I made sure the rational part was in charge when I went back to Blue Hills. So I was actually pleased to find she'd unplugged the machine. They still served popcorn out of it, but the thing was no longer running.

The dragon lady faced me defiantly. "I expressed my displeasure over your actions to your employer," she told me. "And I plan to lodge a complaint with your parent company. This is truly an unseemly action, to prevent a paying exhibitor from running her promotions."

No point in arguing with her. "That's your right, of course," I answered. "But we also have an obligation to prevent actions that might materially harm our exhibitors. I'll be checking back periodically for the rest of the show, so please don't even think about turning it on again."

I left the booth. Behind me the woman continued to mutter protests and threats.

My satisfaction faded when I consulted my watch. It was after three and I'd made no progress toward getting an idea of who might have killed Tim Bethel.

I swung by the G & B booth again.

A young woman recognized me as I approached G & B and stopped me. "They're in a meeting right now," she said. "They said it was important and we shouldn't disturb them unless it's an emergency."

Debating whether to go through with the announcement?

"Could I talk with you a moment?" I asked. We both looked around, but the only customer in the area was talking with one of the other salespeople.

"I guess so," she said.

"Thanks." We moved over to a more private corner. "I understand you were here, helping set up the booth the evening Tim Bethel was killed?"

She gave me an odd stare. "Yes." It was as much question as statement. The doubt showed on her face, too.

I drew a deep breath. "You know that I found his body, right? I just need to get some things straight in my mind. So I can deal with it."

Her expression lightened. "Oh, I see. I'm sorry. That must have been pretty horrible. Even for us, it's pretty unbelievable."

"Yeah, I can imagine, but I'm dealing with it. Looks like you are, too. I just need to know a few things so I can straighten it out in my head."

"Okay."

"You saw him on Wednesday?"

"Yes."

"What time?"

"I guess it was about four. Jason and Taylor and I were talking about taking a break. We'd had an early lunch and we were all getting hungry. We decided to walk across the street to get food. We did that at five and came back shortly before six, to finish setting up. I'm pretty sure I saw him before we went on break."

"Did you see him again later?"

"I didn't, but I think Jason or Taylor did. I know he came by."

"How do you know?"

"He picked up some papers a guy came and left for him. I saw them when we got back. They were on the table with his name on a sticky note. But when we were getting ready to go, they were gone."

"Did you hear or see him argue with anyone on Wednesday?"

She shook her head and started to look troubled again.

"Did the police ask you about this?" I asked.

"Yeah. Detective Gilmore? He talked to each of us."

How far could I push this? Probably not much farther. "When you saw Tim Bethel, did he seem okay? Normal?"

"Pretty much. It's not like I knew him all that well."

She hesitated. I raised my eyebrows and waited.

Air whooshed into her lungs as she sucked in a deep

breath. "He wasn't really very nice. A lot of people didn't like him and they had some good reasons. And he and Mr. Grantwood had some disagreements. Loud ones. But I didn't hear them argue here. This was before. Back in the office."

"They disagreed on selling the company?"

She frowned. "That's not for me to say."

"Fair enough." I considered what she'd told me and what else I'd just learned. Bethel had argued with a woman that afternoon. Odds were it was his wife, but it didn't have to have been. Who else? "How was Mr. Bethel's relationship with Ms. Spencer?"

"Fine, as far as I know. I never heard them argue except once over some marketing thing. That was a long time ago."

Pretty much what I expected. More likely the argument had been with one of the many women Bethel had apparently used and discarded. "Thank you for telling me what you did," I said to her. "It helps. A little."

"Don't let it haunt you. It's done and can't be changed."

I thanked her and scooted away. Grantwood and Spencer still hadn't emerged from their meeting.

Scott had a customer with him, but he made eye contact with me for a moment and frowned in a way that let me know he wanted to talk. I stopped at Chang's booth and tried not to listen as Scott extolled the merits of the candles and vases. He was good. I could see why Chang might want to hire him.

The customer wasn't ready to commit to an order. When he departed, Scott came over. "Where do we stand?" he asked. "Any leads?"

"Not much. I still think Kirshorn's the prime suspect, but I can't prove it. I can't think how we *could* prove it."

"Catching him in the act of threatening Grantwood

would help. But he hasn't been anywhere near the booth today as far as I could tell. Tell me about tonight, Heather. G & B is throwing a party for this announcement, right? Are you invited?"

"They may be ready to rescind it by now, but I have an invitation. You coming?"

"I'll pretend to be your bodyguard," he said. "What time?"

"Starts at seven-thirty. It's at the Shelton."

"Are you going home to change? I was thinking of staying here and keeping an eye on Grantwood after the show. If someone really wants to stop this, they're running out of time."

"I shouldn't need to change."

He grinned as he looked down at me. "You look good. I like the glitter in your hair. It adds a certain dramatic flair. Perfect for a party tonight."

"Oh." I brushed a hand over my head, and a few silver flakes dropped onto my suit. "Drat those angel wings."

His eyebrows rose and the humorous grin took on a wicked glint. It drove a gorgeous groove down one cheek, bracketing his mouth. "I don't doubt they're there, but where? Can't see them."

"They were hanging in the Sandorn & Ackles booth for a promotional event and making a huge mess."

"I heard something about that. People were getting lost in them."

"They were blocking the aisle. I'll stay here this evening, too. There won't be that much time between closing the show floor and the party." I glanced at my watch. Ten to four. "Gotta go. Kirshorn is holding a press conference at four. I assume they're going to announce that they've signed Roberta Harrison to a licensing deal. At least that's the rumor."

"That's the designer G & B is losing, right?"

"Right."

"It sounds as though Kirshorn's winning. Why would he be threatening Grantwood?"

"I'll explain later. Gotta be off."

I got to Kirshorn's at five minutes to four. A small crowd had already gathered. I recognized the editors of two trade publications and three consumer magazines. Sales reps from various companies had come to hear the news. The CEO of a smaller competitor and the designer whose dispute I'd mediated two days before both stood around. I finally dredged up his name out of memory. Tom Rupika.

At the far corner of the booth, on the opposite side of the aisle, stood Ellen Spencer. I suppose I shouldn't have been surprised that someone from Grantwood & Bethel would be there.

Rupika's presence raised some interesting possibilities. He certainly wasn't happy with his current licensing deal and it ran out in a couple of months. Lisa had said he was one of the people G & B might have been courting to replace Roberta Harrison. Before I could pursue the thought, Irv Kirshorn turned from the group he'd been huddled with and stood near an empty table at the edge of their booth. The young woman I'd talked to earlier came out of the back with another man. They dropped stacks of papers on the table. Press releases, I presumed. A pile of CDs and photos went down beside them.

"If I could have your attention," Kirshorn said, loudly enough to silence the people in the vicinity. He waited a moment until the buzz of conversation died down before he continued. "This is a special day for Kirshorn's and for all our employees and partners. For thc last forty years, since my father's days as president and CEO, Kirshorn's has maintained a reputation for providing superb products at irresistible prices."

He rattled on for a while. I listened with half my attention and looked around. Spencer continued to watch. Her gaze never wavered from the man speaking. I couldn't read her expression.

Finally, after going through way too much self-congratulatory recitation of history, he got to the heart of the matter.

"Today I have an announcement to make that gives me immense satisfaction. In the last couple of days, Kirshorn's has signed licensing deals with not one, but *two* top artists, both well known in the field for the quality and appeal of their work. Roberta Harrison will be creating a new line of collectible pet figurines exclusively for Kirshorn's. Those will include a mid-range line of small statuary and an upper-end line of larger, exquisitely detailed animal portraits."

He looked around at us. He stopped a moment to stare at Spencer, but no change of expression betrayed his emotions. I would have expected some smugness, but I didn't see any. Not directed at her anyway. He radiated a general air of triumph—a general celebrating a huge victory—as he said, "Roberta Harrison brings an unparalleled reputation to us. Her long-standing popularity will be an asset to us and to our valued retail partners."

Again he paused for dramatic effect. His stance and the satisfied grin that crossed his face showed how much he was enjoying this. Was he rubbing it in Spencer's face?

"In addition to Ms. Harrison's enormous contributions to Kirshorn's future, artist Tom Rupika will also be lending his sophisticated and elegant design sense to several new lines of accessories, including a series of paintings on glass in the stained-glass tradition and a line of delicate fantasy figures. Tom hasn't been in the industry as long as Roberta Harrison, but he's already built an amazing reputation.

A few gasps of surprise came from the audience and murmurs broke out. Kirshorn waited a few moments for everyone to express shock.

"With the partnership of these two fine artists, Kirshorn's is positioned to become an absolute leader in the collectible-accessories market."

He had more to say, but I didn't hear the rest. My mind churned with possibilities and likelihoods. Kirshorn's had not only lured away one of G & B's most profitable licensees, they'd also locked up the only other available one with a high enough profile to be a viable replacement. Where did that leave G & B? I looked around to check Ellen Spencer's reaction but didn't see her. Most likely she'd charged back to the booth to report on Kirshorn's announcement.

Had they signed Rupika before or after Bethel's death? I was guessing before, based on Bethel's trying to call off the merger with Gaviscelli last week. He'd known they couldn't get the high-profile designer they'd need to prevent some kind of penalty clause from kicking in. But maybe there had been a verbal commitment between Rupika and Kirshorn, and Bethel thought he could change the designer's mind.

What would this mean for the merger with Gaviscelli? Would they still want to go through with it? But Powell had reasons of his own for wanting to do that deal. Reasons that seemed to involve Chloe Bethel. Still, G & B wasn't nearly as attractive an acquisition with only one top designer instead of the two they'd had. And now their main competitor had positioned himself well ahead.

But of course, Powell already expected something of the sort. All his hinting about something triggering certain results should have clued me in. G & B had lost a major asset in Roberta Harrison, and Bethel had failed to replace her. That was why he wanted to pull out of the deal. I suppose it might have cost him his job if the merger went through. Grantwood's, too, but he claimed he wouldn't mind.

It might strengthen Kirshorn's motives, too. It wouldn't be cheap to gear up production on those new designer lines. A partner with deep pockets, like Gaviscelli, would be a major help. If Gaviscelli didn't do the deal with G & B, Kirshorn's would be the next obvious acquisition target. It might just have become a much more attractive target.

My cell phone buzzed again, so I walked off to a quiet area to answer.

"I need to talk to you," Janelle said.

Uh-oh. My stomach twisted. G & B must have talked to her again. "I'll be there in a few minutes," I said.

I stopped by Chang's to tell Scott what had happened at Kirshorn's announcement.

"What does it mean?" he asked after I'd given him the gist. "It still sounds like he's coming out on top."

"It's about capital. It takes money to start up a line, and a lot of money to do several new lines. The word is Kirshorn's doesn't have it."

"This could make him even more desperate for a merger?"

"Exactly. But not with G & B, which is what I thought. He wants the merger with Gaviscelli." I drew a deep breath, bracing myself. "I've got to go. Janelle wants to talk to me." I stopped as it sank in. "I may not have a job anymore."

"Why?"

"I was told earlier to stop asking questions. Apparently, the folks at G & B complained."

"I'll probably be in trouble, too."

I shook my head. "I put you up to it."

His eyes narrowed. He drew a breath and let out some of his tension on a long exhale. "Is there a line to walk?"

"I hope so. I'm going to try to find it."

"And if it's a stop-or-go thing?"

Panic felt like a cold knife twisting in my gut while an icicle dripped chilly water down my back. "I don't know."

"Call or come see me when you're done."

I nodded. My throat was getting tight just thinking about it.

I went to the elevator and stabbed the up button. I'd always been a good girl, a good student, a well-behaved child, a teenager who didn't make waves or get in trouble. Right now it felt as if I'd been sent to the principal's office, something that had never happened to me as a student.

The elevator car arrived and the doors opened. I had to force myself to step in. My finger slid off when I reached for the button marked three. It took two tries to make it light up.

I'd long since stopped noticing that twisting, sinking feeling in my stomach when the car moved, but I felt it that time.

It was even harder to step off and walk down the hall to Janelle's office.

TWELVE

My WISH THAT Janelle might be out proved futile. I hadn't really expected it, but I was trying to find rays of hope to cling to. Maybe she had something else on her mind, a problem of a different sort. Or maybe Detective Gilmont wanted to talk to me again. That was possible.

She was alone in her office. Her expression when she looked up told me all I needed to know. She tried to smile, but it was pinched and showed the effort she'd expended to produce it. "Come in," she said. "Shut the door, if you would."

I couldn't exactly say I'd rather not, so I did as she asked, then sat down in the chair by her desk, feeling more and more like a child facing the school principal.

A pen rolled between her fingers suggested she was as nervous about this as I was. "I'm no good at beating around the bush, Heather. You've probably already figured out I got another complaint from Grantwood & Bethel about your questioning them. Was there a good reason to defy my orders?"

"I don't know if I can explain it well enough. I guess it's a kind of fear. Maybe several kinds of fear."

My fingers knotted together and twisted. I drew a deep breath, hoping I could explain what churned in my heart or mind. "I've never been in a position like this before, and I'm having trouble figuring out how to deal with it. It's like something really, really bad could happen, and I might be able to prevent it. I'm afraid that an innocent woman will be branded a murderer. Afraid for an innocent man—at least I think he is—who might be hurt or worse. Afraid that a killer will walk free, leaving others to pay for his crime. Even afraid of failing the people who think I might be able to do something about it. Though why they think that, I'm not real sure."

"Who thinks you could do something about it? I told Gilmont you might be able to help him, but I certainly didn't say you could do his job for him."

"Not him. At least one person who cares for Chloe Bethel and doesn't believe she did it asked me to make some inquiries he couldn't do himself and see if I could find proof she didn't."

"Who?"

"I promised to keep his identity confidential."

"Is his request more important to you than keeping your job?"

I drew in a sharp breath as pain stabbed through my chest and into my stomach. I braced myself. "His request, no. But justice? Janelle, I don't know how to answer that."

"Justice isn't your business," she said.

"It isn't? Isn't justice everyone's business?"

"On your own time. But it's not what we pay you to do here. We pay you to keep the shows running smoothly and all our clients as happy as possible."

"But when the needs of one exhibitor clash with the needs of others?"

"You consult with me and we figure out how to compromise."

"What would you say about this?"

"I'd say the exhibitor who asked you to do this had no right to make that request."

My stomach felt like the cord on my hair dryer when it started twisting up into knots that pulled tighter and tighter. "What if he did, though? And even if he didn't, if it's true that I might be able to stop something else bad from happening—to one of our exhibitors—isn't there some kind of obligation?"

"Not to you. It's not your job, Heather."

"It's a demand. A need." I shook my head as I struggled to find the words to make her understand. "Here's the thing. If something bad happens, and I stopped trying to find answers, how do I live with knowing I might have made a difference?"

Janelle flipped the pen end over end between her fingers, faster and faster. "There's a big part of me that understands where you're coming from," she said. "A part of me sympathizes. But I've got obligations also. I try hard to support all my employees to the best of my ability. And you know how highly I think of you." Her expression was drawn, tense, and pained. "I'll try to support you in this as best I can. But Roper was here when I got the call from G & B, so he knows about it."

The pen skipped out from between her fingers and clattered on the desk. "You know how I feel about you. I don't want to lose you. But if Roper gets another complaint, it won't matter how much I argue on your behalf."

"I understand. And I'll try hard not to offend anybody."

Janelle nodded. "Are you going to the G & B announcement party tonight?"

"Of course."

"Scott?"

"He's coming with me."

"Good. Can you keep an eye on Grantwood without asking any more questions?"

"I think so."

"Do it, then." She picked up the pen again. "I don't think Chloe Bethel killed her husband, either, and I wouldn't like to see her convicted of it. But have you made any progress in presenting the police a realistic alternative?"

"Not really." I hated making that admission. "I've learned lots of stuff. Some stuff I really didn't want to know, and a lot of it doesn't add up and probably doesn't matter."

"The threats to Grantwood?"

"He thinks they're from Kirshorn, and he's probably right. Whether that makes Kirshorn guilty of anything else, though, is open to debate."

"Sort of depends on whether he follows up the threats with anything more, doesn't it?"

"I think threatening someone is some kind of crime, but yeah, you're right. Except it seems kind of odd to think there would be two people at the show so close to the line of violence. I mean, it's not like there's ever been a problem like that before."

Janelle started tumbling the pen between her fingers again. "Actually, there are usually quite a few people at any given show who are close to the line. We've never had anybody really cross it before, but we've had plenty come close. You had one yourself a day or so ago."

"Oh, heck, the designer. Yeah. He did come close."

"That's why we have a security team. One of the reasons anyway."

"It was a stupid comment on my part. I guess what I meant is most everyone here has too much to lose to step over the line."

"More accurate," she agreed. "Anyway, tomorrow is the last day. If you have to continue to ask questions tomorrow, try to keep it low-key. And stay away from G & B unless it's absolutely necessary. Okay?"

"Okay. Thanks for backing me."

"You're good at this, Heather, and your heart is in the right place. Please don't squeeze me against Roper."

My head felt light as I left the room. After so much worry and dread, the reprieve felt like…well, a reprieve. A cold sweat broke out on my face and neck as I got in the elevator and the doors slid shut. Relief was almost as overwhelming as my worry had been. Until I remembered I still had no answers and only a couple of hours until Grantwood's big announcement.

It was a quarter to six by the time I got down to the show floor. Already people were starting to clean booths and stow things for the evening. A few buyers still roamed the aisles, but most had fled for cocktail parties, dinner meetings, drinks in the bar, or they had left to get ready for the evening events.

I went straight to Chang's, but I didn't see Scott there.

"He said he needed to follow Mr. Grantwood," Martin Chang told me when I asked. "He asked me to tell you he'd give you a call around six."

I thanked him and wandered aimlessly for a few minutes. I found myself checking out the Kirshorn's booth again. The table with the press releases and pictures still sat there, but I didn't see Kirshorn or his assistant. The young man who'd helped tote out the material for the press conference seemed to be manning the booth by himself, though given the few buyers remaining, he wasn't overtaxed.

He recognized me as an employee of the Center, though he had to check my badge for my name before he said hello. In answer to my question, he said Mr. Kirshorn and most of the rest of the staff had left for meetings or just to relax. He didn't expect any of them back again that evening.

I then meandered over to the Gaviscelli booth, looking for Dave Powell, but he, too, had gone.

My stomach, which had unwound a bit after the conversation with Janelle, tightened up again. Time pressed down on me. I had no clue what to do next, and I felt helpless.

As I wandered away from the Gaviscelli booth, my cell phone rang.

"I'm at the Shelton," Scott said. "I followed Grantwood over here and up to his room. He's alone in there now. Want to join me? I'm on the fifth floor. To your left when you get off the elevator, then take a right at the end."

"I'll be there in ten minutes."

I rushed back upstairs to get my purse from my desk and took the stairs down. I didn't want to wait for the elevator, and I needed the activity to use up some of the adrenaline.

Darkness had taken over when I got outside, and the air was cool. I shivered even with my suit jacket on and walked faster, hoping the activity would help warm me up. Naturally, the crossing light at the corner turned red just before I got there. At that time of day too much traffic clogged the street to ignore the signal. I shifted from foot to foot as I waited, more to work off the energy than to keep warm.

The light changed and I charged out into the street. When I reached the other side, I sped up again, until my heel caught in a crack in the sidewalk. I nearly pitched forward on my face, but caught myself on a signpost.

My cell phone rang again as I walked in the front door of the hotel.

"Where are you?" Scott asked.

"Just inside the front door."

"Duck into a corner where you can see the elevators," he told me. "Grantwood's on the way down. I'll be in the next car, but watch and tell me if he gets out at the lobby."

I glanced around and moved back to where a large potted plant would let me keep an eye on the elevator lobby but hide me from sight.

Seconds later the bell pinged, doors opened, and Stan Grantwood emerged from the car. He turned the other way and walked toward the back of the hotel until he got to the entrance to one of the restaurant/bars and went in. I reported that back to Scott.

"I'm on my way down," he said. "Care for a drink?"

"Only if I can get some food with it. I'm starving."

Scott came out of one of the other elevator cars while I was talking. He glanced around.

"Behind the potted palm to your right," I told him.

He grinned as he turned and saw me. "That is *such* a cliché. Couldn't you find a more original place to hide?"

"Time pressure. Had to take whatever cliché presented itself."

"Excuses. Let's go see if he's meeting someone or just having a quiet drink on his own."

We approached carefully and entered the bar just as Grantwood joined several people—Ellen Spencer, Vickie, and Jason among them—at a table near the back corner. The others already had menus and someone handed his to Grantwood when he sat. Following the directions on the sign near the door, Scott and I seated ourselves, choosing a booth in the front corner. In the dim light, the group at the back couldn't easily see us, but we could keep an eye on them. Scott sat facing the door, which meant he had to turn and lean out of the booth to look at the others. We crowded over toward the wall to be out of their line of sight.

This was supposed to be business, but I couldn't help it. I enjoyed being that close to Scott in the booth and being able to watch his face.

A waiter brought menus and we took a moment to study

them. Once we'd ordered, Scott asked, "What happened with Janelle?"

"I still have a job. For the moment. As long as I'm careful not to do anything that will bring another complaint."

"What are you going to do?"

I sighed. "What I have to."

"What does that mean?"

"It means I hope we can settle things tonight."

"And if not?"

"I'll try to be careful about the questions I ask. And who I tackle."

"You'd risk your job to keep pushing on this?"

I turned to look at him. Something in his tone alerted me that this was more than just curiosity.

"I don't want to," I answered. "I really don't want to."

"Why would you, then?"

"Scott, what are you wanting from me?"

A waiter chose that moment to bring us water and a basket of bread. He took our orders and departed.

Scott's drink of water lasted much longer than needed. His gaze flicked over to the table where the G & B people sat, turned briefly to me, and then fixed on a spot on the far wall. Shadows darkened his light eyes, which looked mostly gray and sort of bleak. When he put down the glass he said, "You know I was a cop once."

"You said so."

"I'm sure you've wondered what I'm doing working here." He rubbed circles in a ring of water his glass had left on the table.

"It's crossed my mind."

"I had to make a similar choice to the one you're facing. It's why I'm not a cop anymore. I want you to know that I understand the dilemma, better than you could imagine."

"Would you do it again?"

His expression mirrored his thoughts, changing several times in small, subtle ways; a twitch of the lips here, a narrowing of eyes there, an occasional brow lowering.

I wished he'd talk about what had happened. I hated that there was nothing I could do for him. Or maybe that was wrong. Maybe there was something I could do for him. Learn from him.

He picked up a roll, tore it into several pieces, and began to butter one section. "Yes, I'd do it again. But I'd do it differently. There were things I could have done better. Or more carefully." His tone, the harsh flatness of the words, showed how hard he found it to admit his mistakes. "Because I was sure I was right, I thought it didn't matter how I said things. I stepped on toes I didn't need to step on. Or at least, I stepped on them before I *had* to. I should have been a little less arrogant and sure of myself." He shrugged. "Hindsight. I'm not even sure it's twenty-twenty yet."

"Are you still sure you were right?"

"About the basic issues? Yes. The way I handled it? No. On the other hand, it might not have mattered how I handled it. I might have ended up here anyway."

I cringed, knowing that for him, "ending up here" was a sort of purgatory. Or worse. "If you could go back and do everything right, knowing the outcome would be the same, would you still do it?"

He chewed a piece of roll he'd just put in his mouth and swallowed. All his muscles tensed, as though he braced himself. "I don't know. I like to think I would. But I don't know." He picked up another chunk of bread and began pulling it into ever smaller pieces.

He leaned out to look over at the G & B table again and I followed suit. They'd settled in to eat. I sipped some water before I asked, "Any suggestions?"

"For you? First, you have to accept that you really could

lose your job over it. I'm not sure I believed that until it happened. I stupidly thought that being right was enough to protect me from any bad consequences."

"My nervous stomach and tight chest tell me I've accepted it."

"Second, this *really* isn't your responsibility. It's not your job. No one has any right to ask you to solve a murder. Including you. You're not trained to do this. You weren't hired to do it. You've no experience in doing it. You may, in fact, be interfering with the police's investigation. No matter what happens, you've no reason to feel guilty if you decide to let it go. Understand?"

"Understand, yes. Accepting it is something else."

He glanced around again at the G & B table then turned to face me full on. His eyes were brighter, the gray glowing almost warmly. He took my hand and the heat from his palm flooded me with awareness of him. It offered a sort of comfort, too. "I'm not going to tell you to stop, Heather. If you feel that strongly about it, you can't. And I admire the principles driving you. I just don't like that you could get hurt by it."

I tried for a smile, but I felt it wobble. "I don't like the idea, either. And I'm going to try not to offend anyone any further. I don't know if that will work. But I'm really hoping that after tonight, we won't have to worry about it anymore."

"You think something will happen tonight?"

"Makes sense, doesn't it? If the killer wants to stop the merger, he's running out of time to do it."

A server with no sense of timing chose that moment to deliver our meals. Scott let go of my hand with a wry grin. He frowned as the server departed. Stan Grantwood had risen from his seat. Instead of coming to the front, he headed for the back of the room, following a sign to the restrooms. I let out a sigh of relief. I was hungry and the smell of the big, juicy hamburger on my plate had just reached my nose. It set my taste buds dancing in anticipation.

Scott had ordered a chicken breast with vegetables, and he tackled the vegetables first. "Are you a health freak?" I asked, watching him dig into the green beans.

His eyebrows rose. "I take care of myself. It's important in my line of work. What makes you think I'm a freak about it?"

"You're eating those green beans like you're actually enjoying it."

"I am. What's wrong with green beans?"

"The taste? The texture? The greenness?"

He laughed. "The greenness?"

"Puts me off."

"I like green beans."

"You probably like broccoli, too," I said. "And Brussels sprouts. And turnip greens."

"I like broccoli, tolerate Brussels sprouts, and draw the line at greens of almost any kind."

"Whew. You're human after all."

"You're a mess," he said. "Eat."

I picked up the burger, but after a couple of bites I stopped long enough to ask, "What were you going to say earlier, before the waiter delivered our food?"

"Hold on a minute while my train of thought finds that rail again." He took another drink while he pondered. "I was going to say that the deal isn't done until they sign the papers. My guess is, if they haven't already, they won't be doing it until Monday when all the lawyers can get involved."

"Oh." I should have known that. I probably did know

that. I just didn't want to admit it. "But isn't it as good as done once they've announced it?"

"I don't know what the legal aspects are, but I'm pretty sure it doesn't count until the signatures are on the bottom line."

"I suppose not."

I must have sounded as discouraged as I felt because Scott said, "We'll just take it as it comes. Let's see what tonight brings."

"Too reasonable. I'm considering rescheduling my nervous breakdown for sometime tonight. Then they can cart me off and I won't have to worry about anything else."

"Do people take you seriously when you say things like that?"

"Mostly no. One of these days I'm going to surprise everyone."

"Mind giving me a bit of advance notice?"

"Where's the fun in that?" I asked. "The whole point is the surprise."

"You're a dangerous woman, Heather McNeil."

"Harmless little old me? No way."

"You're not harmless and you're not old. Little, well, yes."

"Hey! I'm five foot four and if I eat any more of this burger, I'm going to weigh five *more* pounds too many."

While I'd chomped my way through half the hamburger and devoured most of the fries, he'd eaten all of the chicken breast and vegetables. He looked over at the G & B table and said, "We're passing on dessert. It looks like they're finishing up."

Scott signaled the waiter and got our check. I insisted on paying since I could put the meal on a Center credit card.

"When the waiter's gone, I want you to crawl under the table to the other side," he said.

"So they can't see us as they leave?"

"Right."

Once the waiter had gone, I ducked down and crawled under the table. I met a stray fry that must have escaped my plate, avoided a blob of dried ketchup, and swerved around a piece of something unidentifiable but unquestionably dead.

Scott made room on the seat for me between his body and the wall. It felt way too good to be so close to him. The piney smell of his cologne teased and the warmth of his body steadied me.

Only moments after I'd clambered up onto the bench on the other side, we heard the G & B party making their way to the exit. Scott leaned forward so that if anyone turned to look back when they got to the door they would see him, but I was sheltered in his shadow. None of them did. They were engrossed in a conversation about a television show.

Once they were out, we got up and followed. It was almost too easy, since they never turned back or even suspected anyone watching them. They went straight to the elevators and someone pressed the down button. We waited until their car had arrived and they were on it before we summoned another elevator. Fortunately, it came within seconds. There were only two levels below. Since the ballroom where they planned to hold the announcement party was on the first of those, that seemed a safe bet.

The right one, too. I hadn't realized it was almost time for the party to begin until we arrived at the door and discovered a group had begun to gather around the bar inside.

The buzz grew louder as people noticed that the Grantwood & Bethel contingent had arrived. Stan Grantwood and Ellen Spencer immediately crossed to the stage area to talk with a couple of men setting up electronic equipment.

The screen and laptop computer suggested a PowerPoint presentation in the offing.

"Circulate for a bit," Scott whispered in my ear when he'd gotten us each a soft drink from the bar. "I'm going to find a place where I can get closer."

I made a round of the room while trying to keep an eye toward the stage. I talked to people. I'm pretty sure I did. I barely remember what I said or who I said it to, but no one seemed to have been offended by my inattention. Every nerve ending in my body jangled with tension. My gut kept screaming that something was going to happen. Something bad.

My gaze kept wandering to the stage area. Dave Powell had come in with some of his staff from Gaviscelli and joined Grantwood. Scott had disappeared, though I was confident he was somewhere close by, watching.

I couldn't help keeping an eye on Grantwood myself, following as he moved back and forth around the stage, talking to various people and helping move items around. I was waiting for something to happen. Grantwood turned to leave the platform and stumbled as he descended the set of four steps, but he righted himself quickly. He walked around to the back and disappeared from my sight. I think I stopped breathing for a few minutes until he reappeared.

Grantwood, Spencer, Powell, and two of the people with Powell climbed onto the stage. After a few minutes of discussion among themselves, Ellen Spencer went to the podium and tapped the microphone.

"Ladies and gentlemen, if you'll take your seats, we'd like to begin our presentation," she said.

A few minutes of noisy chaos followed while everyone settled. I collapsed into an empty chair on the end of a row five back from the platform. The lights went dim and

Grantwood took Spencer's place at the podium. I couldn't escape a crawling tension that curled my stomach into a knot. It almost felt like the air grew thicker in the room, the sense of expectancy gearing up to storm-warning proportions.

"Welcome, all of you," Grantwood said, "and thank you for coming out tonight. I realize that most of you would do just about anything for free food and drink, but listening to me rattling on is probably too high a price even for that. I'm grateful so many of you came anyway."

Laughter broke out around the room, but it seemed tight and forced.

"Seriously, folks, this is an occasion of sadly mixed emotions for me. As most of you know, my partner of many years, Tim Bethel, passed away just a few days ago. His absence leaves a huge hole in so many of our lives and casts a terrible shadow over the joy we should be feeling tonight. We had a long and very serious debate whether to go ahead with holding this party. In choosing to do so, we hope it will be clear that we mean no disrespect to Tim. Rather, we honor his memory.

"In respect to him, we've put together a brief presentation of his life and his career in the industry, culminating in the formation of Grantwood & Bethel, which leads directly to tonight. Before we start, though, I have to thank several members of Tim's family, including his daughter, Julie, and his wife, Chloe, for providing some of the images and information we've used. I'd also like to thank the staff of Grantwood & Bethel who've worked so hard and such long hours to pull this together."

What followed was a standard "Who's Who" sort of recap. The pictures showed a cute kid growing into a good-looking man. Even in college he flashed a hundred-watt grin that probably had girls falling all over him.

It got more interesting when they came to how he and Grantwood met while working at a furniture-importing firm that went out of business years ago. A shared interest in accessories and recognition of their importance led them to form G & B. Their first designer license deal, with Roberta Harrison, put the company on the must-visit list for most retail buyers. Signing Vittorio Angaro as well lifted them into the top tier of accessory manufacturers.

Hard to tell how much of it got cleaned up and given a glossy coat of paint to hide the ugly stains, but it couldn't all have been that neat and pretty. I probably wouldn't have believed a lot of it even if I hadn't heard the stories about Bethel.

It was, as promised, short. The applause that followed owed more to guilt, politeness, and, cynical as it sounds, maybe just a bit of relief. It certainly couldn't have represented a genuine warm respect for Bethel. It lasted long enough to be polite and not a second more.

When the clapping died down, the lights in the room brightened and Grantwood returned to the podium.

"I have two announcements to make this evening," he said. "The first one is that we will be creating a fund for the benefit of Tim Bethel's children and their education. Grantwood & Bethel will start it with a ten-thousand-dollar donation. We invite anyone else who is moved to do so to add a contribution. You can pick up flyers with the information at our booth tomorrow."

He paused for a dramatic moment. "You know, it's both sad and ironic that Tim Bethel isn't here tonight because we're about to announce something that he worked tirelessly for the past year to bring about. For a long time now, Tim has—" He stopped but this pause was unplanned. And disturbing. We could hear him draw several deep, labored breaths before he seemed to get control again.

"Sorry about that," he continued. "I believe some of my dinner might be having an argument with its current environment."

That evoked a ripple of laughter throughout the room.

"As I was saying, Tim has been working toward this goal for a long time. It's simply a tragedy that he's not here tonight to see it come to fruition."

Grantwood let his head sag for a moment in respect. "That said, I think one way to honor his memory is to celebrate the event. So, without further ado, I'd like to announce that Grantwood & Bethel will be merging with The Gaviscelli Company, effective the first of June. The new company will retain the name Gaviscelli, but it will integrate the licenses and lines of Grantwood & Bethel, save for one. We will work out later how to integrate staff and supply lines, but I'm confident we can—"

This pause wasn't for dramatic effect, either. Silence spread like a smothering blanket of horror over the room. We all saw the change in Grantwood's face as it lost all color. His eyes closed and he let out an odd, strangled gasp. Then he took a wobbly step backward, doubled over, folded up, and crashed to the floor of the stage.

THIRTEEN

PEOPLE RUSHED TOWARD him from every side. I didn't. Shock held me in place for a few moments until it occurred to me that as the only official representative of the Center present, I should try to find out what had happened and offer help. I was so scared of what I might learn that I didn't want to do it.

I forced myself to stand up and head to the front, along with the other hundred or so people in the room. I had to push and shove to get close. A group on the stage surrounded him so that all I could see was one knee and a foot. Neither appeared to be moving. Around me others pressed forward to see what was going on and asked each other what they'd seen and what they thought had happened. I shoved my way through the crowd to get a better view.

Scott leaned over the collapsed form. He had a cell phone in one hand and the fingers of the other were on Grantwood's throat. I pushed, wriggled, and climbed my way up to the stage and got close enough to hear him say into the phone, "He's got a pulse."

I let out a breath I didn't realize I'd been holding. Relief compounded by the heat and press of the crowd around me made my head light and spinny.

"Weak but holding," Scott added. After a moment he said, "Good idea. Wait a minute." He looked around and spotted me. "Heather, go ask at the desk if they know of a doctor or nurse in the building."

"Nine-one-one?" I asked, glancing at his phone.

Scott nodded.

I jumped up. This time people moved aside to let me through. In truth, I was thrilled to have something to do. It beat hanging around, waiting and wondering and worrying.

I rushed across the lobby, ran up the escalator rather than wait for an elevator, and hurried to the concierge desk. "Need medical help downstairs," I managed to pant out while struggling to get my breath.

"Is someone injured?" the concierge asked in a voice that didn't convey much concern about the possibility.

"Sick, I think."

"Has anyone called nine-one-one?"

"Yes. I hoped you might know of a doctor or nurse in the hotel."

"I'm sorry, we don't have any medical personnel on the premises, but I'll be happy to try to find one in the phone listings for you."

"That won't help. I was thinking maybe a guest." I turned away but stopped. A siren screeched outside, growing louder. The sound grew clearer as it approached, so I waited near the door. The emergency vehicle pulled up a couple of minutes later.

"Downstairs," I told the man and woman who hopped out and yanked big metal boxes of equipment from a panel in the truck before they came inside.

They followed me down the escalator and into the ballroom. I prayed hard every minute of that trip from the lobby to the stage where Grantwood had collapsed.

Scott looked up as my companions made their way through the crowd. He moved back to give them room.

The male paramedic recognized him. "Scott! Didn't expect to find you here," he said, while his companion snapped on a pair of rubber gloves and knelt down beside

Grantwood. "Heard about what went down with Sandersly and Richland. Bad stuff. Sorry you got caught in the mud. But it looks like you're doing okay." He stared around the room at the beautifully dressed people and up at the elaborate glass chandeliers hanging from the ceiling.

"Could be worse. More later." Scott glanced at the patient and the paramedic got the message.

As the medic leaned over the unconscious form, Scott stood up, turned, saw me, and drew me back, away from the crowd still jammed around Grantwood.

We found a quiet spot against the wall, near the door. He put an arm around my shoulders and said, "Calm down, I think he'll be all right." He wiped a tear off my face. I hadn't realized I was crying.

"We should have been more careful," I said. "We should have watched more closely."

"What do you think happened to him?"

"I don't know. Poison?"

"Possible, but it didn't look like it to me."

"What, then?" It felt good to have his arm around me like that. Supportive and close and warm.

"If I had to speculate, I'd guess he had a heart attack."

"Oh." Shock sent an odd sort of quiver through me. I'd been so focused on the possibility of murder, I hadn't even considered that it might be something natural.

"Could someone induce a heart attack? The timing just seems so convenient."

"It's possible, I suppose. It looked like a genuine heart attack to me, though." His eyes narrowed. "I agree about the timing. It worries me. On the other hand, the stress of the last few days and especially this presentation tonight might have brought it on. He's not in the best of shape, physically."

"What can we do?"

"I'll suggest a deeper tox screen. Ordinarily it would get laughed at, but given that his partner was murdered a few days ago, I think it'll float this time. And I'll suggest extra security for Grantwood's room tonight. Otherwise, we've only got tomorrow to figure it out. If you're still going to pursue it."

My stomach twisted hard enough to send a surge of nausea through me. "After this? You're damned right I'm going to pursue it. I'm just afraid there isn't enough time."

Scott released me and pulled out his cell phone again. Whoever he called didn't answer. I could tell from his tone he was talking to a machine when he said, "Gilmont, Scott Brandon. Need to talk to you about the Bethel murder as soon as possible. Tonight or tomorrow morning. Call back." He gave the number and hung up.

The paramedics had Grantwood on a gurney. As they left, Scott stopped the one he knew and asked where they were taking him.

"You want to go?" Scott asked me after the medic had told him which hospital.

"Need to. At least until we know he's going to make it. We should probably offer a ride to Spencer and other G & B people."

Ellen Spencer looked like she'd been run over by a truck and still hadn't figured out what hit her. "We're going to the hospital," I said. "You want a ride?"

As she said yes, Dave Powell came forward and offered his car, as well.

We all got to the hospital and found our way to the emergency-room waiting area about half past ten. Gilmont returned Scott's call at eleven, but it was my turn to get soft drinks and snacks so I wasn't there when it happened. By the time I got back, Scott had gone off somewhere to talk to him privately.

He returned half an hour later and drew me apart from the others. "Gilmont will meet with us at seven tomorrow morning at the Center. At the door. I told him you could let us into the building. I can't tell what he thinks about it all."

Near midnight a doctor came out to say that he thought Grantwood had suffered a heart attack, but the damage seemed relatively mild. They'd be keeping him in the Cardiac Care Unit for a while, but he expected a full recovery.

Later, when Scott drove me home, I tried to fill him in on everything I knew that might be relevant.

"I'm too tired to think right now," he said as he escorted me to the door. "Maybe if we sleep on it, something will occur to us."

"I hope I can sleep," I admitted as I unlocked the door.

He drew me to him and kissed me. The outdoor light reflected brightly off his blond hair, but it leeched the color from his eyes. Still, when I looked into them, I saw warmth and worry and a fire that raged behind the warmth of his kindness. Tingles ran up and down my back. His breathing became louder and harsher and the fire blazed brighter in his light eyes.

I reached out to rest my hands on his chest, but he stopped me by pushing against my wrists. "Not tonight. Show's over tomorrow. Can I take you out to dinner tomorrow night?"

I actually had to force myself to breathe in. "Yeah. Please. I'd like that. Whatever happens."

"Whatever happens, you'll know you did everything you possibly could." He leaned forward and kissed me again, lightly and quickly. "Sleep. I'll pick you up at six-thirty."

To my surprise, I did fall asleep. The buzz of the alarm clock at five-thirty shocked me out of one of those disturbing dreams where someone is chasing you and you're trying and trying to run away but your feet are mired in mud and you can't move.

I had to drag myself out from under the covers and into the shower. True to his word, Scott showed up at six twenty-nine. I grabbed my purse and a granola bar and went out to meet him. To my surprise and joy, he pulled into the drive-through lane of a Starbucks.

"Thank you, thank you. I don't function well without a good dose of caffeine."

"I noticed. I'm not real clear-headed myself," he admitted. "And I want to be at the top of my game when we meet with Gilmont."

While Scott drove, I called the hospital. Grantwood had spent a comfortable night, I was told, and would likely be moved from the Cardiac Care Unit to a regular room later in the day.

Scott and I reached the Center at five to seven and waited outside for Gilmont. He arrived ten minutes later. I let us all into the building and we went upstairs to the conference room. Scott set the coffees on the table while I got milk and sugar from the break room.

When I returned, Gilmont asked, "Is there a good reason for this meeting?"

"I think so," Scott answered. "Listen to what Heather has to say."

I went through everything I'd learned—the threats to Grantwood, the mergers and desired mergers, the struggle for the high-profile designers, the financial issues, and even the reason for Chloe Bethel's early arrival at the show. I didn't tell him who'd told me.

When I finished, Gilmont sent me a hard look and said, "What did you leave out?"

I stared at him. "What are you talking about?"

He shook his head. "Don't. And by the way, forget about

an acting career if you had any notions that way. You're terrible at it."

"Crap. I never could get away with anything as a kid, either."

He and Scott both grinned.

"So?" Gilmont prompted. "It wouldn't be that guy who overheard Tim Bethel arguing with a woman Wednesday afternoon in the loading-dock area, would it?"

"I told him to call you about it."

"He did. Obviously, you're not subscribing to the Chloe Bethel guilt theory."

"I haven't from the start. I've met her and I don't believe she'd do it. She had no motive to harm Grantwood."

"At this point there's no reason to think Grantwood's collapse was anything but a heart attack. He fits the profile."

"But if it wasn't?"

"You think this guy Kirshorn is a killer?"

"He's my prime suspect, yes."

Gilmont pulled out a notebook and pen and scribbled a few lines before he said, "He's got motive enough, certainly. He didn't like Bethel. And he's passionate about his own company and making it work. But is he passionate enough to kill a rival? Means is no problem. How about opportunity? Have you been able to place him in the loading-dock area around the time of death?"

"What time was that?" I asked.

"Somewhere between five and eight. The coroner thinks it would have been closer to five than to eight but we have one witness who claims to have seen Bethel around seven."

"So after seven, then. I have nothing on where Kirshorn was then. No one in the area saw him. His people don't know where he was around that time. He was supposedly at meetings outside the booth from early afternoon on."

"You haven't been able to ask him?"

"I haven't had the opportunity. If he's at the booth when I get there, he's with clients. If he's not with clients, he's not there."

The detective made another jot in his notebook. "What about Bethel's argument with the woman?"

"What about it?" I asked. "We know plenty of women here hated him."

"So did a lot of the men. All right. It's worth asking a few questions. You have any other ideas?"

I shook my head. Scott did the same. Gilmont rose to go. "Walk me down to my car," he said to Scott. Since he pointedly didn't invite me to accompany them, I said goodbye, went to my desk, flipped on the computer, and sorted through the gazillion emails waiting.

"Did he ask you if I had all my marbles?" I asked when Scott returned.

"Nope. Just wanted to know what a scumbag like me was doing in a classy place like this."

"The burning question we're all asking ourselves."

"Don't waste too many brain cells on it. The answer's easy. It's called a paycheck, and I need one as much as the next guy. The question for now is, do I go back to Chang's and keep an eye on G & B or go back to being Scott Brandon, security guard?"

"Stay at Chang's. I'm not sure why, but until we get some resolution or the show ends, I feel better with you there."

"Whatever the lady wants." Going all-business, he said, "I'd like to go down and check a few things on the show floor before it opens. How can I get in there now?"

I gave him my key and directions. "Make sure you lock the door behind you once you're in. Oh, and do you have your Center credentials as well as the show tag? If any of the temps see you, you'll need them."

He reached into a pocket and brought out his Center ID. "Thanks. I'll bring the key back up before the floor opens."

I had a quiet half hour and managed to take care of most of the email messages and make notes about phone calls to return later.

Janelle arrived at eight-thirty. Although dressed in her usual classy style, her face showed more strain than normal.

"Be glad when this one is over?" I asked after wishing her a good morning. "At least today's the end of it."

"Thank God. This has been the roughest one in years." "You heard what happened last night?"

"At Grantwood's announcement? No. What?"

I followed her into her office and explained about Stan Grantwood's collapse and our trip to the hospital.

"Oh, my God, you're kidding. Is he all right? What was it?"

"The doctor said a heart attack. Scott says there might be things you can give someone to cause one. He's getting the doctors to check. I think Scott has some kind of in with the cops so he can ask them to do things."

"Handy."

"Anyway, I called the hospital this morning, and they said they're moving him from the CCU to a room later, so I guess he's doing as okay as possible."

"Thank heaven." The words were heartfelt. "What now?"

"I'm not sure. For the moment, he's safe enough in the hospital. But that announcement didn't quite get finished, so what happens after the show is over? Is there still a risk?"

Janelle scribbled a few notes on a pad. "I'll try to visit

him later today if they'll let me. I'll suggest that he either get that deal signed right away or postpone it indefinitely. Either one should protect him."

"Good idea. Doesn't help Chloe Bethel, though," I pointed out.

"I've got the best lawyer I know working for her. He told me yesterday he doubts it will ever come to trial. The case is circumstantial and weak."

"I guess that's good. I still feel like we've got this big thing hanging around us, with an unsolved murder."

"It's not great PR," Janelle admitted. "But we may have to learn to live with it. D.C. has a dozen or more murders a month. I don't know what percentage goes unsolved, but I'll bet it's a fair number." She looked at me. "What are you going to do today?"

"I have to check in with Savotsky first. I promised her I would. Yikes. I'm so not interested in her complaints."

"But you promised."

"Right. This elephant never forgets. Almost never anyway."

"And is faithful one hundred percent?" Janelle grinned at me.

"Let's call it ninety percent, okay? I need some margin for error."

"Ninety-five and that's my final offer."

"Sold."

"What else is on for today?"

"I really want to talk to Kirshorn. Every time I've gone to his booth, he's either with a client or not there. I'm going to try harder to catch him today."

Janelle's smile faded into a concerned frown. "Tread as lightly as you can. Please. No more complaints."

"I'll do my best. But I made my decision last night. I really don't want to rock the boat here. Really. But even more, I don't want to risk a killer going free to hurt others and someone else getting blamed for it. I couldn't live with that. Maybe you should just fire me now and get it over with."

Janelle's eyebrows rose and her lips quirked. "No way, lady. You don't get out of working today that easily."

I looked at my watch. "Speaking of which, it's past eight-thirty. Time to get going."

"I've got a couple more things I need you to check on this morning." Janelle handed me a page of notes.

I met Scott in the hall outside our office where he'd just gotten off the elevator. He handed my key back and rode down with me again since that was the only reason he'd come up. "What's on your agenda?" he asked.

"Visit Sue Savotsky, follow up on her complaints, check on the popcorn machine, check on a couple of other things for Janelle, try to talk to Kirshorn, figure out who killed Bethel. All before the show closes at four."

"You don't expect much of yourself."

"Lofty goals."

"How bad is it going to hurt when you don't reach them?"

"You may have a chance to find out tonight. If that's still on?"

"You're not trying to wiggle out of it, are you?" he asked.

"I was trying to make sure I was wiggled into it."

He grinned. "Better believe it."

We reached the entrance to the show. Scott promised we'd talk later and headed off toward Chang's while I went to see Sue Savotsky. I found her in her booth, but something seemed off about her. When she saw me coming, she didn't get excited or act irritated or pleased. She just looked sort of morose, shoulders slumped, moving slowly, face set in a frown. No matter how grumpy or combative she got, I'd never seen her look…depressed.

"What's wrong?" I asked when a close-up confirmed my impression of her sad humor.

She shook her head. "I swear, sometimes I wonder why I even keep trying. It's so pointless. So futile. Nothing ever works out for me."

"What happened?"

"It's been a terrible market and I'm not sure it's worth it to continue."

I questioned her some more, but she wouldn't tell me anything more specific than that. Whatever had happened—if it was anything specific and not just a quick glance at her bottom line—she wasn't ready to talk about it.

She gave me her list, but it had only two names on it.

"This is all?"

Her shrug had the same air of melancholy resignation. "No point in bothering," she answered.

"Okay. I hope you feel better later."

"I doubt it," she said as I walked away.

Did she suffer from bipolar disorder? This seemed so out of character for the feisty, aggressive, perhaps somewhat delusional woman I thought I knew. I actually felt stirrings of sympathy but had no idea what I could do to help.

I glanced at the two names on the list. One was new to me, the other familiar. I took the new one first and went to a booth at the far end of the aisle. Again I wondered about Savotsky's sanity in thinking of these people as rivals. Their collection of beaded silk and satin throw pillows, bed linens, and wall hangings bore no resemblance to anything she offered.

I dutifully visited the company president and delivered

the same brief speech I had several times the day before. She grinned at the end and thanked me, but a customer approached and our conversation halted quickly.

Dan and Joanne greeted me like the old friend I was close to becoming. "You here for Savotsky again?" he asked, before I even had time to launch into the spiel.

I nodded. "She's obviously worried about you. Maybe you're too successful?"

Dan grinned. "It's been a good show for us. I don't have to resort to underhanded tactics to bring in customers. We promote like crazy, but we don't steal other peoples' business. But hey—did you hear about what happened to her?" His smile grew broader, but then he deliberately tried to shut it off. Not too successfully, though.

"No. What?"

Joanne didn't bother to try to hide her smile, but Dan did manage a measure of sobriety as he said, "I'm really not the kind of guy who enjoys other peoples' misfortunes. Really, I'm not. It's just that she's been such a thorn in our side. Still, it's kind of tragic in its way."

"What? Tell me!"

"A couple of buyers from a big discount mart wandered up this way yesterday morning, but they didn't identify themselves. Said they were just checking out some new things for a local store. Savotsky blew them off. Didn't think they were important enough to bother with. Then later they came back and signed some nice orders with a couple of vendors. And yes, us, too. You can imagine her face when she realized what she'd done."

So that accounted for her depression.

"I really do feel kind of badly for her, even if she was reaping what she sowed," Dan added.

"Maybe she'll learn something from it," I ventured.

"Would be good, but I don't believe it," Joanne said.

Dan shrugged. "As much of a pain as she is, I can't really want bad things to happen to her."

"You're way too nice for your own good," Joanne told him.

"Nope. I believe that what goes around comes around. Which is why I try to be nice to everyone. And hey, did it work for us with the mart buyers?"

"Well, yeah."

"Congratulations on that sale," I told them.

"It's huge," Dan admitted. "Now we've got to see about ramping up production. We never anticipated something like this could happen."

"A good problem to have."

"No kidding," he said. The grin broke out again.

"Good luck to you," I said. "Have a safe trip back if I don't see you again today. I'll see you at future shows, I hope."

"You can bet on it."

I walked off, heading toward Kirshorn's booth, hoping to find him available. On the way, though, I couldn't help thinking about Sue Savotsky. The woman really was a pain. To me. To everyone. No doubt, she'd had this coming. Still, I couldn't help feeling sorry for her and hoping she'd learn a lesson. I wondered, though, if she'd even realize there was one. Should I try to find a way to tell her?

I passed the Popcorn Aisle and diverted from the straight path to Kirshorn's booth. It actually disappointed me to see the popcorn machine sitting in a back corner, unused. I wanted a confrontation. I had this urge to argue with someone.

When I got to Kirshorn's, I encountered two complete strangers, though they identified themselves as employees. They had no idea where Mr. Kirshorn was, but he wasn't in the booth.

I went by Grantwood & Bethel. Ellen Spencer was there and didn't seem all that pleased to see me.

"I just wanted to stop by and say how sorry I was about what happened last night," I said. "Also to ask if you've heard how Mr. Grantwood is doing?"

Ellen pushed back a strand of chestnut hair with an unsteady hand. "According to the hospital, he's doing okay. They may release him in a day or so."

"I'm glad to hear that. It was such a shock when he collapsed last night. I think we were all holding our breath."

"It was a shock to all of us."

"I didn't realize he had heart problems. I suppose that explains some things."

"He didn't, at least as far as any of us knew. Of course, we knew he had high blood pressure. He took medication for it, but I thought that pretty much took care of it."

I wanted to push her on the question of whether the deal would go through and how soon, but she looked ready to fall apart. With Bethel dead and Grantwood out of commission, that probably left her to run the operation here. All the stresses of the past week had taken a toll on her.

Plus, she was the one who'd complained about my questions before. So I let it go. "Let us know if we can be of any help to you," I told her.

"Thank you." Her tone, more than the words, told me it would be a chilly day in the netherworld before she made any requests of me.

Scott watched as I left the G & B booth so I went over to him. "Any progress?" he asked.

"Not really."

"I talked to that other kid who was here on Wednesday. Jason. He has no idea who Bethel talked to that day, said he was gone most of the day. He definitely saw him around four and thought he might have seen him again later but isn't sure of the time. Not much help."

"No." I would have loved to spend the rest of the day with Scott, but I was on the clock.

I left and went to check on the other things on Janelle's list. They proved mostly routine. I got maintenance to take care of a corner of carpet that refused to lay flat and was tripping people, mediated another territorial dispute, and gave directions to the airport to a couple of different people. As I was finishing the last one and heading back to the Kirshorn booth, I began to detect a familiar aroma. Burnt popcorn?

I followed the smell, and sure enough it led me back to the Popcorn Aisle. I halted near the end of it, peering around the corner to check it out as I'd done the day before.

Darned if that woman didn't have the machine running again.

I got on the phone and summoned security and maintenance.

The dragon lady saw me coming and straightened her spine, bracing for a fight.

I didn't say a word to her, but stalked directly to the outlet and pulled the plug.

"What do you think you're doing?" She stood over me and turned a fierce glare my way. I swear if she'd had a weapon handy, she might have used it.

"I warned you yesterday what would happen if I found this thing running again. I don't make promises I don't intend to keep."

"You don't have the right. This is our display and we choose what equipment we use and how we organize it. It's in the agreement."

"Did you keep reading down to the part where the Center reserves the right to remove any display deemed haz-

ardous or in violation of fire or building safety codes? It's
in there. Trust me. And this monster is decidedly in violation of all sorts of safety codes."

"Heather?" Mark and Sam approached. Howie was right
behind them.

"Can you get this thing out of here?" I asked them. "It's
become a nuisance, and the only way I can think of to resolve it is to remove it from the show floor."

The dragon lady ranted, fumed, raged, and swore in
language I hadn't heard even in college.

But as my guys began to roll the machine off the carpet
and into the aisle, I heard an amazing sound.

Clapping.

Exhibitors from all the neighboring booths had gathered to watch, and they burst into applause as the machine
made its dramatic exit.

It's almost embarrassing to admit how good that felt. I
had to resist the urge to take a bow. No point in rubbing it
in too hard with the dragon lady. But oh, boy, did I enjoy
it. I accepted thanks from several people as I walked away.

My stomach grumbled a complaint that the granola bar
I'd had for breakfast was too far in the past. It was one-
fifteen, so I headed down to the snack bar.

The hot dog didn't sit well, and I'm pretty sure it had
nothing to do with the chili. My stomach had been getting
tighter and tenser all morning as time ran out with no progress toward finding Bethel's murderer. I was down to only
a couple of hours, with nothing more than a vague suspect and no idea how to prove anything. It looked like I'd
have to live without any resolution. That thought twisted
my insides into a knot. Worse yet, Grantwood and Chloe
Bethel might still be in danger.

I threw away the last third of the hot dog when my

stomach refused to process any more food, went back up to the show floor, and headed for Kirshorn's again.

On the way I ran into Lisa, almost literally because I was so lost in thought I wasn't watching where I was going.

"Hey, lady," she said, catching me by the arms before I crashed into her. "You okay?"

I drew a deep breath and willed myself to calm. "Yes, barely."

"Just a couple more hours. Hang on."

"You look cheerful," I said. "Had a good show?"

"Not bad, but that's not really it." Her face broke into a glowing smile. "I got an email from my guy in the army!"

"Obviously, good news."

"He'll be back stateside in a week or so. And he asked me to arrange a getaway for us in April. Somewhere romantic. I'm so excited."

I had to restrain a twinge of petty jealousy. I really was happy for her. I was. "Fantastic news. I'm thrilled for you. This has been so hard for you, not knowing where he was."

"Maybe he'll get transferred back here permanently. We'll see. But I can hardly wait for April." She paused then said, "I heard about Grantwood. What a shame. Will he be all right?"

"I think so."

"It wasn't a murder attempt? I heard they thought heart attack."

"That seems to be the verdict."

"And you and Mr. Tall, Blond, and Gorgeous?"

"Have a date tonight."

"Way to go, girl!" she said and gave me a high five. "Gotta run now. I'll give you a buzz next week."

I nodded and resumed my trip to Kirshorn's, taking it slower and watching where I was going. Though it hadn't solved any of my problems, the conversation lifted my mood.

Nancy, the girl I'd talked to yesterday, was at the booth again, along with a couple of other sales reps, but I didn't see Kirshorn. "He's off somewhere," she said. "I'm sorry you're having such a hard time getting to see him."

I shrugged. "That's the way it goes, sometimes."

"He should be back soon, though," she said. "He has a three-o'clock meeting here."

"Good. I'll wait for him." I'd planned to hang around and wait for him no matter how long it took. He was my last chance to get anything definite on Bethel's murder.

"Can I get you something?" Nancy said as a pair of buyers approached the booth.

I spent a few minutes looking around at the merchandise. The village scenes attracted me for no reason that I could explain. There was just something fascinating about all that tiny detail—the miniaturized buildings, the tree models, the little streetlights, even the small people who effortlessly negotiated the cotton-snow-covered sidewalks of the carefully landscaped display. Although the pieces were painted and some had brightly colored detail, white predominated throughout the scene, creating an atmosphere of peace and purity. It created a tug of yearning in me for a life so simple and clean and uncomplicated.

The Halloween setup produced the opposite effect. Dark colors dominated, with blacks and dark grays and deep blues everywhere. I didn't see any tiny people in this display. Not living ones, at least. Skeletons hung from spidery branches of leafless trees and out the windows of the decrepit houses. Ghosts oozed from chimneys and windows and up from the graves in the poorly kept cemetery, whose headstones suggested an array of jagged teeth.

Oddly enough, I liked it, too. It appealed to the part of me that had once been addicted to Stephen King and Clive Barker novels and old horror flicks.

From there I moved on to the vases and the statuary, but none of it did much for me. Frankly, I thought it all looked cheap, and most of it either tried too hard to be cutesy or failed to achieve the elegance it strove for. I checked out a bunch of glass wall plaques and wasn't inspired by the inspirational messages.

I kept looking around for Kirshorn and glancing at my watch. At ten to three he still hadn't appeared. I worried that Nancy might have gotten her information wrong, or he might have rearranged the schedule and wouldn't appear.

I drifted over to the jewelry racks. I wasn't really a jewelry person. I generally wore plain gold or silver hoops in my ears unless the occasion called for something dressier. I'd put on a necklace if the outfit demanded it, but I really didn't like bracelets and rings. They always seemed to be getting in the way of whatever I was trying to do.

On the other hand, if I could afford really good jewelry I might feel differently.

The stuff Kirshorn's featured wasn't top-end, real-gold-and-gemstones stuff, but some of it was attractive. A sign said all pieces were designed by Cleanna Hulton—a name I vaguely recognized—exclusively for Kirshorn's, and they included genuine Swarovski crystals. The display lights were positioned to make those stones shine.

I didn't realize I liked glittery, glitzy jewelry until I looked at those. Several of the pendants drew my attention and held it. Big, colorful crystals sat in elegantly wrought settings that would complement almost any outfit. Some nice pins hung on the display, as well. A couple of Christmas trees with gorgeously embedded crystal decorations could tempt me to reconsider my disinterest in wearing pins despite the current mania for them.

Another series also intrigued me, a group of nature-themed ones—flowers of various sorts, trees, butterflies, birds, insects, and—

One stopped me dead in my tracks. It looked so familiar. I'd seen it, or one like it, recently.

It took a moment, but I remembered where. A link slammed into place in my mind. Like a series of dominoes falling, more links dropped together until I knew. I knew who'd killed Tim Bethel. And why.

I didn't know what to do next or how to prove it, though. I stood there staring at that pin for several minutes while I debated my next move.

Nancy came over and said, "I see Mr. Kirshorn coming this way now."

It broke the spell of discovery and forced me to act. I glanced at my watch and said, "I've got to go. I'll talk to him later."

I ran down the aisle and across the floor to Chang's booth. Scott had no customers with him, thank heaven. "Come with me," I said, tugging at his arm.

"What's up? Where are we going?" he asked, though he kept pace as I sped down the aisle toward the lobby.

"Upstairs." I was so breathless I had a hard time getting that word out. Fortunately, an elevator car waited, doors open. "I know who—"

Just as the doors were closing, someone else got in with us, squeezing through the narrowing entrance. A strange buzzing noise suddenly filled the car, echoing off the walls as the door slid shut.

Scott's eyes widened. He let out a strangled half-shout

that was almost a scream. Then he collapsed, sagging to his knees first and crumpling sideways to the floor as the car began to rise.

FOURTEEN

SHOCK HELD ME frozen for a moment, before I started to bend down.

"Don't move," Ellen Spencer said. "He's not hurt. Just knocked out for a while. The guy who sold this to me swore it didn't do any real harm." Her right hand rose to show me a small black box with some metal pieces sticking out of the end. A red LED light glowed on the side.

"Stun gun?" I ventured.

She nodded. "I saw you at Kirshorn's, looking at the jewelry. I could see it on your face when you realized."

I glanced at the elevator's control panel, but she stood between me and it. No way I could reach the alarm button without her zapping me. She pressed the button for the sixth floor, the highest number on the panel.

"What are you going to do?" I asked.

"Shut up. I don't know."

We reached the third floor. When the door started to open, she pressed the close button, and it immediately started to shut again.

"It was self-defense, wasn't it?" I said.

"Yes. He would have strangled me."

"He found out you'd told Kirshorn that Rupika was available?"

"I've never seen Tim so livid. He was capable of murder. I could tell."

"Why didn't you use that?" I gestured toward the stun gun.

"I didn't have it with me. I went to the loading dock to find a missing box. I didn't think I'd run into any trouble there."

"So you picked up whatever weapon was handy to defend yourself—the crowbar."

The car reached the sixth floor and the doors opened. The top floor was just a small area, featuring doors out to the roof on both the left and right.

"Pull him out," Spenser told me.

I considered my options, but none looked like good choices. The best I could come up with would be to drag Scott halfway out of the car and leave him while I ran for the stairway entrance behind the elevator shaft. With any luck she'd trip over Scott, giving me a crucial head start. It would leave Scott at her mercy, but he was no danger to her. He'd gone down so fast, he probably had no idea who'd done it or how.

Unfortunately, as I leaned down to grab Scott's arms, she moved to the car's entrance and held the door open with one arm, guarding the passage with the hand holding the stun gun.

If I could heft Scott up to his feet, I might push him into her, which would also give me a chance to get away. Unfortunately just dragging his limp body was proving a challenge. He wasn't a huge man, but he had a good bit of muscle packed on that lean, six-foot-one frame. None of it wanted to slide easily across the gap between the car's door and the floor of the building. It took all my efforts to get him partway out of the car.

I dropped his arms. "I don't think I can do this. I don't have the benefit of any big pieces of cardboard to slide him on. That's how you got Tim's body to the trash bin, isn't it?"

"I was lucky he fell on it." Her face crumpled. "I never

intended to kill him. I didn't even mean to hurt him. I just wanted him to go away and leave me alone. But he wouldn't." She shook her head and her eyes narrowed. "Try again. Get him off the elevator."

I yanked on Scott's arms again and succeeded in moving him about a foot before I was huffing and puffing and my shoulders hurt from the strain. I was so going to get back to working out at the gym regularly when this was over.

"Can't…do it," I said. "Give me a hand."

She reached down and took one of Scott's arms. As soon as she leaned back and started to pull, I dropped the arm I held and ran for the staircase. I got away before she could zap me. As I yanked the door open, she said, "I'll kill him. Come back right now or I'll hold this thing against him until he dies from it."

I hesitated. Could a stun gun really do that? I thought I'd read somewhere that they were safe. Harmless. But what if they weren't? Would she really kill him? Could I take that chance with his life?

I went back. "You wouldn't do it, really, would you?"

Her eyes narrowed and lips pressed together. "Want to find out?"

For all her bravado, I heard something that made me think she was trying to convince herself as much as me, but I wasn't ready to risk Scott's life on it.

"What now?" I asked.

"Outside."

Together, we dragged Scott over to the door. I tried to make my brain work, to formulate a plan, any kind of plan, but my neurons seemed to be shorting out. Spencer leaned into the door out to the roof, shoving it until the automatic catch engaged to hold it open. The sun shone down brightly but the breeze blowing across the area was chilly enough to be uncomfortable. I shivered. My stomach did flip-flops in time to the pounding of my heart. We pulled Scott's still-limp form out onto the graveled roof. Cloth tore as we lugged him across the rough surface.

"Where are we going?" I asked.

"Over to the wall."

I got it then, what she planned to do. I dropped Scott's arm. "No."

She held the stun gun toward me.

My breath almost quit working entirely, but I got out the words. "I won't do it."

"I'll zap you and take care of it myself."

Anger rose and it wiped away some of the fear, thank goodness. "If you really think you can personally throw us both off the roof, use that stun gun on me right now." I looked her in the eye. "I don't think you can. Look at him, Ellen." I nodded toward Scott. "He's a man. Still fairly young. Thirty-one years old. He's got problems. He's made mistakes and taken chances, and he's paid a heavy price for some of them. But he's trying to get it back together. He's got plans. Dreams. A future. Are you really prepared to take that from him? To end his life?"

She narrowed her eyes against the glare of the sun. "You're in love with him."

"No. I don't know. Maybe. I like him. It could turn into love, but I don't know him well enough yet to say it will. Are you going to deny *me* that chance? Any chance to ever fall in love with a man? That's what started all of this, isn't it? Your love for a man. You wanted Kirshorn's business to flourish so you two could continue to meet."

I stabbed her with the sharpest look I could manage. "You're not a killer, Ellen. You never have been. You were only trying to defend yourself against Tim. The cops know it. I promise they do. Detective Gilmont told me they had some evidence that his death wasn't murder. He knows. He understands what happened. You panicked. You're doing it again now. But you don't have to. I swear you don't." I prayed Ellen couldn't see through me as easily as Gilmont did.

She stood still, watching me, shaking a little.

"You didn't intend to harm Tim when you picked up the crowbar. You just wanted to keep him from hurting you. People will understand that. You did what you had to. But if you do *this,* you turn yourself into a cold-blooded murderer. You're not a murderer, Ellen. You're just a woman who made a mistake and did something horrible and has been in agony ever since."

Her face started to crumple and a tear leaked out, but then she pulled herself together. "I just wanted a chance to be with Irv. This was going to be it. He wanted to get the business taken care of so we could have more time for us. He had the designers, but he needed a merger to get the capital. Gaviscelli was courting him, or he was courting them, until Tim decided to horn in on it."

Scott began to stir, moving his hands and legs, grunting something I couldn't understand. Ellen looked down at him, then glanced around, her wide-eyed expression wild and panicked. Before I realized what she intended, she'd leaned over and zapped him a second time. Scott subsided again with a strangled groan.

"God," I said as fear surged through me, almost as sharp and electrical as the current she'd poured into Scott. What if she'd killed him? I leaned down to touch his throat. I could see him twitching, but I worried about the effects of the voltage on his system. Beneath my fingers, his pulse beat strong and regular enough to reassure me. Sweat beaded on his skin and his face pulled into a rictus of pain.

My stomach had twisted into a tight ball, making my insides churn. Nausea threatened, but I pushed it back down. I couldn't afford distraction. What to do next? I ran over the options in my mind. Confront her or try to run away. Try to get help? I still had the cell phone in my purse, but I thought she'd zap me before I could press a speed dial. Trying to run was my best option, but it left Scott at her mercy again.

I stared at her, struggling for the words to bring her back to reason. A thought occurred to me. Her weakness. My strength. "Tell me about you and Irv Kirshorn. When did that happen? How did you meet? What attracted you to him?"

Her brown eyes looked lighter in daylight. The breeze lifted strands of her chestnut hair and the sun picked out red glints. I shivered in the chilly air but she didn't seem to notice the cool temperature.

She lifted the stun gun and pushed it toward me but didn't touch the trigger. Her hand shook, though, and her expression changed, some of the wildness fading. She wanted to talk about it; I knew she did. She and Irv had hidden their relationship for a long time. It burned inside her to tell someone about it.

"He's an attractive man," I ventured. "Especially when he smiles. He doesn't do it often enough." I looked her in the eye and invited her confidence.

I don't know how much rational thought was going on, but her hesitation indicated that at some level she recognized the ploy. Part of her wanted to resist it. The wilder, more panicky part. The other part of her wanted to talk, wanted me to recognize the relationship, wanted to reclaim something of her life, maybe try to salvage something from the wreckage.

"He doesn't smile often enough," she agreed, finally,

as some of the tension went out of her. "He's got so much responsibility, and it's been so hard to keep things going."

She sighed. "We met a couple of years ago. At this show, in fact. The heel of my shoe got caught between the floor and the car, getting into the elevator in the hotel. He was right behind me and he helped me get it loose. He was such a gentleman. Later I saw him in the bar at the hotel, sitting by himself in a back corner, so I joined him and bought him a drink. To thank him."

I wanted to drop my gaze, to see where the stun gun was and if I could grab it, but I didn't dare break eye contact. Not yet.

"We ended up talking until late that night," Ellen continued. "We'd both been recently divorced and were struggling with where we were going. We began to see each other. Of course, we had to keep it completely secret. I knew it was risky, since his company was a competitor, but I really did try to keep business out of our relationship and vice versa. We were very discreet. I don't think anyone suspected a thing.

"This thing with the designer was the first time I'd ever let our relationship cross over into business. Honestly. The only time. I wanted a future for us. Together. God, it's such a mess now."

Tears shined in her eyes again. I recognized my cue. "It's not irretrievable. Yes, it's a mess, but we can sort it out. You have friends who'll help. It won't be fun, but it can be worked out. I bet Irv will stand by you and help, too. Others you might not even know will help."

Dave Powell was going to, for sure. He owed me a big one. If I survived.

"Give me the stun gun," I pleaded, "and let's go back downstairs. We'll have a talk with the police. I promise you we'll do everything we can to help you."

"Do you think I'll go to jail?"

I needed to handle this carefully. It was going my way but was not there yet. "Maybe, briefly, if they charge you. Maybe not. But we'll bail you out if you're charged. We'll get the best lawyer we know to defend you. I don't know exactly what the cops have, but I really do think they're leaning toward viewing it as self-defense. And if not, I'll do my damnedest to convince them of it."

I held my hand out.

She stood there, desperate and undecided. "My life will be ruined," she said. "I don't know what I'll do."

"Will your life be better if you kill us? Can you even live with it? Tim was an accident that happened while you were defending yourself. If you kill us, it will be cold-blooded murder. You're not that kind of person, Ellen."

I felt Scott beginning to stir again, but I shuffled a foot against his chest to keep him from making a wrong move and tipping a delicate situation the wrong way.

"It hasn't been easy having Tim on your conscience, has it?" I asked. "How will it feel to have two more deaths on your mind?"

Ellen's hands were shaking and it spread to the rest of her body. I pressed on. "This time you'd have to live with knowing it wasn't even an accident. You did it deliberately. You killed us, just to cover up an accident. Cold-blooded murder. Can you really live with that? I don't think so. It'll haunt you. Every moment of every day for the rest of your life. You won't have a good night's sleep ever again."

"God," she said. Tears ran down her face. "God, no. I can't do it. You're right."

She held out the stun gun.

I tried not to be too obvious about the huge sigh I heaved as I took the thing from her and slid it into one of my jacket pockets. I extended my hand again. "Let's go down and get a cup of coffee before we talk to the cops. Okay?"

She swallowed hard, nodded, and laid her hand in mine.

"Help me get Scott on his feet. I think he's starting to come around," I said.

Between the two of us, we hoisted him to an upright position. "Damn," he said, his voice still sounding thick. "That hurt like bloody hell. What hit me?"

"Trust me and I'll explain later," I said.

He closed his eyes, opened them, and glared at Ellen. "You! You did something."

"Scott, please shut up for now," I said. "Please."

He wobbled on his feet as we guided him toward the elevator. "Can't think straight anyway."

"You'll be all right in a few minutes. We're going downstairs to get some coffee."

We took a quiet ride back down to the third floor. By the time the door opened again, Scott had recovered enough to walk without help. We headed for one of the conference rooms.

"I need to call downstairs and let the guys in the booth know to go ahead and start closing up," Ellen said. "Also, I'd like to talk to Irv. Is that okay?"

"Why don't you ask him to come up here where you can be private?"

She made the calls. I left her with Scott while I went into Janelle's empty office to call Craig. I told him it was an emergency and to send every available security person up to the third floor. I wasn't taking any chances. Ellen could change her mind about facing the future, and I had no idea what Kirshorn might do.

Soon four security people took up posts around the lobby and office.

As Kirshorn got off the elevator, he gave me a cold

look. I directed him to the conference room. Scott came out right away, leaving him alone with Ellen. Scott and I went to the break room to make coffee.

"You handled that beautifully," he said. "I don't know how anyone could have done better."

"I was a wreck inside, though. She could have gone off the deep end at any moment."

"You had a handle on her. You knew she wouldn't."

"I didn't think she would. You could hear it?"

"Over the buzzing in my ears...most of the time. Except right after she zapped me. I just couldn't make my body do anything for a while after that."

"You were faking it those last few minutes, weren't you?"

"I wasn't exactly in top shape. But yeah, a bit. If she didn't buy it or changed her mind, I was ready to tackle her. I'm just as glad that wasn't put to the test. I might have fallen flat on my face. If I could have even got up off the ground. Damn. Never been zapped that way before. Stun gun?"

I nodded.

"Where is it now?"

"In my pocket."

"Get rid of it. They're not legal in D.C."

"What do I do with it?"

"Trash can's over there." He pointed. "I recommend a decent burial among the coffee grounds and Styrofoam cups."

I did as he suggested before I found a tray in one of the cabinets and loaded it with the coffee makings.

"Have you called Gilmont yet?" he asked.

"No. I better do that now."

Scott waited quietly while I made the call.

"He's on his way," I said.

"There's enough time for you to tell me how you knew it was Ellen. And let's not wait until he gets here for the coffee. I need a cup. Now."

"It was seeing the pin at Kirshorn's booth," I said, pouring a cup for both of us. "One of their product lines is designer crystal jewelry. I was looking at the display and saw a dragonfly. I realized I'd seen one like it before. It took me a minute to remember it had fallen out of Ellen Spencer's purse when I bumped into her the other morning. She wrapped it up very carefully when I gave the pin back to her, like it was precious to her. And it was a designer line, exclusive to Kirshorn's, so there was only one place she could have gotten it."

"From Kirshorn himself?"

"I should have guessed something like that when I realized she wasn't wearing it, but I thought she didn't have it on because it didn't go with her outfit. I'd caught her watching him often enough, but she masked her feelings well. I thought she was worried about what he might do to Grantwood."

I sighed as I inhaled the fragrance of the coffee. It was office coffee, too, not exactly a high-quality brand, which shows how desperate I was. "When I realized what the pin meant, it was like everything else fell into place. Lisa had told me the rumor that Ellen was having a show affair, although Lisa didn't know who it was with. And I'd seen her watching Kirshorn at the benefit dinner Thursday night. I thought at the time she was afraid of him, but I think she was afraid for him. Afraid that he was digging himself in too deeply. Afraid that if Gaviscelli did merge with G & B, Kirshorn would be out of business. She'd already done what she could for him, but he still had to come up with the financing."

"Done what she could?"

"You must have still been out of it when she admitted killing Tim Bethel. I'm pretty sure now she was the woman Tim called a traitorous bitch. He'd just discovered she'd told Kirshorn that Tom Rupika was available. Remember Grantwood told me that Bethel knew another top-name designer they could sign? One who was unhappy with his contract? No one else knew about it. Keep in mind there aren't that many designers with the kind of cachet they needed. In fact, my friend Lisa could only think of two, and she's in touch with the industry. But of the two she named, I already knew Kristian Grange was signed by Andy Tarantoro, so that left Rupika. Bethel had somehow learned he was unhappy well before everyone else found out. I think Rupika turned him down at first, but Bethel was sure he could convince him to sign on when he got here. Instead he found out Kirshorn had beat him to it. Which spelled disaster for Bethel."

"It devalued the company."

"That, yes. But Powell hinted that other consequences could be triggered. My guess is one of those was that executive-level employees might not be welcome in the merged company as a result. Grantwood didn't care. Bethel cared a lot."

Scott stared at me. "No wonder he was in a murderous rage when he found out."

"Ellen picked up the crowbar to defend herself. When she realized he was dead, she panicked, dragged him to the trash bin, and tossed him in. Probably thought it was appropriate, too, except that I'm not sure she was thinking rationally at all by then. She got lucky that he fell on the cardboard. Most of the blood seems to have stayed on it and she didn't have to touch him to move him."

"The threats to Grantwood?"

"Ellen and Kirshorn still had a problem. Kirshorn had

the designers, but he didn't have the capital. I don't know for sure, but I'll bet Kirshorn's is pretty overextended debt-wise, so his only real hope of getting the money was a merger. And Gaviscelli was the perfect partner. Except for the inconvenient detail that they already planned to acquire G & B. So Ellen arranged for some mild threats to Grantwood, hoping to at least get him to delay signing the agreement."

"And what about Grantwood's collapse last night?"

"That I don't know," I admitted. "I really, *really* hope it was a coincidence."

"So do I. Initial tox screens came back negative, by the way, other than a blood alcohol of point zero three. We know he had a glass of wine. If there *was* anything else, it would be harder to find. Maybe impossible."

"Ellen would know that the announcement itself wasn't particularly significant."

"The timing might have been coincidence. Doesn't mean the event was."

"I know. But I think I can live with not knowing this one for sure. I doubt it will matter now."

"Probably not. But if there was something more than natural causes, the full tox screen should show it. I think we can—"

The elevator pinged and Janelle got off. She saw the two of us but her attention focused on me and "furious" doesn't begin to describe it. "Where have you been? The show's closing down, Ellen Spencer has disappeared, the G & B people are going nuts, I got a complaint that you've stolen a popcorn machine, and someone else said you'd run off the show floor, dragging Scott along with you. What's going on?"

"A lot," I said, "but Gilmont will be here any minute and we might as well go through it all once for everyone.

By the way, Ellen Spencer is in the conference room with Irv Kirshorn. Very likely they're discussing how much to tell Gilmont."

Janelle looked from me to Scott and back. Her stance relaxed just the tiniest bit. "Spill it," she ordered.

"Ellen Spencer killed Tim Bethel. Probably in self-defense, but that's not my call." I barely got the last word out. All of a sudden, my heart started pounding a mile a minute and I couldn't seem to catch my breath. I felt as though a huge wave had just broken over me and I was drowning. My eyes burned and my head felt swimmy.

"Heather?" Scott was at my side, taking the coffee from me. "Sit down." He guided me into the nearest chair and pushed my head down between my knees until the dizziness cleared.

"I almost wish I hadn't found out." I shook my head, fighting off tears. "None of this was ever my problem. So why did I let it get to me so badly?"

"Because you care so much," Janelle answered. "It's a strength and a weakness, but in you it's more strength. You just have to watch out for it or it'll lure you into trouble."

"And you probably saved an innocent woman from going to trial." In a blatant effort to lighten the atmosphere, Scott raised one eyebrow. "You stole a popcorn machine?"

"Long story."

The door to the conference room opened. Kirshorn looked out and gestured for us to join him.

The elevator pinged at almost exactly the same moment. Detective Gilmont and another man in plain clothes got off. While Scott and Janelle escorted them into the conference room, I grabbed a few more coffee cups, set up the spare pot, and put the nearly full one on the tray.

Ellen Spencer's eyes were red and swollen, and she

clutched a damp tissue in one hand. The other was enclosed in Irv Kirshorn's.

Once we were all seated and supplied with coffee, Gilmont looked around the room. "Someone want to tell me why we've called this meeting?"

After a moment of silence, Ellen said, "I do."

FIFTEEN

ELLEN SPENCER told her story to the police and answered a few questions. Then she and Irv Kirshorn went with Gilmont and his cohort to their office to give formal statements. Scott and I followed Janelle into her office.

Janelle called the lawyer she'd hired for Chloe and asked him to meet Ellen Spencer at the police station.

"Do I still have a job here?" I asked.

Her brows went all the way up to her hairline. "You doubt it? Of course you do. You know I couldn't manage without you."

I breathed a sigh of relief. "I wasn't sure. I didn't exactly keep a low profile."

"You did exactly what was needed. How did you figure out it was Ellen?"

I related the same sequence of things I'd told Scott about earlier. A lot more slowly this time because I still felt shaky. It took a while. When I finished, I added, "I had a lot of luck, seeing that pin the morning I accidentally ran into her and knocked her purse loose. If it hadn't been for that, I never would have put her together with Kirshorn."

Janelle shook her head. "That was the *only* bit of luck. The rest of it was you, digging for information, knowing our business, and figuring out what the various pieces meant and how they fit together."

"And my stubborn refusal to believe Chloe Bethel was guilty despite all the evidence. And I'd met the woman once and talked to her for maybe fifteen minutes, total."

"Did I hear my name?" Chloe Bethel looked as beautifully elegant in her simple gray-and-blue, two-piece dress as a model straight off the runway. Dave Powell stood behind her.

"Come in," Janelle said and introduced Scott to both of them.

"We've got to go make arrangements for Tim's funeral, but I had to stop by and thank you for your efforts on my behalf," Chloe said. "And I'm so glad to find Heather here because I have so much to thank her for. When the detective told me they were dropping all charges against me, he also told me what you'd done. And what you'd risked."

I tried to deny I'd done all that much, but Chloe insisted on taking my hand and kissing me on the cheek. Powell also shook my hand. I'd talk to him later about helping Ellen Spencer, if she needed it. He definitely owed me. His eyes silently acknowledged the debt.

By the time they left, it was close to six. Janelle said, "Let's get out of here. It's way past quitting time. By the way, sleep in tomorrow. We don't need to get started early." She looked at Scott and said, "I'll tell Craig."

"Sounds good to me," he answered. "I'll be back to plain old security guard again."

"Are you going to continue working here?" I asked. "Most of our shows are exciting in their own way, but not like this one. I'm afraid it will be boring for you."

He looked at me. "You're going to continue working here, right?"

"Of course."

"It won't be boring, then."

I made a mental note to call Chris tomorrow and tell him our on-again, off-again relationship was now permanently off.

* * * * *

REQUEST YOUR FREE BOOKS!

2 FREE NOVELS
PLUS 2 FREE GIFTS!

Your Partner in Crime

YES! Please send me 2 FREE novels from the Worldwide Library® series and my 2 FREE gifts (gifts are worth about $10). After receiving them, if I don't wish to receive any more books, I can return the shipping statement marked "cancel." If I don't cancel, I will receive 4 brand-new novels every month and be billed just $5.24 per book in the U.S. or $6.24 per book in Canada. That's a saving of at least 34% off the cover price. It's quite a bargain! Shipping and handling is just 50¢ per book in the U.S. and 75¢ per book in Canada.* I understand that accepting the 2 free books and gifts places me under no obligation to buy anything. I can always return a shipment and cancel at any time. Even if I never buy another book, the two free books and gifts are mine to keep forever.

414/424 WDN FEJ3

Name	(PLEASE PRINT)

Address	Apt. #

City	State/Prov.	Zip/Postal Code

Signature (if under 18, a parent or guardian must sign)

Mail to the **Reader Service:**
IN U.S.A.: P.O. Box 1867, Buffalo, NY 14240-1867
IN CANADA: P.O. Box 609, Fort Erie, Ontario L2A 5X3

Not valid for current subscribers to the Worldwide Library series.

Want to try two free books from another line?
Call 1-800-873-8635 or visit www.ReaderService.com.

* Terms and prices subject to change without notice. Prices do not include applicable taxes. Sales tax applicable in N.Y. Canadian residents will be charged applicable taxes. Offer not valid in Quebec. This offer is limited to one order per household. All orders subject to credit approval. Credit or debit balances in a customer's account(s) may be offset by any other outstanding balance owed by or to the customer. Please allow 4 to 6 weeks for delivery. Offer available while quantities last.

Your Privacy—The Reader Service is committed to protecting your privacy. Our Privacy Policy is available online at www.ReaderService.com or upon request from the Reader Service.

We make a portion of our mailing list available to reputable third parties that offer products we believe may interest you. If you prefer that we not exchange your name with third parties, or if you wish to clarify or modify your communication preferences, please visit us at www.ReaderService.com/consumerchoice or write to us at Reader Service Preference Service, P.O. Box 9062, Buffalo, NY 14269. Include your complete name and address.

WWL11B